More Critical Praise for Arthur Nersesian

For *dogrun*

"Nersesian's writing is beautiful, especially when it is about women and love."
—Jennifer Belle, author of *High Maintenance*

"A rich parody of the all-girl punk band."   —*New York Times Book Review*

"Nersesian's blackly comic urban comi
paragraph."

"Darkly comic . . . It's Nersesian's love a
pages afire."

For *Chinese Takeout*

"Not since Henry Miller has a writer so successfully captured the trials and tribu-
lations of a struggling artist . . . A masterly image."
—*Library Journal* (starred review)

"One of the best books I've read about the artist's life. Nersesian captures the ob-
session one needs to keep going under tough odds . . . trying to stay true to himself,
and his struggle against the odds makes for a compelling read."

"Nersesian weaves a heartfelt,
myth of Orpheus and Eurydic
the hip squalor of this milieu
lyrical celebration of an evane

"Capturing in words the energ
is a definite achievement. Setti
degradation, and hope, and ma
in a novel confirms Nersesian's
art and of life, and of the creat
to put down."

For *Manhattan Loverboy*

"Best Book for the Beach, Summer 2000." —*Jane Magazine*

"Best Indie Novel of 2000." —*Montreal Mirror*

"Part Lewis Carroll, part Franz Kafka, Nersesian leads us down a maze of false leads and dead ends . . . told with wit and compassion, drawing the reader into a world of paranoia and coincidence while illuminating questions of free will and destiny. Highly recommended." —*Library Journal*

"A tawdry and fantastic tale . . . Nersesian renders Gotham's unique cocktail of wealth, poverty, crime, glamour, and brutality spectacularly." —*Rain Taxi Review of Books*

"*MLB* sits somewhere between Kafka, DeLillo, and Lovecraft—a terribly frightening, funny, and all too possible place." —*Literary Review of Canada*

For *The Fuck-Up*

"For those who remember that the '80s were as much about destitute grit as they were about the decadent glitz described in the novels of Bret Easton Ellis and Jay McInerney, this book will come as a fast-paced reminder." —*Time Out New York*

"*The Fuck-Up* is *Trainspotting* without drugs, New York style." —Hal Sirowitz, author of *Mother Said*

"Touted as the bottled essence of early-'80s East Village living, *The Fuck-Up* is, refreshingly, nothing nearly so limited . . . A cult favorite since its first, obscure printing in 1991, I'd say it's ready to become a legitimate religion." —*Smug Magazine*

"Not since *The Catcher in the Rye*, or John Knowles's *A Separate Peace*, have I read such a beautifully written book . . . Nersesian's powerful, sure-footed narrative alone is so believably human in its poignancy . . . I couldn't put this book down." —*Grid Magazine*

MESOPOTAMIA

by **ARTHUR NERSESIAN**

9-10
16⁰⁰

This is a work of fiction. All names, characters, places, and incidents are the product of the author's imagination. Any resemblance to real events or persons, living or dead, is entirely coincidental.

Published by Akashic Books
©2010 by Arthur Nersesian

ISBN-13: 978-1-936070-08-4
Library of Congress Control Number: 2009939081
First Printing

Akashic Books
PO Box 1456
New York, NY 10009
info@akashicbooks.com
www.akashicbooks.com

Printed in Canada

to my uncles

Richard A. Burke
Patrick G. Burke
Thomas P. Burke
Michael F. Burke
Stephen U. Burke

MESOPOTAMIA

It turns out I was right.
But nothing has come of it.
And this is my robe, slightly singed.
And this is my prophet's junk.
And this is my twisted face.
A face that didn't know it could be beautiful.
—*Soliloquy for Cassandra*,
Wislawa Szymborska

ACCUSED TEACHER
HANGS SELF
IN FRONT OF HIS SCHOOL!!

BY CASSANDRA BLOOMGARTEN
NY ♡ NY

"HIS DEATH WAS EXCRUCIATINGLY SLOW," said the M.E. "The drop was not far enough to snap any of his cervical vertebrae, which customarily causes instant paralysis." After fourth period, a high school biology teacher walked to the scaffolding in front of his school and took out five feet of 3/8" braided rope. He bound a noose around his neck, climbed up to the eight-foot crossbar of the outdoor shed, knotted the free end to the bar, and jumped. If I had to grade his suicide, I would've given him an F for failing to snap his neck. Well, maybe a D- for slowly strangling himself. He had been accused of molesting a student, a charge that was never substantiated.

FRUSTRATED WRITER
SLITS JUGULAR

SCANDALIZED POLITICIAN
JUMPS TO HIS DEATH!

I remember a state politician who I interviewed while I was an intern. A few years later he was **CAUGHT IN A STING WITH A HIGH-PRICED CALL GIRL.** Once he got out on bail, he went home, opened a window, and jumped twenty-two flights, deciding to throw himself to the mercy of the courtyard. 🏛

While in college, I wrote a piece for the school newspaper about a visiting journalist. Weeks later, upon returning home, he found himself in political hot water in his Eastern Bloc nation. He slipped into a tub of hot water with a saber in his hand, and cut open his own neck. Unfortunately, the Berlin Wall fell a few years later, proving that things are rarely as bad as they seem.

CHAPTER ONE

. . . those were all the suicides that I could remember, all sad males (as I envisioned in tabloid headlines—an occupational hazard of working in this business). Women tend to be more passive in their self-annihilation. Accidental overdoses gradually slowing down their broken little hearts. Repeatedly peeking into ovens, à la Sylvia Plath, where the gas delicately overwhelms the oxygen and their last thoughts are regretting not using a better oven cleaner. Stressful jobs, loveless marriages, bad food—most people kill themselves slowly every day.

When I got fired from my marriage and divorced from my job, I found myself getting drunk and passing out too early. Then I'd wake up around two in the morning with only the unbearable emptiness of my miserable failure to keep me company. That was when I started with the sleeping pills.

None of this had anything to do with the seemingly happy, successful life of one Thucydides Scrubbs. His comely young wife Missy was probably too dumb to kill herself. At thirty-eight years old the African American tax attorney probably slept as soundly as the dead. At least he slept well until that fateful day in July 2005 when he returned to his posh two-million-dollar estate outside of Memphis, Tennessee, to find his allegedly pregnant, white teenage bride, Missy Scrubbs, missing. Four days after her disappearance, her mother notified the police. When they asked Thucydides why he didn't call them, he replied that he simply thought she was visiting some friends upstate. Apparently she was from some podunk town between Memphis and Nashville, and this was where I started paying attention as I was raised in that very same area.

When the police examined Thucydides's bank records, they discovered that a million dollars had been withdrawn from his account a few days before she vanished. He had no explanation and was an automatic suspect.

When they learned from the neighbors that Thucydides and his wife had been fighting on a regular basis, the police considered he might have used that money to hire a hit man. But a murder didn't cost nearly that much. Some hypothesized that it might be a kidnapping. If that was the case, then Thucydides had probably been warned that if he involved the police, little Missy would be executed.

They interrogated Scrubbs at length. First alone, then with his nerdy counsel. When a local reporter broke the story that Scrubbs had been cheating on Missy with an even hotter, dumber blonde who worked on Beale Street, the gossip hit a fever pitch.

The titillating detail that tipped the story into the circus tent of tabloid land was something Missy's middle-trash mother had done ten years earlier. She had entered little Missy into every children's beauty pageant from Texarkana, Texas, to Biloxi, Mississippi. As fate would have it, she looked uncannily like Jon-Benét Ramsey. That, along with the fact that Scrubbs looked vaguely like a short, stocky O.J. Simpson, didn't help. Aspects of these two highly publicized cases with poorly resolved endings were natural fodder for the always hungry 'bloids.

Within a matter of weeks, as the case cauliflowered into this year's most sensational crime investigation, a quiet suburb in Memphis became the newest journalistic Mecca. People weren't sure whether this was a case of a runaway bride, or another Laci Peterson story, or, best of all, an old-fashioned kidnapping. It all came down to one question: where the hell was Missy Scrubbs?

Ninety-nine percent of my supermarket stories dealt with high-profile hookups of Tomkat, Bennifer (as in J-Lo), Bennifer

II (as in Garner), and Brangelina—moronic celebrity romances. Eventually they all turned into *marri-vorces*. Last year I had reason to suspect my husband was cheating on me, but I pretended not to know. Soon he would only show up for a change of clothes. I tried to get out of the house on tabloid assignments, but before long I had taken to drinking on the job and was given a pink slip. Since my husband actually owned our classic eight apartment at the Ansonia—and I didn't want a divorce lawyer telling me to move—I took the initiative, locating a barely affordable studio in Hell's Kitchen. And there I slept; spring turned into summer . . . By early August I was deep in debt, and unless I wanted to continue my hibernation in some ATM bank card cave, I had to get out of bed.

One day shortly after the move, when my answering machine clicked on, I groggily heard the faint voice of A. Paul O'Hurly, my soon-to-be-ex-husband, asking how I was. I ignored it. Some time later, I was awoken by another click of some reporter I knew in Washington quickly saying that she wished she could help with my pet project, an article about the Homeland Security reorganization. She said if I wanted to write it for some distant blog she knew . . . blah . . . blah . . . blah . . . I was holding out for print. I retreated deeper into the black sludge of sleep. It took a third louder, longer phone message to batter through the three tablets of Ambien and two Valium I had taken ten hours earlier.

"Miss Bloomgarten, this is Jericho Riggs, editor of the *Rocket*. You were recommended by Mr. Benoit to cover the Thucydides Scrubbs saga. He said you know the area and the reporter who I hired has turned up AWOL."

I snatched up the phone to learn that some naïve young editor was accidentally giving me a small break. The *National Enquirer*, the *Star*, *Weekly World News*—after burning my bridges at each of those fine institutions, I thought I was done with tabloid news (or vice versa). Now, thanks to my old friend Gustavo Benoit, I was being offered a freelance gig with a kill fee.

For me this job could potentially kill three annoying birds with one small stone: Aside from its therapeutic effects on my slowly smothering depression, the job could also earn me some desperately needed cash. More importantly, though, it would put me near to my deservedly neglected mama from Mesopotamia, Tennessee. I was going to drive from one land between the rivers to another in hope of borrowing yet more money.

I cleared my throat so that Jerry Riggs wouldn't sense I was severely hungover and had been sleeping for ten hours, and said, "Great."

"They just indicted Scrubbs, so I need you to go down there and dredge up anything related to the case." He wanted a small but steady news feed so he could put large colorful photos over them and sensational headlines above that. Riggs said that Gustavo was already down there if I needed help, and that he was expecting my first clump of words by tomorrow. *Click.*

I was once a real reporter. Even though I was no longer on any masthead—perhaps out of habit—I was still pushing and checking in on stories that I felt needed to be out there.

Last December, Gustavo Benoit invited me to a Washington "insider Christmas party" where I quickly got waylaid by some old bore named Silas who confused my ear with a spittoon. As he jabbered on and on, I searched for an escape route, but even Gustavo, who had brought me there, had vanished.

Though Silas's speech was slurred and too filled with facts and figures to be very engrossing, I slowly realized that the man was actually sitting on an important story. He had been prematurely retired from FEMA where he had worked for years as a meteorologist. The Federal Emergency Management Agency had just been absorbed into the growing swamp of the "Homeless Insecurity Department."

"Problem is, it's not nearly as effective now, and this is a really bad time to be ineffective," Silas explained.

"How exactly is it ineffective?"

He casually described how the agency had been scaled down. Time-tested protocols had been scrapped, making responsibility far fuzzier and the chain of command very murky. More specifically, budget, staff, everything had been dramatically reduced.

"And it's a really bad time to do this because we're heading into severe hurricane activity, not to mention the fact that this is a very different world."

"Different how?"

"Biologically," Silas said. "There's a recent theory that this global warming wave is incubating countless dormant bacteria and viruses, allowing them to jump from various animals to human hosts. And I'm not just talking about some bird flu."

On and on he went, detailing how we currently had a perfect mating of mediocre politics with an abusive mother nature.

CHAPTER TWO

When I finally woke up from my Hell's Kitchen hell five hours later, I realized that I was supposed to be in Memphis, Tennessee, this very same day.

Too achy to reach the top shelf of my undusted closet for my tasteful toting luggage, I tossed the same unlaundered pile of clothes from my last assignment—a celebrity wedding stakeout six months ago—into two shopping bags. I stumbled downstairs and headed west to my river-adjacent car garage. It was only after my car rolled out of the Holland Tunnel like a tired torpedo that I began to feel myself emerging from my stupor.

I had been raised in a small town an hour and half northeast of Memphis and ran away at a young age. Though I eventually reconciled with Rodmilla, the annoying woman who had adopted me from a Korean orphanage, I managed to keep her at arm's length. I had paid her final installments on a mortgage she had taken out to help raise her biological family, but she and my debts were both moving up in years. She and her husband owned a huge house next to a defunct old mill situated behind one of the two narrow rivers that defined the town (Mesopotamia literally means *land between the rivers*). Soon after I had been adopted, she gave birth to two healthy twin girls. Shortly afterward her husband dropped dead, but she was one of those "crisis in Chinese means opportunity" types. Instead of moving back in with her parents, she mortgaged the house and converted the empty mill into a general store—the Ziggurat. (Since the locals were unaware that she was making a play on the original Mesopotamia, everyone soon called it ZigRat's.) She hired the local Boo Radley guy, a Vietnam vet named Pete, to run the place and within three months was making a little dough.

The store's steady success allowed her to start a local freebie newspaper, the *Mesopotamian Cuneiform*, which my two sisters and I wrote for when we were growing up. That little twelve-page rag got me infected with the journalistic bug while I was still in my teens. I learned more about writing, editing, and general production during those postpubescent days than in all of journalism school.

Unfortunately, the last time I had spoken to Rodmilla, a few months ago, it sounded like she was losing it. The sharp old coot that used to criticize my every move had grown noticeably dull. Only with the help of Pete was she still able to keep the store going.

Twelve hours and hundreds of miles later, having blasted through eight big bags of Doritos, several gallons of water, and all of my CDs twice, I washed up in that reportorial flood zone of Memphis. Over the past few unemployed months, in the wake of my chat with Silas, the retired meteorologist, I had become a one-woman lobbyist, trying to attract some big-name reporter or magazine to follow up on the story of the new FEMA being ill-prepared. After pitching it to a couple dozen reporters and editors I knew, I had only succeeded in becoming a pariah.

As I gathered with the other reporters covering the Scrubbs case, I learned that our just-indicted target, Thucydides, had not been seen for over a week. Rumor was he had traveled to Europe just before the D.A. announced he was going before the grand jury and the suspected wife killer wouldn't be back for another week or so.

From across the magnolia-lined thoroughfare, behind a forgotten Confederate solider statue, under the swaying and dappled shadows of redundant maple leaves, in his dirty white seersucker suit and clownish panama hat, leaning against a rented white compact, was the gentleman alcoholic and friend extraordinaire, Gustavo Benoit. If Sydney Greenstreet and Peter Lorre ever shared a quadroon mistress, Gustavo might well have been the result.

When I crossed the street and joined him, he put a Styrofoam cup in my hand and before I could pretend that I was on the wagon, he poured some tempting single malt.

"It's Lara Croft, tomb raider, in our sleepy little Bayou-burg," he said in a retractable Southern drawl.

"If you're expecting me to thank you for getting me this awful job, forget it," I replied, gulping down the whiskey so as to quickly get to that always better second cup.

"Actually, you could compensate me by joining me for a drink at one of the local boy bars." He flung his hat into his car.

Gay Gustavo would always pay my tab at such pubs, where he used me to entice cute young men who he would attempt to intoxicate and seduce. But that was when Clinton was president and we still thought of ourselves as old youths. Despite our obvious decline—measured by the intake of liquid ounces—Gustavo was still as sharp as a rusty tack.

"I'm too broke to have fun," I said, finishing the Scotch, "so unless you can loan me a grand I'm going to have to pay a visit to the ruins in Mesopotamia."

"Sorry," he answered, impoverished.

As the expensive Scotch started to do its magic, I opened the back door of his car for a place to sit. Out fell a pair of battery-operated devil horns. His entire backseat was covered with odd party favors: hook-on rabbit ears, a shotgun that unfolded into an umbrella, a strap-on parrot beak, a Groucho Marx eyeglasses-nose-mustache, and under a George W. Bush mask I spotted Bozo, a clown scalp that I pulled over my own hair.

While I rooted around for the attachable nose, Gustavo filled me in: "This Scrubbs dude isn't coming back to town for at least a week, so now's a good time to have your big maternal reconciliation."

"You're sure?" I asked, fixing the round red nose on. "I'll never get another assignment if I miss him."

"I'll call you if his bulbous head pops up," Gustavo replied. "You're going up near Nashville, right?"

"About midway between here and there."

"Anywhere near . . ." he peeked in his notebook, "Doomland, Tennessee?"

"*Daumland*," I corrected. "It's ten minutes away. Why?"

"That's where the Scrubbs child bride hails from: Daumland."

"Any names or addresses?"

"I tried," Gustavo said, trying to light a second cigarette from the first. "All I could get was the town's gloomy's name."

"You know, if you think you're going to fool any doormen or security guards with this stuff . . ." I kidded, referring to the novelty items in the backseat.

"These orphans were rescued from a fire in Screwy Louie's Novelty Shop yesterday. I found most of them in the garbage bin out back. I just couldn't resist." He reached in and pulled out a flat Frankenstein top that he clipped over his coiffed scalp, then sipped his Scotch.

After thanking Gustavo for three cups of booze and all the 4-1-1, I got back in my jalopy and called editor Riggs, giving him an update on Scrubbs: he was out of town while the D.A. was convening a grand jury.

"I can write a decent little piece that suggests he might be fleeing the country."

"We're going to print in roughly an hour, have it by then."

"Fine, but since nothing else is going on here, I thought maybe I should dash up to Daumland, Tennessee, and see if I can dig up anything on Missy's family."

"Sounds good, but don't go too far in case I need you back down in Memphis."

I stopped at a Starbucks, fired up my laptop, made a couple of calls, and whipped out my first new item in over four months.

It played up the fact that T. Scrubbs was about to be a fugitive from the law. I e-mailed it to Riggs and made a quick grand. Now I only owed nineteen thousand dollars.

When I pulled into the driveway of my mom's shop an hour and a half later, I stopped in to say hi to old Pete, but he was busy doing checkout for an impatient line. As I walked around to the back of the big empty house, it was difficult not to remember my teenage years when this place was crawling with kids.

Rodmilla answered the door. She made a big show of hugging and kissing me, her prodigal daughter. She led me into her huge kitchen.

Like a living newsletter she updated me on the successes of her two real daughters. Ludmilla and Bella had married and re-produced. Three and four children respectively. Both were com-fortably situated in suburban Atlanta where they were living in elegant homes and prescribing to Rachael Ray's hasty vision of domestic bliss.

Finally, as she tore her garden-grown mint leaves into her etched-crystal pitcher, she asked about Paul, my wonderful blond husband.

"He was fine last time I saw him."

"When exactly was that, dear?" she asked, delicately placing her large decanter of mint julep and glasses on an antique silver tray and carrying it out onto the veranda.

"About six months ago, when he forgot his way home." I sat on her new antique patio set. Although I had no intention of drinking alcohol, I didn't want to offend her, so I asked for just a small glass.

"What exactly are you saying?"

"I packed up and moved out a few months ago." I swigged down the drink.

She sighed and poured me a second helping. "Did you *try* working it out?"

I shrugged and finished the second glass quickly, which she politely refilled.

"I don't know what to say." She looked off dismally and took a sip of her mint julep.

"Also, I haven't gotten much work lately and was hoping for a little loan." Life was easy once you learned to deaden the shame.

"How much is a little?"

"About three grand should do it." It sounded like a lot, but was only a fraction of what I had given her over the years.

"You know I thought Paul was a prince." That was the first leak in her levy. "In fact, to be quite frank, I thought *he* could've done better."

"Oh, he did a lot better—with every young intern in his office."

"I find that difficult to believe. He used to dote on you like no man I ever saw."

"Too bad you couldn't adopt him," I said as I refilled my glass.

Paul was currently the executive producer of the highest-rated local news show in the tristate area. It was difficult to imagine what more he could've accomplished.

"You come here to announce you're getting a divorce and you're broke and—"

"If you don't want to loan me anything, that's fine, but please don't kick me when I'm down."

"Sandy, I don't have much time left," she began. "My veins are clogged with a lifetime of fat. My lungs are congested with tar and nicotine. And when any one of my old body parts finally conks out, the rest of me is eager to follow."

"People live for a long time nowadays."

"Didn't you tell me and your sisters that as someone who was rejected by her own biological parents, you wanted a child more than anything else?"

"I haven't spoken to my sisters in ten years, but yes, I told you that. And thanks for not letting me forget that I'm a middle-aged, dried-up Asian adoptee with a failed marriage and a drinking problem."

"Though I wasn't going to mention it, you clearly do have a drinking problem." She pointed to the nearly empty crystal pitcher. Rodmilla had put it out simply to test me. Of course I failed.

"Look, Ma . . ."

"You can move back into your old room. Other than that I simply have nothing for you."

I apologized for wasting her time and walked out into the darkness. Being born an orphan was hard enough, but being air-lifted halfway around the world from Panmunjom, Korea, and adopted by a liberal Jewish household in Tennessee was just plain awkward. When I wasn't called a kike, I was a gook—Gustavo actually merged the two words and called me a kook.

Five minutes after I left her, only a few blocks away, I decided to hell with the Scrubbs case, I was going back to New York. Drunkenly I missed a turn and went through a bank of bushes. Luckily there was no serious damage, but I was starved for sleep. Pushing back my seat, I covered myself with every piece of clothing I could find and passed out.

Awaking groggily several hours later, I turned the key and got back on Highway 21.

I drove for a short time before I heard some rattling around in my glove compartment. When I popped it open I found a mini bottle of Scotch just sitting there. Without even thinking, I used my teeth to twist open the top and sucked it down just as quickly. While looking out at rolling hills of dark green maple trees, I passed an old *Welcome to Daumland* sign, population two thousand something. Just then, my cell phone chimed.

"Cassandra?"

"Who is this, please?"

"Debra Blake . . . with the *New York Times*."

Suddenly my faith in good journalism rose. Someone had finally responded to my endless e-mailings. "Okay, I met this guy at a party last December, a meteorologist from FEMA," I explained. "He told me that this is an active hurricane year."

"Active how?"

"Apparently the 1970s, '80s, and '90s were inactive, until the late '90s. It's a cycle and we're in the middle of a really active period that could last another twenty years."

"Cassie, the thing is—"

"Now, I didn't really believe him, but the hurricane season started so early this year and—"

"Early?"

"Oh yeah," I said and rattled them off: "June 9, tropical storm Arlene. June 28, Bret, and Cindy was next. Then on July 10 the first hurricane, Dennis, a category three hit Florida—"

"Wow!"

"Then hurricane Emily, which was a category four. Franklin and Gertrude at the end of July."

"But—"

"Harvey came next, and as we speak Irene is still active, off the coast of New Jersey. And it's only the beginning of August."

"This is all quite fascinating but—"

"This is just the weather. I mean, it could be an earthquake, a flood, you name it—the real story is FEMA."

"You mean the Federal Regulatory—"

"The Emergency Management Agency. It was just reshuffled under Homeland Security and they've completely stripped it down and so that—"

"Cassandra, the reason I called is—"

"No one even heard of the guy who heads it," I managed to squeeze out.

"Hold it."

"I know, I should be talking to your editor or something, but I've tried to get this story out and no one's going anywhere near it. It'll just take one of these hurricanes—"

"Didn't you just move into that old building on the northeast corner of 50th Street and Ninth Avenue?" she finally elbowed in.

"Yeah, why?" The last time I had seen her was when I was moving into my new bachelorette pad.

"Cause I'm walking by it right now and I saw the fire trucks and police barricades and just wanted to make sure you were okay."

"Huh?" It was a solid brick building. How could it catch fire?

She continued: "Also, I'm a fashion reporter. I don't know anyone in politics."

"Could you do me a teeny favor?" I asked. "I'm on an assignment down South. Could you ask someone what happened?"

"There's actually a sign right on the front door." Then, clearing her throat as if about to audition for an anchorwoman spot, she read, "The heading says, *Department of Buildings, City of New York*, then in big red letters it says, *Vacate, do not enter.* Underneath that it says, *The Department of Buildings has determined that conditions in these premises are imminently perilous to life. These premises have been vacated and reentry is prohibited until such condition has been eliminated to the satisfaction of the Department. Violators of this vacate order are subject to arrest.*"

"FUCK!" Five minutes ago I just needed a little cash, now I was homeless. "Debra, thanks a lot for everything and if you want a good fashion tip for next season, look into hazmat gear."

I quickly located the phone number of my downstairs neighbor, Wanda Basall—I remembered her because her name rhymes with asshole—in my address book. She picked up after the first ring.

"Hi, this is your upstairs neighbor. You'll pardon me for calling, but I'm out of town."

"No problem."

"Some woman just told me our building was condemned, but I'm sure there's a mistake."

"If there was a mistake," she replied, "I probably wouldn't be talking to you from an army cot on the gym floor of Cardinal

Spellman High School in the Bronx that was set up by Disaster Services of the American Red Cross."

She then explained what had happened. Our landlord Mr. Wolfe, one of the last of the great slumlords, had hired three Mexican workers to do some construction. He was trying to convert the former corner bodega into a new Starbucks, every landlord's wet dream. Apparently, too intimidated by Wolfe to confirm his vague instructions, the workers had accidentally torn down a load-bearing wall. When the entire building suddenly sagged down the center, someone called the fire department. They in turn notified the Department of Buildings, who instantly condemned the premises.

"Now the landlord has to get a building permit to get a licensed contractor to fix the problem and then they have to get the building inspector back in there to give it some seal of approval. According to one person I spoke to," Basall concluded, "that could take months."

"Where the hell am I suppose to live until then?"

"There's an empty cot next to me."

"What about all our things! And the rent?"

She explained that the landlord was prorating everything. All rents would be suspended until the place was livable again.

It was then I heard a faint siren slowly growing closer. I thanked her and clicked off. When the cop car closed in, I pulled over and realized my breath probably still smelled of liquor.

I could live with a DUI on my record; I didn't even mind the prospect of being locked up for the night in some uriney small-town jail cell. The horror was that the only person in the county with the cash to bail me out was the very last person I ever wanted to see again—dear old Ma.

As the corpulent officer with the ninth-grade education slowly walked the short distance from his cruiser to mine, I fruitlessly searched for a Tic-Tac.

"You know why I pulled you over, don't you, ma'am?" he asked, employing the mandatory patronizing tone.

"Was I speeding, officer?"

"Probably. But you missed a stop sign a couple of miles back. Driver's license, please."

Inasmuch as he still hadn't detected the booze on my breath, I frantically flipped through my purse and knew I'd be lucky if he just wrote me the damn ticket and cut me loose.

Just when I realized I had left my license and registration at home—another citation—his radio blared, "*A homicide at Blue Suede's.*" The small-town dispatcher didn't even bother with police code.

"I'm there," the cop replied on his remote, then, leaning into my car, he said, "I'll let you off with a warning, but the next time this happens, you'll get a ticket."

Before I could thank him, he raced back to his vehicle and zoomed about fifty yards down the road and spun to the right into a tangle of untrimmed trees. Of course I followed him. It opened up into a parking lot for some large pub. Having worked for several years as an investigative reporter at the city desk of the *Daily News*, I had covered more homicides than could fill the town's cemetery, certainly more than this Quick Draw McGraw. He appeared to be first on the scene. I saw him pull to a stop at the back of the lot at the base of a hill. I discreetly slipped my vehicle between a pink Cadillac covered with silly decals and an old, dilapidated wooden garage.

CHAPTER THREE

I reached into my shopping bag and did a quick change into country casuals: an old pair of worn cowboy boots and a faded dungaree jacket. Then I lassoed my hair in a red checker scarf. To hide my Asian squinters, I pulled on a pair of sunglasses. The dark, dirty roadhouse had a large vintage sign obscured by trees that read, *Blue Suede Shoes Tavern.* Under it was a black silhouette of Elvis's huge pompadour. I sat in my car and just waited. When the cop came back down the hill with another man and vanished inside the pub, I figured they must've just returned from the murder scene.

Since the coast seemed clear I cut right through the foliage and headed up that verdant hill, until I noticed a large old antebellum mansion through the trees. Hiking up further toward it, I spotted some yellow police tape and, just beyond that, the protruding heels from a large pair of boots belonging to a corpse. Suddenly, though, I found myself sinking into a brown rectangle of newly plowed dirt. I quickly slipped through the dirt and could now see that the vic was a large bruiser of a man lying flat on his back. Taking out my cell phone/camera, I carefully crouched close to his face—which struck me as oddly peaceful—and snapped a couple photos. His mouth and eyes were slightly open. Despite the fact that he looked to be in his late fifties, he had an inky black, triple-decker pompadour with thick, clownish mutton-chops. The wide collar on his outdated jacket was yanked up in the back. His white shirt had light pink ruffles down the button line. His black dungarees were caked with mud as were his red alligator-skin cowboy boots. A large, serrated circle had turned the center of his chest into dark red pulp. It was either a ten- or twelve-gauge blast at close range.

At that moment I heard approaching footsteps. Ducking behind an oak, I listened to a second cop asking a haggard-looking man questions as they trudged around the body, corrupting the crime scene.

"Musta been late last night, during the storm. My night man, Vern, heard someone trying to break into the front door shortly after closing. Vern warned that he had a gun and whoever was back there should desist. When the guy kept working his crowbar, Ricky put a hole through the door."

"That's a pretty thick door, Snake," the officer countered.

"If you look at the door, Nick, you'll see he put a shot through the one square where a piece of cardboard was covering the gap that was a missing lock cylinder."

"Bad luck. Why didn't you call us last night when all this transpired?"

"I did. In fact, both Ricky and Officer Shutes looked around, but they didn't see no one. We all figured he just got away."

"No moon last night," the cop added.

"Yeah, it was dark. This clown musta took it in the chest and staggered up here."

"So you called."

"Leon only spotted him here about ten minutes ago, when we called you."

"Who the hell is he?"

"The ID in his wallet said some goofy-ass name, Pappy East."

"Anyone know who he is?"

"Nope, spent the evening drinking, keeping his own company. Left around one, after last call." Sunlight glinted off the barkeep's silver-capped front teeth.

"Wonder why he decided to break in last night."

"Could just be a coincidence, but we didn't do the night drop Sunday so we had two big deposits."

"To know that would make it an inside job, wouldn't it?" The cop reached down and picked up a stick that he used to delicately lift the bottom of the victim's loose shirt. Under it, the handle of what appeared to a .38-caliber pistol protruded from the man's belt.

"Looks like he was packing," the man named Snake said.

After several moments of quiet, the cop asked, "How's your boy doing?"

"He's a little jittery," the old fellow answered. When their forensic expert showed up and started examining the body, taking photographs, I crept further uphill and hid behind a weeping willow. When the men retreated I circled wide and headed back down to the old roadhouse.

A small, quiet diner in the front opened into a much noisier beer hall in the back. A line of old guys seemed permanently attached to the bar, drinking, chatting, watching some game on TV. A minute later the metal-fanged man from out back entered and walked right by me into a large empty room that turned out to be an auditorium. He vanished behind an old door that was probably the bathroom.

I took a table adjacent to the empty stage. A yellowing banner above it read, *Sing Like the King—Elvis In-Person-Ators Contest.*

When a waitress asked what I wanted, I employed my best Tennessee twang: "A cup of coffee and slice of shoo-fly pie, please."

When the old boy finished his business and came back out through the door, I said, "Wasn't that poor guy one of the Elvis impersonators?"

"Huh?"

"The body out back, any idea who shot him?"

"Who the fuck are you?" He squinted his veiny eyes at me.

"No one, I was just coming in and saw him." It was the

middle of the afternoon and they had an open diner; it wasn't far-fetched.

"But you must've climbed up the hill if you saw him that clearly," he fired back.

"I overheard someone say it was an Elvis impersonator. And I've always loved the King, so yeah, I did go up there to check it out, but I didn't mean anything by it."

"Sing the King, do you?" he changed his tone.

"Sorta," I replied, without thinking. "I need a drink. Can I buy you one?"

"I don't feel right about a pretty girl buying me a drink."

"How about I'll ask you a couple questions in return?"

"You're not one of them snoop reporters here about that Missy Scrubbs tramp, are you?" I remembered that Gustavo said she was from around these parts.

"I am, but I'm more interested in the body out back."

"Well, if that's all you wanna know, follow me out to my office," he said and started walking. I told him that my Uncle Hymie from Vegas took me to see Elvis in concert for my Bat Mitzvah thirty years ago, which was absolutely true.

"You wouldn't happen to remember when that was, would ya?"

"Around the week of my thirteenth birthday—September, 1975. I remember him doing karate moves and rambling on about his ex-wife and how they were still dear friends."

"It's true, he did a lot of rambling back then . . . So, can you carry any of his tunes?"

"When I was in high school I had to learn 'Love Me Tender.' I was pretty good at it, but I haven't hummed in years."

"Well, in a little less than two weeks we have our annual Sing the King contest, which comes with a big cash prize."

"But I'm not even a guy, let alone white," I said removing my sunglasses.

My host took the last stool at the bar, next to six other barflies. "Hey everyone, this is . . . What's your name, dear?" All of them appeared to be above two hundred and fifty pounds, and over sixty years of age—except one.

"Sandra."

"I'm Snake Major." Who the hell willfully calls himself Snake? "These guys are a band called the Evils." He reached up over the counter for a mug and slipped it under the spout. He tipped the tap and filled me a frothy glass.

"It's an anagram for Elvis," one explained. "We're an Elvis tribute band."

"You from here, doll?" another of them asked.

"I'm from the next town over, Mesopotamia. How 'bout you guys?"

"We're retired," one muttered, choosing to interpret it as a question about employment.

"Actually, we only perform for the Sing the King contest," clarified another. "Till then we drink."

With that as a cue, they all took sips of their beers.

"So, y'all from Tennessee?"

"I guess, so, 'cept I ain't in the band," replied the younger man, standing up from a stool at the end of the bar.

"What singer are you impersonating?" I asked. He sported a Roy Rogers cowboy shirt with a patriotic red and blue motif in the upper panels and a white ten-gallon hat.

"I'm what you might call a Jesus impersonator," he replied with a smile. "Have you heard the beautiful voice of the Son of God, sister?"

"Only once," I said. "He sung to me that I was on my own." Several of the Evils chuckled.

"This is Minister Morton Beaucheete," Snake Major introduced.

"I assure you that He has a lot more to sing to you," said the muscular young preacherman. "Why don't you come by my church and I'll be glad to fill you in?"

"The minister can definitely fill you in," muttered one of the Evils lecherously.

"I'm at the Fifth Baptist Church, down on Makataka Road," the minister said, looking at his watch, "and I got to scoot."

"It was a pleasure," I replied, and he left.

"So what brings you to us?" an Evil asked.

"I was just wondering about the vic out back," I said, heaving myself up on the barstool.

"His name weren't Vic," corrected another Evil.

"We're now welcoming multicultural, multisexual Elvises . . . Hell, we even have some transgender Elviras."

"That means they got no dicky," clarified another, wagging a loose finger.

"Shoot, the Asian thing'll work straight to your 'vantage on account'a this being the year of Affirmative Action Elvis. *Elvis-clusiveness* they're calling it. In fact, I'll tell you a big secret: the judges'll be partial to a minority Elvis."

"Yeah, you could be like a Clarence Thomas Elvis," one joked.

"I'm not really much of a singer."

"Go *ahhhh*—" He sang a note that sounded like a D-flat. I did likewise.

"See there, just as I thought, you have the same natural register that the King had. I know that cause I worked for the man himself."

"No one ever said I could sing."

"Well, there's a big cash prize."

"The grand prize is ten thousand dollars," said Snake, "and there are smaller prizes also."

"When exactly is this again?"

"Next week is the deadline for registration and the following week is the actual contest."

"I'll think about it. And about the body out back . . ."

"You buying beer for the boys, are you?" Snake asked, implying cooperation.

"Course."

"How about Bushmill chasers?" someone suggested as the bartender came over. I nodded yes, and smudged shot glasses were deposited in front of each of them.

"Make it a double for me," I said, "I have woes of my own."

"What kind?"

"I just got into a fight with my mother. That's why I'm out here now."

"You have mommy problems, do you?" another old man said and belched.

"Don't ask."

"Hey, we all got mothers, don't we?"

"Elvis adored Gladys," said one. "She was his mammy."

"A mother can be a boy's best friend," a third hypothesized.

"In my case she's my worst enemy." I took a deep sip of my beer. "It might just be a cultural problem."

"What? Is she white and you're Chinese?" asked a man with chipped teeth.

"Wow! How'd you know that?" Chinese and Korean, white and Jewish were all the same in these parts. Before chipped teeth could answer, another barfly flew into a racially insensitive joke ending with the punchline: "Two Wongs don't make a white." All guffawed and more beer was brought over.

With each added pitcher, I faded slowly into the brownish wallpaper. As I listened to them yak about the wars in Iraq and Afghanistan and other news items, I waited for some comments about the dead Elvis out back. Although they did refer to him a few times, there was no real story there. A dead B&E perp didn't merit the tabloids, even if he was an Elvis impersonator. And the fact is, he looked more like Kenny Rogers. At some point I finally started asking if anyone knew anything about Missy or her relatives.

"Who's missing?" one misheard me.

"Missy Scrubbs, the missing bride from Memphis, she's from around these parts, isn't she?"

"She hung out here years ago," Snake spoke up. "Diddled one of the younger fellas and was shooed off. No one's seen her since."

"She must've been in her midteens," I pointed out.

"Yeah," Snake replied. "That's why we eighty-sixed her."

"Any idea where she lived?"

"Yeah, with her family down the road. They all up and moved to Memphis when she did and the shotgun shack they lived in burnt down."

So much for any new leads on Missy Scrubbs. The highlight of the day was when the old station wagon from the county morgue eventually arrived. All the men grabbed their mugs and moseyed over to the window to watch as the two skinny guys bagged the body, hauled him down the hill, and loaded him into the back of the meat wagon.

The rest of the evening flaked away like a smoldering cigarette. I had no one waiting for me and the prospect of being homeless in New York kept me rooted to my stool. Still, the drinks kept coming and floated me into the land of drunken burnouts. After the last call, some of the burly beer-soaked men half-walked, half-carried me out into the cold night air where I was deposited into my car and I duly passed out.

CHAPTER FOUR

When my car door popped open, I awoke, still drunk. My hands fumbled through my purse. But they weren't my hands. They had to belong to someone else. At some point I realized it wasn't my purse they were fumbling through—it was me. Hands were crawling up my shirt, and trying to unbuckle my pants.

I shoved the man backward into a bush outside and locked the car door, but a second guy, some slick-haired kid I hadn't seen earlier, pulled me out through the passenger door. Then he shoved me backward into my backseat.

"Just calm down," he said tensely. "We gonna help you get that story about Missy."

"Fuck off!"

As I fumbled with his hands, the bushed one raced around to the other door just in time for my firm kick to his balls.

That was when the one in the car walloped me across the jaw and I knew I was in trouble. Yet before he could hit me again, the hand of God seemed to reach into the backseat and yank him out by the neck, throwing him out on his ass. While I was struggling to buckle up my pants, I heard God say, "Haven't you had enough, Roscoe?!"

"Bitch karated Zek and tried to rob me!" the backseat bandit said.

"Oh, is that why you were on top of her?"

"Ain't like that, sir," said Zek, still holding his nuts. "Vern said this chinky chick came by asking questions."

"What kind of questions? And don't lie, cause I'll check."

"Mainly looking into the dead dude, but she was asking about my business too. She got drunk off her ass, so—"

"I gave you my old car for a reason. Your dad said you had to scat pronto. I thought you were long gone, son."

"I was, I just came back for my passport and thought I'd grab a little Chinese takeout."

"That little tail you got is all over the place, boy. Now here you are with a drunken reporter, playing with a possible rape and assault charge. Normally I don't try to come between a fool and his foolishness, but you're crapping where I eat."

In a moment both men were gone.

"Okay young lady," the voice announced, "now it's your turn. Off to bed."

I tried to get up, only to collapse drowsily back in the seat. But the big hand snatched me up.

For the first time, I saw his face and instantly sobered up. He was truly hideous. Scarred and stitched, it looked as though he were Frankensteined together from a series of dead faces. Underneath it all, though, were baby-blue eyes and a thick wave of iron-gray hair. His back was bent and he had a pronounced limp in his right leg, but he was strong as he carefully lifted me out of my car.

"What do you think you're doing?" I asked, trying to keep the world from spinning.

"Even if you are a no-good reporter, you're too drunk to drive and it's too cold to sleep here, so you can spend the night in the big house."

"Where you'll rape me like some farm animal in a canoe," I drunkenly mixed my *Deliverance* motifs.

"If I were going to do that, I woulda just got on the line, wouldn't I?"

He sounded reasonable enough and I was too out of it to resist. Wet leaves, earth, and dark sky curled around me as he carried me up the hill to the large old mansion at the top. Eventually he pushed open a door and set me down on a cozy couch in a vast living room. The interior of the house was dark. Candlelights, or lights no brighter than candles, seemed to fill the old palace. Thick dark velvet curtains, wooden furniture, black walls, old creaky floors—all very goth. I tiredly watched the brutish, heavy-set man squatting at the fireplace, assembling a small log cabin of kindling. He struck a match and it went up like a midget's funeral pyre.

"This is your house?"

"No, I'm just the butler."

When he stepped out of the room I located my cell and speed dialed Gustavo. It seemed like a healthy precaution to tell him where I was in the event that Jeeves turned out to be a Quasimodo serial murderer.

"Listen," I whispered when he picked up.

"No, you listen! We fucked up!"

"What's the matter?"

"Little Earl's dead." Earl was his nineteen-year-old nephew. Through tears and curses, he drunkenly explained that Earl had become "the latest casualty in a war conducted by one U.S. president intent on outdoing another—who happened to be his wuss daddy."

"I'm so sorry, Gus."

"If just one national magazine or influential newspaper stood up to those liars in the White House, there would be no war in Iraq," he ranted. "If the New York Times or Washington Post wrote headlines that said, No Proof of WMDs, if just one real muckerfucker wrote a piece on the simple truth, those cowards Cheney and Bush would've lost their nerve! Other papers would've joined in. Public support would've vanished overnight and over a hundred thousand lives, not to mention a trillion dollars, would've been spared . . ."

"I'm so sorry."

"Some fucking IUD blew him into a million pieces." He meant IED, but I didn't correct him and he kept on ranting. Even if I hadn't been mentally incapacitated, there was nothing I could say, so when Jeeves returned, I gently switched off my phone.

When he stepped into the flickering light of the fireplace, I got an even better look at the misshapen man. He resembled a human ampersand. Despite his monstrous face, however, there was something oddly familiar about him.

"I'm kinda the caretaker here," he said softly.

"Well, Jeeves, I'm Cassandra."

Something below his thick and turbulent skin radiated outward, a kind of profound yet gentle sadness. He spoke in a low raspy voice. "Are you okay, Cassie?" I nodded yes. "You can stay the night, but you have to leave early."

"Why, do you turn into a handsome prince?"

"No, but the lord of the manor returns. Okay?"

"Sure, thanks."

"Y'hungry? Anything I can get for you?"

"I wouldn't mind another Scotch."

He went to the far side of the room, took out a glass, and only poured a drink for me, neat. He held the glass in one hand and a twenty-five-year-old Scotch bottle in the other. As he hobbled over to me, seesawing his body up and down, I was reminded of a sort of sexy, virile Elephant Man. Though he had been mangled by nature's barbaric sense of humor, I sensed a very thoughtful and delicate spirit locked within.

Despite my initial reaction, I quickly found his distorted face truly alluring. Usually pain is deep and hidden, but here it was right on the surface. It was as though each twisted little contour was a tiny sad face of its own—a trapped audience in that fleshy arena. Narcissistically, all I could think was that he looked how I felt, cracked up yet held together by a modicum of wit and dignity.

"I know I shouldn't say this," he began, plunking down next

to me, "but you might be the prettiest girl to ever grace this old room." When I smiled, he added, "And I'm probably the ugliest thing that ever set foot in here."

"Probably," I kidded. He laughed.

"Just for the record, I didn't always look this way. Truth be told, I was once a young prince."

"What happened?"

"I went through about a dozen windshields and just kept a-goin'." Pointing to a picture frame on an end table, he added, "That's what I resembled before."

A handsome younger face with the same eyes and hair greeted me. "Hello, sexy."

"In a way I'm glad to have left him behind."

"Why's that?"

"When you're young, you're handsome and horny, so you screw through everything in sight. No one is ever good enough. After so much empty sex, you're kind of ruined for any one girl. Then you reach middle age and guess what, you're lonely anyway and now you always will be."

"Yeah," I replied facetiously, "who wants to be young and sexy?"

"You think I'm kidding, but sex appeal is a curse. If you got it, hallelujah. But I'm telling you, everything comes with a price."

"That sounds a bit like how I feel about my family," I said as he leaned forward to re-Scotch me. "I was grateful to be adopted, but I spent most of my life wondering if the orphanage in Panmunjom really would've been that bad."

"So you're a reporter?"

"A reporter without a story." I decided not to mention the dumb Scrubbs case. "I mean, I just got into this big fight with my mother in Mesopotamia. I was heading back up to New York when I got a call that my apartment building in Manhattan has just been condemned. Then a cop pulled me over and I heard on his radio that there was a homicide here."

"Oh, down the hill."

"Yeah, but there's no story." A headache in my frontal lobe started clawing toward a migraine.

"There's always a story, just rarely the one you're looking for."

"Not for me, I'm cursed plain and simple," I said.

"Wanna hear cursed? I got drunk one day, slammed into a retaining wall going a hundred miles an hour, died on the operating table, was brought back, ended up losing my family, got a botched face-lift, and . . ." He let out an exasperated sigh. "It gets worse from there."

"I'll raise your lost family and wall collision with a stillborn child, a failed marriage, and a kamikazeed career." Focusing on his face, I saw tears in his big beautiful eyes. This painfully twisted and brutally damaged man was crying for me!

I leaned in to give him a comforting hug. No one ever wins at misery poker.

A desperate consolation, as if we both believed we were the last two people alive, started snowballing into something much more. His large strong hands, which were holding my throbbing skull, proceeded down along my tense neck and knotted shoulders. He had no idea of the waves of ecstasy he was releasing. It felt so utterly soothing that after just minute my headache lifted away. A few more minutes, as his hands climbed down the tiny ladder of my back, and I just melted into vapor.

I didn't even know when his large fingers breached the borders of zippers and elastic bands. I found myself swooning under his unstoppable flow. Strangely, his grotesqueness unhinged all self-consciousness. As clothes came off and our affections manifested themselves physically, our combined sense of grief made for a desperate variety of love. Though his handicaps limited certain motion, hip thrustings, finger probings, and tongue twirling were not among them. Indeed, the man was bottomless well of energy. Soon, in this bizarro world, I found that each ejaculation only seemed to energize him further.

Afterward, lying in that wonderful healing bed, he asked me more about my woebegone past: How could any husband leave someone as beautiful as me? Couldn't I rebuild my shattered career? Why did I need to drink so much?

Maybe it was the booze, but I couldn't recall feeling quite so wonderful in a long while, and though these tender topics were something I usually recoiled from, he steadily lured me out, compelling me to tell him more messy details about myself:

After journalism school and landing a great job for the *Daily News*, I hit the pavement, writing solid, simple features, working up a street beat, slowly positioning myself to get ever better assignments. After ten years of writing, still in my thirties, I networked with other reporters in the city. When I was offered the editorship of the City desk, I gladly grabbed it. And that was my first mistake. I loved writing and hated office politics. Yet my type-A personality was simply not programmed to retreat. I kept pushing myself at a job I wasn't particularly good at. That's when I started washing pills down with the morning coffee. Then doing shots to unwind at night.

During my last few years at the *News*, I made the novice's mistake of having a fling with a senior editor, Paul, who had been covering for all my little fuck-ups. Unlike me, he was one of those people who grew stronger under adversity. His star seemed to be rising as mine fell. This always made me wonder if it was really love or just pity he had for me.

In the course of our very first date, he voiced his desire to have a family, but for the remainder of our thirties we kept running on our little hamster wheels, sixty hours a week, barely taking vacations, burning up our fertile years in the grind of our jobs. As one of the new breed of sensitive men, he respected my career.

When I turned thirty-eight, we finally married and soon afterward he was offered an opportunity as an assistant producer for a syndicated television news show. Less than a year later he was snatched up by a nearby Fox-affiliated news show where he quickly rose to executive producer.

Around then, I found myself screwing up twice as much and taking triple the blame for it. Slowly little duties were reassigned. The bigger problem was the fact that the sun was setting on the newspaper industry: people's increasing dependency on the Internet—BlackBerries, iPhones, and laptops—was steadily killing it. Old dailies were folding one after another all over the country. Operating costs were being reduced to a trickle. It was all just a matter of time.

Late one night, on the eve of turning forty, I woke up in the little hours with an acute bout of morning sickness. That's when I realized, hallelujah, I was pregnant! I had the best face-saving excuse to quit my job and start working freelance gigs with a morsel of my dignity still intact. And Paul couldn't be happier. His wish had been fulfilled. He was making more than enough to support his new family.

Unbeknownst to me, my pregnancy became the first part of a two-year descent into maternity hell. That pregnancy went to full-term, but the little girl, who we were going to name Jeane, was stillborn. Over the next year I had two miscarriages. The next time I got pregnant, the amniocentesis revealed that the fetus had Down syndrome. That's when Paul and I had the first major battle of our marriage. He wanted to keep the child.

"You never see a sad kid with Down's," he argued.

I simply didn't think I had the strength to raise a baby with that kind of adversity.

We argued about it right up until the legal deadline, before I finally got the abortion. After a series of painful blood tests, my gynecologist explained that it appeared I was incapable of ever getting pregnant again. We went to a fertility clinic and kept trying, but nothing stuck. We talked about a third-world adoption, but as a charity import myself, I found myself shuddering at the thought of it. When Paul wasn't taking a business trip, he was working late. Eventually I heard the rumor that he was having an affair with an intern and felt too pathetic to blame him. We had taken on way too much water. Tensions built up to such a point that simply a strange glance would set off a shock-and-awe of explosive fights.

"Kids are always where things get tricky," Jeeves consoled.

Our conversation lapsed into silence. Like two panicky swimmers, we hugged each other until we drowned into sleep.

CHAPTER FIVE

Early the next morning, still intoxicated, Big Jeeves gently woke me with a soft kiss on my rosy cheek. He informed me that the lord of the manor was about to arrive. I had to scat or he'd lose his job.

"The only problem is," I explained catatonically, "I can't move."

He made me a cup of coffee (which I was too drunk to even hold), helped me dress, then led me to my car and drove me to a nearby motel. The Inn & Out was several miles down the main road. Walking me to the front office, he said, "Spend the day here and sleep it off. It's cheap and the rooms are so cold, even the bed bugs don't stay."

I thanked him for the sympathetic ear and the great internal workout. He handed me my car keys. Before he left I asked him if he knew anything about Missy Scrubbs or her family. He shrugged and just started walking into the woods like some old bear.

I knocked on the motel door for a while until an older woman, the desk clerk, opened up. She introduced herself as Rose. I handed over my credit card and she assigned me a rathole at the farthest end of the old building.

The room was an undocumented catalog of fungi and mildew, but I was too tired to care. Flipping on the light, I saw that it was also covered with dust. I kicked off my shoes, jumped in the mossy bed, and fell right to sleep.

That afternoon, waking with a slight hangover, I swallowed

some aspirin without water, then staggered into the tiny bathroom and under the icy shower, which was covered with cobwebs. I gulped down about a gallon of water and collapsed back in bed. I told myself that except for the few bruises and near rape, temporarily losing my condemned New York apartment was not an altogether bad thing. I couldn't afford the past two months of back rent, let alone any of the future costs. And the owners couldn't start eviction proceedings while their building was condemned. Perhaps in the time that it took them to repair the building I could return to Memphis and dig up some more details about Scrubbs, enough to cobble together a few crappy articles and work off my debt. Either way, it destroyed the option of racing back to New York and just hiding under my overpriced shell.

When the earth slowly stopped spinning, I located my cell phone and turned it on. Among the new messages were three from my editor Jericho Riggs. First: had I come across anything juicy? Any good photos, like of Scrubbs burying his pregnant wife? Then, "Where are you?" and finally, "Where the fuck did you vanish off to?" The next message was from good old Gustavo, who groggily asked if I had called him last night. He was just waking up from a terrible hangover himself.

"I did call you last night," I said, upon ringing him back.

"I suppose I mentioned Earl." His poor nephew, the war casualty.

"Yeah, and you said the war in Iraq was our fault."

"I tried to be a good uncle, but the last time I saw him, he asked me why I never had a girlfriend."

"I remember." Gustavo had told me how he'd come out of the closet only to have his nephew verbally assault him until he was forced to leave his sister Clementina's house. Gus had intended to just let his nephew calm down, but that was nearly a year ago, and in the interim Earl had joined the army and their growing list of KIAs.

"So where are you anyway?" he asked, eager to move on. "I just learned from the *National Enquirer* guy that the Monster of Memphis will be back in two days."

"I had a terrible fight with the Madame of Mesopotamia. And I was about to drive back to New York."

"Don't be silly. I got a lead." He lowered his voice as if he were surrounded by other reporters. "I've located a great connection— a plumber with a big leak."

Gustavo was nice enough, but he was also lonely. His tips and leads were always in doubt. He once introduced me to some garage mechanic who claimed to have sex photos of Tom Cruise in some youthful gay tryst. Gustavo assured me that the guy always delivered the goods. After doling five hundred bucks out of my own pocket, I was given what amounted to a page from a high school yearbook, specifically on Greco-Roman wrestling matches. Any kid on that page could've been the handsome Scientologist.

"I'm just not in great shape now," I explained. Dumpster diving through the trashy lives of contemptible celebrities, bribing their maids and servants for whatever crap they might've overheard, following them to gyms, clothing stores, and airports, going through their garbage cans in the early-morning hours, renting hotel rooms across from them and camouflaging the zoom lens—it was all too much.

"As one of the walking wounded myself," Gustavo sympathized, "I know what it's like to just want to stop forever. Death looks better every day. But until then, what choice have we, my dear?"

I thanked him and hung up. Like me, Gustavo had gone to the Ivy League, then graduated from a top journalism school and became a promising reporter for a prestigious city paper. Eventually he was appointed a features editor. Unlike me he did a fabulous job—until he discovered that one of his sparking young protégés had fabricated details on a big serial piece.

"My sexy own Jayson Blair," he called the young reporter,

referring to the fraudulent *New York Times* writer. The problem was that Gustavo had an affair with the youth, and the series was selling a lot of papers. So he covered it up. But all scandals are eventually revealed and this one was no exception. Everything, including Gustavo's indiscretions, was discovered and it cost him his job and reputation. The anguish of his failure was directly related to the vertiginous height to which he had risen. After losing his post, he drank his way down. Like me, he rarely got too messy when drunk. We were just never really sober anymore.

At the Inn & Out I exited my room in search of the countrified concierge. I needed some coffee. Rose, the desk clerk, gave me a short list of local eateries which included the Blue Suede Shoes.

"I was there last night," I explained. "They had a murder. The victim was dressed like Elvis."

"Goodness gracious," she said. "Another dead Elvis?"

"Huh?"

"If I ain't mistaken this makes their second."

One Elvis impersonator killed during a break-in did not a tabloid story make, but two was a whole different ballgame.

"Was the first Elvis impersonator also breaking and entering?"

"No, he done got himself blown up. Must've been about three months back. He didn't even make it to the Ding-a-ling singing contest."

"Is someone named Major the organizer?"

"Yeah, he started it with this other guy, years ago."

"Who?"

"Not sure of his name, I think it was Carpenter. A rich businessman from Memphis. He took over the old Daum estate about twenty years back. The mansion and the dilapidated barnhouse at the base of the hill. They converted it to the Blue Suede Shoes tavern. It brought a lot of money into the county. That Elvis contest is the biggest thing in these parts."

"I heard. It's next week, isn't it?"

"In two weeks," she explained, "August 16, held on the anniversary of Elvis's demise."

"Ever been to it?"

"I don't much go in for that sort of thing," she said in her twangy Southern accent.

Returning to my car, I got my Dell out of the trunk and brought it back to the hotel room. There I plugged into the phone jack and dipped into the virus-filled river of cyber sewage. I typed *Dead + Elvis + Impersonators* into Google and found no mention of the recent death Rose had told me about.

After surfing through dozens of pages of references to Elvis, I did locate one mention of a John Carpenter who was a coowner of the Elvis tribute saloon, the Blue Suede Shoes. There was also surprising news about the freshly deceased Pappy East. Apparently, along with his brother, he had cowritten a scandalous tell-all entitled, *Elvis, Why?* The book was published roughly a month before the King's accidental overdose and reached the top of the *New York Times* best-seller list.

On the Elvis tribute web site, All the King's Men, I came across an obituary of one Floyd Loyd who did work on the impersonator circuit. He had only Elvised publicly for a few months—this was the man who Rose had mentioned. The detail that surprised me most was that his primary job had been private investigation. He had died a little more than three months ago. His death was listed as an accident. The piece concluded: *He left behind a young wife and seven kids.*

I called information and found four phone numbers in the area with his last name. The third name down, one Wilma Loyd, turned out to be sister to the deceased.

"Floyd's wife Vinetta now goes under her maiden name, Compton, cause Loyd's credit wasn't too good," Wilma said. "Why you want her anyways?"

After I explained that I was investigating his death, she said,

"Vinetta always insisted he was murdered but no one believed her."

"I'd like to help her."

"All she has is that old trailer park, and once the pig farm reclaims it . . . Well, let me give you her number."

When I called Miss Compton, I introduced myself as an investigative reporter, and said that I was looking into her husband's untimely demise.

"I told Sheriff Nick that he was killed," she said, "but he's just a lazy old bastard."

I let her know where I was staying and she gave me directions to her house: "Drive straight down Makataka Road till you pass the church. A few minutes later you'll see Tornado Alley Trailer Park."

This was close to the western edge of the Appalachians and as I bumpily drove along an old fence line, the wooden posts stitched together with rusty barbed wire, past dented old vehicles and dilapidated homes, I began descending into that great gulch of entrenched rural poverty.

It was three o'clock when I drove by the old church, then made a sharp left turn onto the dirt road of Tornado Alley Trailer Park. The place was covered with various types of debris, large and small, scattered upon cracked tracts of weed-strewn concrete slabs. Toward the rear of the property there appeared to be a very large breadbox, which I realized was a grouping of antique recreational vehicles.

A clearing of yellow grass was encircled by an old wooden fence and inside were a slew of youngins. Crawling in the mud, running in the high grass, swinging from trees, kicking each other, sneezing all over, climbing on a broken jungle gym, and dangling from a rusty bar that once held a swingset—kids. The place was like a human puppy mill. As I pulled up, two floppy-eared dogs came galloping up to my car and started barking.

I sat in my vehicle and waited for the dog's owner, checking out this strange improvised domicile. Up close, it appeared to be winched and rigged together from the salvaged parts of several old trailers.

The wheels had been replaced with cinder blocks and the seams of the trailers were hammered and wrapped together with duct tape. Two small shacks that resembled outhouses were tagged onto each side of the place. It sort of looked like two aluminum railroad cars that had slammed into each other, with square wooden barbells at either end. Parked out front was a weathered pickup truck.

"Buck! Henry! Down!" I heard a young woman shout from afar. The two dogs, which turned out to be quite sweet, meandered back to the children.

Vinetta was edging out behind the trailer frantically engaged in some activity. It took a moment to realize she was hastily plucking laundry—diapers, colorful onesies, and little jumpers—from the zigzagging line that seemed to snare every tree within the property. With a long blond ponytail that came down past her butt, Vinetta Compton was photogenically adorable. She was also surprisingly slim considering all the babies that had shot out of her.

Setting her large blue laundry basket down just inside her front door, she finally came over. As she moved across the crab grass, she mindlessly plucked toys out of children's mouths, collected garbage, and snatched up a couple of bawling babes on the way—a multitasking parent machine permanently stuck on high-speed autopilot.

CHAPTER SIX

The batteries of my handheld digital recorders were long dead, which was fine as I didn't want to make her nervous. I grabbed a pen and pad as I stepped out of my car.

"Hi, I'm Sandra Bloomgarten, the reporter."

"Oh cheesewhiz! Not Cass-andra Bloomgarten, the gossip columnist!"

"Well I never had a column—"

"Reading celebrity rags is one of the few joys I got left." She led me into her house and pulled an old tabloid off a small stack. Flipping through it she pointed to an ancient story I had written about the early hints of romance between Angelina and Brad while on the set of their film *Mr. and Mrs. Smith*.

"I didn't know anyone noticed the bylines of tabloids."

"With a name like Cassandra Bloomgarten, how could I not remember it? My god, I got a telescope to the stars right here in my living room!" she said, compelling me to chuckle. Instantaneously, an adorable little girl behind me started crying.

"Ohhh! What's da matter?" Mama asked in a playful voice.

"He stole my dolly doll!" She pointed to a darling little blond boy right behind her. He was dressed in a bright purple jumper with a shiny black belt, and was holding a cloth doll by its head.

"Sterling, can this even be true?"

"No ma'am . . ." He casually dropped the evidence behind him.

"Is that yours?"

"No, but . . ." He looked down at the dolly doll.

"How would you like it if she stole your Tonka truck?"

"I wouldn't," he responded earnestly, then picked up the tattered Cabbage Patch rip-off and shoved it back into her sticky little fingers.

"Okay, Evil Elvis, give me a 'Hound Dog,'" she said dolefully.

Suddenly the little boy, who couldn't've been older than four, silently started mouthing something.

"Do it loud so the nice lady can hear you."

In his tiny whiny voice, he yodeled: "*Ainnotin buttahunda, cryin allda-tine, aintnotin buttahunda, cryin alldatine. Ain caughtna rabid anya ainno frena-mines.*" Even at that slight age, he was able to ham it up with pelvic gyrations and air guitar strumming. Upon completion he took a deep bow, and in a perfect juvenile Elvis, he said, "Thankya very mush."

"Now leave the building," sexy Mama said, even though they were already outside. The child dashed off.

"What the hell was that?" It was the most entertaining form of child humiliation I had ever witnessed.

"When I was growing up, when we did something wrong, we used to have to say Our Fathers and Hail Marys. They were kind of our timeouts. But since the church has become a haven for hypocrites and pedophiles, I make my kids do Evil Elvis instead. The girls do Evil Elviras."

"You must get sick of hearing 'Hound Dog' all day."

"Each of them have a different Elvis number. That way I can tell them apart. And unless I'm drunk or entertaining I make them do it at a whisper so I don't have to hear it anymore."

"Well, you should call Colonel Parker, because if each of these kids can do that in an Elvis onesie, you could definitely get on the *Tonight Show*."

"Much as I could use the money, the only thing worse would be a half a dozen little prima don and donnas."

"I'm here about your late husband's death," I said, getting to it.

"Of course," she said, leading me through the house as kids seemed to be tumbling out of the woodwork. The place reminded me of a story I did on exploited Asian illegal aliens who were packed into a barrackslike basement in Chinatown.

Elvis was the single motif running through that never-ending trailer: an Elvis wall clock, two Elvis lamps, velvet Vegas Elvis needlepoints. Although the place looked sufficiently child-proofed, I could see she was living under obvious duress. The three electrical outlets I could see—though located six feet above the ground, beyond all their little reaches—were octopussed with what looked like more plugs than the circuits could handle. Yet that was the least of her problems. Vinetta, the nonstop mother-machine, was clearly on overload herself. Another girl, little Eugenia, suddenly earned an Evil Elvira for roping her face in her mother's bright orange lipstick and was told to perform her act of contrition—a soft and abbreviated "Fallin in Love wit Yous."

"Gosh, even at a whisper that can be annoying."

"You have to zone them out. Particularly when a group of them misbehave." She paused a moment. "Earlier today I had five of them doing Elvis songs at the same time. What a screechfest that was."

"What is this place exactly?"

"Used to be a trailer park till a tornado struck last year. Everyone moved out except for us. We couldn't afford to, so we're alone here now."

"How can all these kids be yours ?" She looked no older than twenty-five.

"I got two rows of nipples and drop them four at a time," she said with a straight face.

When I widened my eyes thinking of what a great story it would make, she let out a cackle. It was then that I looked up and spotted something in a small plain frame. It looked simply like a fine line, and the frame was placed high on the wall, almost up near the ceiling.

"What's that?" I asked.

"A lock of Elvis's hair," she said. "I put it up there so that none of the youngins can ever get to it."

"Elvis Presley's hair?"

"Yes sir-ee," she said. "It's the only holy thing that Floyd left me. We got into a big fight over it, cause we really couldn't afford it. But he bought it off the Internet with a letter of authenticity and I ain't never selling it."

A duet of giggles pulled us to a distant corner of her human puppy mill. She introduced me to her adorable pair of twins who were watching TV. "Rufus and Cotton, say hi."

"Hi," they chimed in perfect unison without removing their twinkling eyes from the fourteen-inch black-and-white screen.

"Come on, boys, sing Mama a tune," she said, then turned to me. "This one does 'Jailhouse Rock' and that one does a powerful 'Burning Love.'"

"But we didn't do nothing wrong, Mama," one of them responded.

"TV's on," the other added.

"I'm asking you, not telling you. For the nice lady."

Too focused on their cartoon, they weren't taking requests.

"First Floyd had two from a prior marriage. His first wife, a tweaker, ran off on him, dumping him with the seven-year-old, Urleen, and eight-year-old, Floyd Jr. Then we had three of our own—the twins and their older brother. Then my dear sister passed with lupus earlier this year so I got her two, Sterling and Eugenia, who are two and three . . . Give me a moment," she said, as she began putting together some kind of just-add-water gruel for her many hungry mouths.

"Do you work?"

"Every waking moment," she replied tiredly. "Unfortunately, I don't get a salary, but between my sister's life insurance, my husband's Social Security checks, and modest savings, as well as clothes from the donation bins and food from the local church pantry, I scrape by."

A boring adult commercial must've come on the TV because both twins looked up at the exact same time. Probably confounded by the first squinty-eyed Jewess they had ever seen, they stared for another moment, then smiled. It took me a moment to recognize that I was feeling a strange form of maternal envy. About a year ago, giving birth to just one little premature baby would've saved my marriage.

"So when did Floyd take up an interest in Elvis?"

"Well, you know in these parts Elvis is a big thing, so he was always interested, but Floyd kinda went off the deep end late last year. First he bought that strand of Elvis's hair just when we adopted my sister's kids. I mean, we always loved Elvis, collected his paraphernalia, had the kids sing his tunes and all, but for him to suddenly decide to be an Elvis impersonator . . . I still can't bring myself to throw it out."

She opened up a tight closet and took out a big cardboard box. Lifting the flaps, she reached inside and removed an ensemble that could only be called Elvis Presley Vegas Wear. The outfit even included a cape with electrical wires. When Vinetta plugged it in, the entire suit lit up like a chubby Christmas tree.

"Wow!"

"I stitched this together myself."

"How exactly did Loyd die?"

"Floyd was murdered," she corrected, "because he was on to something really big."

"What?"

She took a deep breath and nervously looked to the twins who were staring back at their toons. "He had reason to suspect that the owner of the Blue Suede was instrumental in . . . in some way—and I know this is going to sound harebrained, cause I thought it was harebrained right up to the instant Floyd was killed—but he believed John Carpenter was involved in Elvis Presley's untimely death."

"Elvis OD'd with a truckload of pills in his system."

"I know it sounds insane, but Floyd found something big, I think."

"What exactly did he find?"

"He said that Carpenter had the motive, the resources, and he thinks he more than had the opportunity while working for him."

"Okay," I bit, since I was there anyway, "what resources and motives did he find?"

"That I don't know. I never touched Floyd's papers."

"Then I guess that ends our investigation."

"Hold on. He actually did leave a diagram. Just follow me."

"Look," I said, as it was now nearly dark and growing cold outside, "why don't I come back in the morning?"

"Nonsense. You can stay in his office. It has a cot and electricity so you can read as late as you like."

Before I could consent or reject, she led me out of the house and past several screaming babes. As we walked across the dark field something smelled rank.

"Watch it over there!"

At the very end of their property I could see a large pile of burnt planks that looked like a toolshed that had caught on fire. Between where we stood and the pile of scorched wood, the odiferous earth seemed to erupt with feces like a herniated diaper.

"Septic tank's on the fritz," Vinetta explained. "I've been meaning to fix that."

She led me upwind and uphill until we came to a door that was camouflaged the same color as one of those cracked concrete slabs. She opened it then led me down a few creaky steps into the storm cellar, where she opened a second door.

"This is where we run when the tornado monster's on the loose," said a sticky little girl by her side.

"If anyone knew that Floyd stored his files in here, they would've torched this place too," Vinetta said, pulling a small drawer string, flipping on a naked bulb dangling overhead. Aside from various small articles of junky furniture were several beat-up file cabinets pushed every which way. Magnetized to their metallic sides were drawings and spelling quizzes as well as math assignments with gold stars. Apparently Floyd Jr., the oldest kid, was a good student. Packs of disposable diapers were stacked in the corner.

Against the far wall was a single metal cot. Above it was a homemade chart that appeared to be the product of a paranoid mind.

Dusty knitting twine ran along the wall connecting several fuzzy photos of men to other ill-focused photos of men. It resembled a hierarchical structure that the FBI would create to relate members of a crime family. In this case, the central image that all other photos revolved around was a shadowy photograph under which was the caption: *John Carpenter*, the mysterious coowner of the Blue Suede.

Looking carefully at the picture of Carpenter—a large man walking in the woods—it reminded me of an infamous Big Foot photo from the early 1970s.

"When the toolshed blew up, everyone assumed the files went too, but they were all down here," she explained, pointing to the dented cabinets. Before she left, it struck me to ask why she didn't notify the police immediately with all this "evidence." But not wanting to look a gift horse in the mouth, I kept quiet.

For the first few hours, I fitfully searched through the filing cabinet for that one smoking gun—a clear and simple document that would reveal that some murky figure named Carpenter had murdered the King of Rock and Roll.

As the hours tediously unraveled, though, the files only released more smoke. It was a landfill of documentations, utility bills, credit card offers, bank statements, and endless receipts. Unfortunately, nothing on that twine-lined wall explained anything. There were no neat Pelican Briefs, no Deep Throats, not even any manila files with carefully printed headings. Mostly they were filled with curling scraps of yellowing papers. A phone number here, an illegible marking there. I could feel my hands slowly drying up, just begging for moisturizer. At one point, after hours of skimming, a wave of itchiness hit as though hordes of dust mites had swarmed up my arms. Eventually I found a handmade flier regarding the 2004 annual Sing the King contest at the Blue Suede. On the back, I saw various names followed by hastily drawn question marks. For the most part, the handwriting was unreadable.

All papers I found led to a single overwhelming conclusion: Loyd was one phenomenal pack rat. Along the back wall, behind an old poster of Farrah Fawcett, I made an odd discovery. In a stack of half a dozen Florsheim shoe boxes were hundreds of different-sized photographs. There were also lots of negatives, and when I held a few of them up to the single bulb, I could make out voyeuristic closeups of intertwined black-and-white ghosts.

Usually the photos showed couples. Frequently they were poorly lit and ill-focused, probably taken with a broken zoom lens. Precisely who these people were or what their significance was remained a mystery. One photo in particular caught my eye: a sleazy-looking guy and a younger, cute blond girl. Something about the girl's cowboy boots and longhorn belt buckle grabbed me. In one slightly clearer photo she appeared to be giving him a blowjob, but I could only see the top of her head. Something about the guy gave me the willies, I didn't know why.

By two or three in the morning, I had checked out all but two rusty filing cabinets buried in the back like a pair of upright metal coffins. I leveraged my body around one, spinning it, then pried open the top drawer. It was packed with yet more trash. In the middle drawer, however, I made an exciting find—a half bottle of Jack Daniel's. There in the bottom drawer, I made an even more surprising discovery—emptiness. Odd in that hoarder's paradise. I just couldn't help sensing that something had been covertly removed from it.

Inasmuch as alcohol sped up time and opened part of my brain, allowing me to read deeper into things, I took enhancing sips from Mr. Jack Daniel's. Eventually, though, looking through more shoe boxes I collapsed on the rickety old mattress. Before passing out, I noticed that three of the four legs of the wooden cot had snapped. On the floor I also spotted what I initially thought to be a short, fat snake skin. It wasn't until I delicately picked it up that I realized it was actually lambskin—a used condom.

After shrieking and tossing it in the air, I realized that dear departed Floyd wasn't quite so innocent. Perhaps to get away from all the little screamers, he and the misses would sneak down here for a little privacy. Yet in a family of seven children, where family planning was God's work, I just couldn't imagine him ever unraveling a condom. Looking further under the bed, I saw that even more cardboard boxes were holding it up. Inside them was yet more clerical garbage. Rifling through one, I spotted "case history forms." The boxes held files of divorce cases Floyd Loyd had worked on.

I skimmed through dozens of copies of these case histories loaded with phrases like *subject seen going into* and *signs of intimacy evident. Photographic evidence of infidelity included* was the one phrase frequently at the bottom of them. It painfully reminded me of Paul's infidelities toward the end of our marriage. Feeling increasingly crappy, I finally slugged down the remainder of the Jack Daniel's and knocked myself out.

When I woke up late the next day, my drooling face was submerged in a pile of his canceled checks from the late 1990s. Despite a severe crick in my neck, the only thing I could take away from this endeavor was the answer why Vinetta hadn't gone to the police: Loyd had nothing. No leads, no motives, no real suspects. Nada. For that matter, other than a colorful wall and Vinetta's accusation, I found only evidence of a garbage-driven life.

I clutched my throbbing head and staggered outside. As I opened the busted screen door to the trailer, I was treated to an Alvin and the Chipmunks rendition of "Don't Be Cruel." Some minor miscreant was screeching out his amends.

"Who the heck are you?" asked some pint-sized terror blocking my path. It must've been the boy genius, Floyd Jr.

"She's here to help me find your daddy's killers," Mama yelled from the next room. Floyd Jr. grabbed one of the other kids and led him outside.

Continuing on to the narrow living room, I found that Mama was dressed in a strange sequin dress with a silver tiara and star-tipped wand. She was supposed to be a fairy godmother. There was a plastic drop cloth on the ground and she was surrounded by a circle of four high chairs. Vinetta was playfully feeding the four youngest.

"You've got an amazing level of concentration," she said between spoonfuls.

"Huh?"

"I peaked down there this morning and saw you with your head in the pages so I didn't disturb you."

I smiled politely.

"If you have coffee anywhere . . ." I would've even chewed down some old grounds.

"There's still some on the stove."

I poured myself a cold, thick cup. She had no blue Equal packets but offered me a spoonful of molasses as sweetener.

"You ain't trying to take my mother for some ride, are you?" the eight-year-old asked, returning to the kitchen.

"Huh?"

"We got no money if that's your game," Floyd Jr. said as his sister went through the kitchen cabinets and shouted out items in stock. He was compiling a grocery list.

"I'm not asking for anything," I assured him.

Mama entered still dressed in her outfit and led me into the living room. "They fear the fairy godmother," she said, "makes them easier to handle."

"Can you talk a moment?"

"I'm always starved for adult conversation," she replied as she tried to spoon more food into their tiny mouths.

"I remember reading on the Internet that Loyd died in some accident."

"Yeah, but it wasn't an accident. They blew him up."

"Tell me about it?"

"They wired the shed with explosives and when he went in to get a rake, *kerblam!*"

"Why did the article say it was an accident?"

"Probably cause Sheriff Nick works for Carpenter."

"Floyd was a private investigator?"

"Yep."

"What exactly did he investigate?"

"His bread-and-butter work was for divorce lawyers. Tracking down cheating husbands and such. He was good at it too. He got hired all over the western part of the state. It wasn't exactly glamorous, but it paid steadily and there's a lot of skunks out there."

"Maybe a divorced husband or wife who got a bad settlement killed him," I suggested.

"No, that wall chart says it all—Carpenter did it."

"You really should have gone through his papers before asking me or anyone else to do it."

"I would've, but frankly I was afraid to screw something up."

"That's like screwing up an oil spill. Your husband seems to have saved every shred of paper he ever came across. Unfortunately, nothing really leads to anything."

"Nothing?" she asked, holding her serving spoon in midair for the first time. I let out a hopeless sigh.

"If there's a method to his madness, I don't see it."

"But you're a reporter, you're not telling me you never did an investigative piece before."

"Good reporters know their turf, they slowly build up an investigation. You get to know your players, you have a thread of mystery that you work toward."

"I'm telling you, it's this Carpenter guy! He's your thread!"

"Even if I had a better idea of what was going on, I just don't have a lot of time and cash to pursue this."

"Look, I know the area and people. I can bring you up to speed, and you can stay here. I'll feed you while you're working on the case." She accidentally dipped her magic wand into her food bowl. "In return I can grant a wish."

I went back to my car, got my cell phone and battery recharger, plugged it into a wall outlet, and to my amazement I got a signal. I checked my messages. First my editor Riggs called and again asked where the hell I was. Then Gustavo called to say I should get my ass down to Memphis pronto. Scrubbs was back in town and rumors of his infidelities were swirling like dust devils.

Before returning the calls, I phoned the sheriff's office.

"Can I speak to the investigator who handled the Floyd Loyd case?"

"That would probably be me."

"May I ask your name?"

"Everyone calls me Sheriff Nick, but let me just say there wasn't really a case," he replied. "Floyd died when his crystal lab blew up. The coroner ruled him out of his skull on fumes." My entire body tensed up.

"Crystal *meth*?"

"He had a long list of priors. He had been arrested for using, for manufacturing, and for selling."

I let out a deep sigh. "His wife didn't say a thing about that. May I ask the date of his last drug arrest?"

"Now we both know I can't release that kind of information, but to save us both some time, I'll say it was all about ten years ago."

"So he wasn't convicted recently?"

"No, but we found evidence of the lab all over his property after the fire."

"Where was this lab?"

"It's a burnt-out shack on the edge of the trailer park."

"And you looked for evidence of foul play?"

After a bit of a pause he said, "Vinetta hired you, didn't she?"

"I'm conducting an informal inquiry for her, yes."

"Well, ma'am, I've gone down this road before with Vinetta and some other investigator. Her husband had a sizable life insurance policy. The fact that he got blown up invalidated it. And believe me, if there was even a remote possibility that he wasn't at fault, I would've found it. I think the world of Vinetta, I really do. I've known her since she was a girl, and I know she's under great hardship. But it was a simple case. Open and shut. Some of the locals testified that he would regularly sell ice in the B.S. parking lot. Others from the local mall saw him loading a box of cough medicine into his trunk. Hell, someone else at the Home Depot in the Murphy County Mall testified that a week prior to the explosion he bought two five-gallon canisters of propane."

"Who discovered Floyd's body? Vinetta?"

"No, she was away with the kids. It was his neighbor, the minister. He heard the boom. Like I say, it's really all open and shut, but in the last three months Vinetta has gone on a letter-writing campaign. She's begged and borrowed from everyone who crosses her path, telling some hullabaloo about Elvis Presley to try to enlist any aide she can to reopen the case—but there is no case."

I thanked him for his time and clicked off my cell. Searching through the root cellar the night before, I had seen no traces of ingredients that might be used to cook meth. Still, it was time to move on. Gus was trying to help and Riggs was on the verge of replacing me, just as he had replaced the last reporter.

Making a quick excursion through the ruptured field of shit to the burnt planks where the toolshed once stood, I now noticed little scraps of yellow police tape flapping around the former crime scene. Cannisters of paint thinner, plastic containers of starter fluid, and boxes of cold or diet medicines were all missing. There was no sign of hosing or metal pots to cook the ingredients in. I picked up one of the fire-singed wooden boards and sniffed it deeply. No sweet ammonia scent, customary for such labs.

Still, I was pissed that Vinetta hadn't disclosed this to me. I marched back into that giant beat-up breadbox, where I was about to scold her for wasting my time. But I saw something that jabbed the final toothpick through my martini olive of indignation: Minister Mo Beaucheete—that sleazebag I had met at the bar who allegedly called the police when he found Floyd's dead body—was cradling the widow in his arms and they were both giggling. Suddenly I sensed who had broken that bed in the storm cellar. Disgusted, I sized up that hypocritical lamb of God, who had left those soiled lambskins on the cellar floor.

"Well, looky here," Beaucheete said as I entered. "It's the girl who God forgot."

"She's researching poor Floyd's case."

"Oh really," he said. "Did you discover anything?" They both had this air of concern that made me feel like the world's biggest idiot.

"Unfortunately, I did not," I replied loud and clear.

"Well, you'll have to excuse me. There's never enough time to prepare for a good sermon." And with that, the strapping man of the cloth was gone.

"Vinetta, I got to go too," I concluded.

"You seemed a little rattled to see the minister here."

"I saw him the other day at Blue Suede."

"All the fellas in town hang out at the B.S. and Minister Beaucheete has helped me in infinite ways since Floyd's passing. We go to his church for Sunday services."

"I just heard from the sheriff that he was the one who heard the explosion and found Floyd's body."

"That's cause he's right across the field," she replied. After a short pause, she both divined my thoughts and answered them: "I hardly think he'd kill a man a stone's throw from his own church."

Silently, I looked at my watch and said, "My editor is screaming at me. I got to get back to my story down in Memphis or I'll get fired."

"I really need your help," she muttered sadly.

"Tell you what," I said to pacify her, "I'll try to make some inquiries about Floyd from Memphis."

"Please call me with anything you find." Her eyes were misting up.

I bade her and her band of balladeering children a fond farewell and drove out of Babyland, and back through the maternal hell of Mesopotamia southward.

I didn't know if she, he, or both of them were in on it, but seeing that large lusty preacher cradling that cute little widow spelled out ample motive to eliminate a tired pack rat husband. The only thing missing from their plan was the insurance money, and I guess she figured that if I—a desperate Elvis-baited tabloid reporter—could come up with a weird murder motive, just an iota of evidential doubt, they could all live happily ever after.

CHAPTER SEVEN

En route back down to Memphis, after a forty-eight-hour absence, I finally called Jericho Riggs, boy editor.

"Where the fuck have you been? I've called everywhere in Memphis looking for your drunken ass!"

"Please don't use that kind of language with me," I said. "I told you I left Memphis."

"And then you vanished for an entire day! Christ, I thought you were dead!"

"I was up in Daumland, Tennessee, investigating Missy's family and I stumbled on something big."

"What?"

"Well, it's more of a hunch really," I said without a clue of what I was going to say next.

"You had better tell me something good, and if you fake bad cell phone reception, don't call back." He had anticipated my next move.

"I have reason to suspect," I took a deep breath, "that Missy Scrubs might still be alive." I pulled the lie right out of my ass hoping it might just cut me a little more slack.

"What reason?"

"A tip."

"From who?"

"Just give me some time."

"Give me a name—who?"

"The wife of a dead private investigator."

"What's the private investigator's name?"

"Floyd Loyd," I said.

"You're kidding."

"I'm dead serious."

"All right," he said, "I'm going to Google that ridiculous name and if nothing turns up you're not just fired, I'll have you blackballed."

"He's dead. They said it was accidental."

"Did he live down there?"

"Yes, in Murphy County," I replied, utilizing one fuck-up to cover another.

"If this clown died down around there, I'll give you twenty-four hours, then I'm calling up the next brilliant out-of-work twelve-stepper who desperately needs another chance." He hung up. Life was only getting easier. I called Gustavo to get some idea of what lay ahead.

"Oh my lawd," he said, "I was certain you'd be retreating back through the Holland Tunnel by now."

"I would but my home has been condemned. I have no where to go but Memphis."

"Glad to hear it. I have to return my car to the rental agency by tonight, but my paper actually gave me just enough to stay in a cozy motel. My room has twin beds and a blue movie channel," he invited. "Also, I did find out some juicy goings-on about our Mr. Scrubbs."

I told him I'd see him soon.

We were a partnership by chemistry. Unless he was intoxicated he couldn't work. Though I found it difficult to write while drunk, I could still drive. Mutually imbibed, he said we jointly had the capabilities of one mediocre journalist.

After the long drive back to Memphis, I dragged my shopping bags up to his motel, a Comfort Inn, and knocked on his door. He greeted me with a smile and showed me inside. On his bed was a large brand-new metallic suitcase. Flipping the tiny combination lock, he snapped the latches open. The contents resembled an assassin's rifle case, complete with crisp cut-out cushions. It held a variety of photographic equipment—two digital cameras, a Polaroid with zoom lens, and a heavy-duty tripod attachment.

"Where'd you get all this?"

"Won it in a poker game from a drunken photographer during my last big story."

"Why'd you bring it?"

"Let's face it, they only really care about the pictures. And we got to shake a leg, so grab a camera and let's go."

"With all this technology, you can probably take photos of the future," I said, prying one of his cameras loose from its form-fitting foam. A tiny digital camera with an enormous zoom lens looked like a robotic pygmy with a large steel erection. He grabbed the Polaroid. "So, where we going?"

"Thucydides Scrubbs is back home!"

We jumped into his rent-a-wreck and he had me drive to the Scrubbs estate as he loaded film into the Polaroid and checked his minirecorder.

"What exactly did you discover?"

"That Scrubbs could be innocent."

"What proof?"

"Just a vibe."

"That's probably the DTs from all your drinking."

"I spoke to everyone I could who met the guy and learned he doesn't have a temper. He's not jealous. He's got no history of violence. He's been divorced before. No one's ever heard him raise his voice. He's even been cuckolded before and remained friends with the wife who cheated on him. By all accounts he was cynical about this relationship from the very start. He even had a prenup." Too bad you can't sell a vibe.

As we pulled up to his neatly manicured estate, we saw the ever-multiplying swarm of photographers converging in his rolling driveway. Scrubbs was just exiting his place.

"Return to Camp O.J.," Gustavo said, and holding his camera

like a pistol, he joined the fray. It was like an army of fire ants going after a stray dung beetle. The crowd pelted Scrubbs with questions, shoving their cameras tightly toward his face.

"Why'd you kill your wife?"

"Has she been kidnapped? Why don't you tell the police?"

"Where'd you bury her?"

"Did you strangle her? Did you cut her up?"

"Do you think she's dead?"

"Who do you think killed her?"

"Where's the million dollars missing from your account?"

A thousand questions simultaneously buffeted the middle-aged man as he attempted to act as if it were just another day. I tried my best to shove into that mosh pit, holding Gustavo's pygmy camera above my head, hoping to get a single photo if only to show to Jericho Riggs that I was in Memphis, doing my sober best. Unfortunately, nothing worked. I couldn't get the miniscreen to light up. I was techno-illiterate.

When Scrubbs finally closed the door of his SUV and drove off, a few followed in slow pursuit.

We just stood there with the rest of the First Amendment mob. Gustavo finally grabbed a sterling silver flask from his back pocket and took a deep swig. Then he explained that the grand jury was expected to be filing charges against him imminently.

"I thought he was already indicted."

"Not yet . . . Hey, you should try these, they really mellow you out." He pulled out a burnt-orange container of pills and rattled it.

Right then my phone chirped, with Vinetta's name on the display. I let it go to voice mail. Without asking what the pills were, I gulped down two without water. "Did you say that you had some sort of scoop or lead or whatever they call it nowadays?"

"Yeah, I've tracked down someone who worked for Scrubbs."

"Who?"

"I spoke to a gardener at a neighbor's house who said he knew a plumber who had worked for Scrubbs, and he said the plumber claimed to know or see something hot, or at least warm."

"And you called this plumber?"

"Course. He said it was actually a friend of his, some electrician who learned some vital detail and wouldn't be available until this afternoon." A typical Gustavo convolution.

"What vital detail does he know?"

"Wouldn't say."

"How much does he want?"

"He said eight hundred for him and two hundred for this electrician who had the goods. But we're not supposed to tell the electrician that we were paying the plumber more."

"Unfortunately, I'm broke."

"Me too." He delicately poured more bourbon down his throat.

"Did he say anything at all about Scrubbs?"

"Not a word, but he didn't sound dumb."

"So we're just supposed to just cough up a grand?"

"Well, I thought we could get him down to six, then maybe we can each ask our editors for three hundred apiece and do different spins on the same item." We had done this once before, but we had to keep it behind the editors' backs. They didn't like shared sources for exclusives.

"Does this plumber think you're calling him back?"

"He didn't actually give me his number, but I know where he's working."

"Where?"

"At Graceland later this afternoon," Gustavo said as he nervously opened the trunk of his car. He took out a new gallon-size bottle of Jim Beam and brought it to the backseat of his car. "Maybe I can get the information out of him some other way."

He carefully twisted open his little flask. I watched him trying to control the tremor in one hand as he poured the firewater from the big bottle into his monogrammed flask. We were at the broad bottom of the achievement pyramid, far below the pointy tip of great success. Each little battle strengthened or weakened us for the next one. If Gustavo could successfully fill his flat metal container, even though half of it was dribbling onto the frayed carpet of his rental, it would improve his confidence in dealing with the plumber. While he continued to struggle with the golden liquid, I asked someone for directions.

"Take 240 East to 55 South past the Elvis Presley RV Park." From there we could drive over to the tacky wilds of Graceland.

After briefly getting lost, we followed a packed tourist bus all the way to Presley's infamous digs.

We walked up from the outside gate where we bought tickets. Then, along with a group of roughly twenty-five heavyset people, we were slowly ushered from room to room and spoon-fed tidbits of Presley's colorful life. During the tour we looked for a plumber, but seeing none, I spent the time telling Gus about last night's trailer park saga and the murdered Elvis impersonator who may have been knocked off by his cheating wife.

"That was the only time I ever killed a paying story," he mumbled.

"What are you talking about?"

"I had a terrific lead on Ginnie Laden."

"Any relation to Osama bin?"

"No, she was the last girl the King was dating when he dropped dead off the toilet throne," Gustavo explained. "I was going to sell it for the twenty-fifth anniversary of his death. She had moved to New Orleans about twenty years earlier and married an Armenian rug merchant. Get this, she was living under the name Ginnie Ginnalian."

"Whoa! What did she say?"

"When I tracked her down she was working for the hubby. It was Fourth of July just a few years ago. I followed from a distance taking photos and stuff, and then I saw her go into a Dunkin' Donuts. She bought a cup of coffee and was just heading outside when some kid grabbed her purse and dashed off, knocking hot coffee all over her."

"You're kidding."

"As the guy ran toward my car, I whipped open my door. *Wham!* He didn't even see it coming."

"Wow! You're Starsky *and* Hutch!"

"Actually, I'm Shaft," he corrected. "Anyway, I picked up the purse and brought it over to her. She looked like she was on the verge of a nervous breakdown. Everyone was just ignoring her. We ended up sitting in a booth and talking for about an hour."

"Oh my God, that sounds like a perfect headline story."

"I know, but I saw myself in her pain, with life at its worst. Though I desperately tried to lift my leg and kick her when she was down," he looked off distantly, "I just couldn't do it."

Possibly in homage to the King, Gustavo fingered his shirt pocket and popped down a flurry of little red and blue pills.

"What are those?"

"Dietary supplements," he replied softly.

Our tour brought us to the infamous Jungle Room where the guide, some skinny kid with a hoarse voice, pointed to a fountain and mentioned how it used to repeatedly flood into the living room.

"In fact, it flooded just yesterday," he added.

It was then I noticed some young fellow in a light blue jump-suit. He was squatting near the gaudy waterworks, wrenching on a pipe.

"Is that him?" I asked Gustavo, who was smiling at everyone and everything.

"Who?"

"The plumber."

"Oh yeah, that's him," Gustavo replied, giggling to himself.

"Pardon me, did you work at the Scrubbs home awhile ago?" I asked, taking the initiative.

"No, that was my dad," the young man answered, then, rising nearly seven feet tall, he asked, "Why?"

"Is he here?"

"Pa's at the office. Want his number?"

"Please." As he gave me the nine digits, I typed them into my cell phone. I thanked him as he returned to his leaky pipe, then grabbed Gustavo, led him outside, deposited him in his car, and pushed call on my cell phone.

"Yo," answered the pipe fitter.

"Hi," I said in my best Diane Sawyer voice, "my name is Sandra Bloomgarten, I work for ABC. Maybe you heard of me?"

"ABC, the convenience store on Route 9?"

"No, the TV network. I'm doing a piece for *Dateline* on plumbers to the criminals."

"Isn't *Dateline* NBC?" he asked, surprisingly informed.

"That's what I said."

"I heard ABC, like the convenience store."

"Was my source wrong or did you unplug Ted Bundy's drain when he was living in Memphis?"

"Why, is he complaining?"

"No. He killed over two dozen women. He was executed a few years back."

"That's good, cause I don't give refunds."

When you are not connecting at all, it's difficult to con someone, so I just asked him, "Did you ever work on the pipes in the Scrubbs home?"

"What of it?"

"See anything unusual?"

"Yeah, I saw a bunch of red stuff that could have been blood in the shower."

"Did you tell the police?" I was having trouble gauging his level of sarcasm.

"Yeah, when the wifey disappeared."

A five-thousand-dollar story could be written on this alone if we had photos.

"How well did you know Thucydides Scrubbs?"

"Sid would call me whenever there was a plumbing problem. But I know someone who saw something more. Something that ain't in the papers."

"What?"

"Well hold on now," he wizened up. "I talked to some other fella about this recently. We talked money."

"I don't know anything about that. I'm just trying to get to the truth for the sake of justice."

I could hear the pipes in his head rumbling. "Give me some justice and I'll give you some truth," he finally replied.

"Two hundred bucks for the number."

"Five hundred," he countered. It was half of what Gustavo had been told, but I simply didn't have it.

"Two-fifty."

"What do you think I am, some Okie? You TV folks are loaded."

"Look, why don't we get together and talk in person?"

He gave me his address and directions. I hung up and started the car; I knew I could be more persuasive face-to-face.

"You look like . . . like a caterpillar that ate the contrary," Gustavo slurred. The "diet" pills had reduced the weight of his brain.

After five minutes of weaving and screeching through the streets of Memphis, we were in front of the plumber's garage.

We pulled into an unweeded yard loaded with torn-out branches of old copper piping and several rusty water heaters. A dented pickup was sitting in the driveway. Gustavo was too out of it to budge. As soon as I started walking up the untrimmed driveway, the deep bellow of an old hound dog greeted us. In another moment, the Georgia bloodhound raced up with ears flopping, jowls flapping, and drool lacing behind. Gustavo locked his car door as I stood my ground.

CHAPTER EIGHT

The dog jumped up on me and started licking my face and nose. While I battled with his slobbering tongue, the plumber came out of the house, a short, fat man in filthy overalls. He grabbed his loose hound and peeled it off of me.

"Sure, I remember you. You used to read the news with Dan Rather." He thought I was Connie Chung.

"That's me," I said, even though I probably looked more like Margaret Cho. "You got your buddy's phone number?"

"Sure thing." The plumber made no pretense about inspecting the curves of my body, which were really just clumps of clothing. "So you got my two grand?"

"Chinese people get paid a lot less here than real people."

"Well, maybe you should ask your husband. He's got that pregnancy and lie detector show. Always solving the squabbles of trailer trash and whatnot." I never knew what Connie saw in Maury Povich.

"Unfortunately, we're squabbling too," I replied.

"I'm right sorry to hear that. Good day, hon."

"Can't you bring that price down a bit?"

"'Xactly how much is a bit?"

I counted all twelve of my twenties and fanned them out for him: "Two hundred and forty bucks."

"Tell you what I'll do, pretty lady," he said, ogling the lumpy stretch of pickled organs that made up my torso. Lowering his voice, he continued, "I'll take your two-forty, but you also gotta show me those scrumptious ta-tas, then I'll get that guy on the phone fer ya."

"Why don't I just lay back and shoot ping-pong balls out over your house?"

"And I bet you can, sweetie, I just bet you can," he said, retreating.

"Give me his number first," I demanded, bringing him to a halt.

"I ain't giving out no numbers. I'll dial him up and hand you my phone, but first I want to see yer twins."

I sighed in audible disgust, compelling him to turn away yet again.

"All right!" I shouted before the lecher could walk out of my life forever. "Here's what I'll do. Call him on your phone and let me speak to him, just to see that you're not bullshitting me. Then, if I get something out of it, I'll go inside my car and flash you my breasts."

"Can't see nothing from inside no car."

"Well I ain't letting you near my nudity."

"Tell you what," he countered, "you can stand on the far side of your vehicle."

"Fair enough." I replied, "providing this isn't bullshit."

Despite my Ivy League education, undoing my shirt and flashing my skeeterbites to this miserable man for a possible scoop was more than I could turn down.

"Hold on now," he said. "If I let you talk to him, what's to keep you from just getting the info and driving off?"

I took the most valuable thing I had out of my handbag—Gus's pygmy digital camera—and handed it to him. "If I drive off, you keep that."

"All right," he said, turning it on and zooming its lens like a pro, "but I will keep it." Even he knew how to work the damn thing.

"Fine, now call him!"

"First I'm going upstairs to get my Polaroid."

"Your what!"

"What what?"

"I didn't say you could take a photo."

"The only way I'm going to make up the cash that you're cost-ing me is by selling pictures of you to my buddies."

"Buddies?"

"My bosom buddies," he said, as if it should be obvious to me. "They'll pay big bucks to see Connie Chung's whatnots." He opened the splintery door to his weathered house. "Unless you want to bail out now, I'll be right back."

When I kept silent, he headed inside his dump. If I could make a living selling nude photos of myself, I would've given up journalism ages ago. I pulled open the backseat to find that Gus-tavo had nearly passed out.

"Mission almost accomplished."

"What mission?" he grumbled.

"Just tell me if you see him coming." Pushing Gustavo's sleepy body to one side, I went through the various novelty items—the rubber chicken, the fake vomit . . . and there they were: the poly-urethane double-D boobs with long brown nipples that looked like they had been suckled by a litter of baby hippos.

Totally unlike mine, these rubber breasts were huge and per-fectly shaped. To have a jutting pair of udders like these would've required stilt-supports, but I bet on the plumber's robust libido that he wouldn't notice little inconsistencies like the fact that they were cocoa-brown, while I was a sickly lotus hue. When men are horny, the necessary shot of blood for clear thinking heads right to their peckers. I pulled open my billowy shirt, squeezed the monster boobs over my flat brassiere, and buttoned up, then I tied a red scarf over the rubbery seam where it met my neck.

In another moment the plumber came down the stairs and I met him at his garage door. He was holding an ancient Polaroid camera in one hand and a phone in the other.

"So let's see them panda bears," he charmed.

"First let me speak to your connection."

"I will, but just to warn you, you try running . . ." He held up Gus's micro digital camera. Then he dialed a number and pushed the speaker button so we could both hear it ringing. A moment passed before someone answered.

"Tungston, that you, boy?"

"Yeah."

"Repeat to me what you told me about that Scrubbs fella."

"'Bout six months back, I see this blond teeny-bopper making out with some skinny dude at the Murphy County Mall . . ." I could hear a TV squawking in the background and imagined Tungston parked in front of it in his torn boxers balancing a cold forty-ounce on his knee. "Anyhow, later I realized it was Scrubbs's wife on account of we worked there together and all." The Murphy County Mall was roughly ten miles south of Mesopotamia.

"Why didn't you tell the police about this?" I asked.

"Who the hell are you?" he asked, hearing my voice for the first time.

"Answer her, boy, there's money in it for you," the plumber said.

"Why didn't you call the police?" I repeated.

"How much money?" Tungston asked.

"She's giving you twenty-five bucks," the plumber replied.

"It was two weeks before she even disappeared. And what's wrong with lip wrestling a little? I don't want to get no one in any hot water, cause Lord knows, I've done more than my share of casual smooching."

Interesting as it all was, that Missy was capable of cheating was something I could've figured out on my own. Tungston was giving me nothing.

"Tell me about the guy who she was kissing."

"Don't really remember, to be honest. Just skinny, good-looking, black hair, a little flavor-saver under his lip." He was referring to a soul patch.

"You think he might've worked at the Murphy County Mall?" I asked, hoping that maybe I could use that as a place to start from.

"Probably not. Looked too slick to be pulling down one of those miniwage jobs. But come to think of it, you know what I do remember? He was driving an old pink Cadillac covered with decals and doodads; one of them was a big profile of Elvis."

"A portrait?" I asked.

"Yeah, wait, it was just his hair, I think."

The next moment he had to go. The plumber slapped the phone shut and grinned. It was time to pay the pipe fitter.

"He gave me very little to go on," I said earnestly.

"You got your information. Now you put up or you ain't getting your little camera back." He held it up. "And I know it's worth more than five hundred dollars, so that's fine with me."

"Shit," I relented, as I started heading to the far side of Gus's car. When he began to follow I said, "You were going to let me stand on the opposing side of my car."

"Go on then."

I walked around to the passenger side, where I gave a disgusted expression as I slowly, reluctantly undid the middle buttons of my shirt, leaving the top and bottom buttons fastened. Leaning up on the top of Gustavo's borrowed jalopy and checking both ways, I pulled open my shirt, sending the double-D rubber breasts shooting out like a pair of baby aliens.

"Holy shit!" the plumber marveled, without wondering why I wasn't wearing a bra.

I had to grab hold of that double-headed monster to keep the entire prosthetic from falling out of my shirt. As I squeezed and fumbled to control them, I appeared lustier than if I had just displayed them.

I could see his hands tremble and sweat trickle from his brow as he focused his twenty-year-old camera from the other side of the car, snapping photo after photo of Connie Chung's massive gazongas.

"No one is going to believe this!" he said as he snapped off a fifth and sixth shot. He tossed each photo to the ground without even waiting for them to develop. After his ninth photograph, to my nervous relief, the fool was all out of film. As he carefully re-trieved his prized pictures from the weedy driveway, I squeezed the hot rubbery twins back into my shirt and buttoned up.

"My camera, please," I requested. He took a deep breath to steady himself and slid it over the roof of Gustavo's car.

"You drive safe, dear. I'm going to watch your channel for now on." I didn't have the heart to tell him that Connie had been off the air for a couple of years.

For effect, I slammed the door indignantly as I got in. Gus-tavo stirred when I turned the key and sped away.

"Did we win?" Gus muttered groggily.

"He thought I was Chesty Chung, Connie Chung's volup-tuous sister."

"Huh?"

"I got to speak to his connection for only two hundred and forty bucks plus all the rubber he could photograph."

"Suppose he discovered the hoax you were perpetrating," Gustavo mumbled as he watched me yank the ridiculous pros-thetic out of my shirt.

"Then I would've flashed the real ones, which were less than a hundredth the size of his man boobies. Hell, I did him a big favor. He's going to be in his shower all night, plunging his own drain."

"So what exactly did all that get you?" Gustavo had pulled the rubbery boobs over his own droopy chest.

"A one-way ticket back up to Daumland."

"What do you mean?"

"I thought I saw her in his photographs, but it seemed too far-fetched."

"Whose photos?"

"I think Scrubbs knew Missy was cheating on him. After all, he hired him."

"Who hired who? What in the Fallujah are you talking about!"

"I told you. Last night I got suckered into checking out a possible homicide up in Daumland."

"I'm lost."

"The plumber's friend said he saw Missy Scrubbs with some rural Romeo who drove an old pink Caddy."

"Yeah, so?"

"I saw a pink Cadillac yesterday parked behind the bar called the Blue Suede Shoes—and a cutout of the Elvis pompadour is the logo on their sign."

"So?"

"We're going up to a small town near my mom's house to find the car owned by the guy who Missy Scrubbs was kissing a few weeks ago."

"Well," he mused philosophically, "I guess getting drunk up there is no different than getting drunk down here."

We drove to his motel where he cleaned out his room.

"Be careful if you're driving tonight," said the cordial hotel clerk before we exited. "The weather gal says the remnants of Hurricane Irene are passing through."

After Gustavo dumped all his belongings into the trunk of my car, I followed him to the rental agency and he returned his vehicle.

He came out of the office, staring down the boulevard away from me. When I honked, he turned his large granite head and I could see tears in his eyes.

"You okay?" I called out.

"I tried to be a father to that boy, I swear."

As the sunset faded and the sky grew darker, neither of us spoke for a while as I headed northeast along Interstate 40.

Daumland is loosely a midpoint between Memphis and Nashville. Since he seemed to be in mourning, I tried my cell phone, but couldn't get any signal.

I broke the silence after an hour or so: "There's this young widow who lives up here in Daumland with seven kids."

"Seven, wow! I don't think I've even ejaculated that many times."

"Her husband got drunk and blew himself up a few months back while cooking crank, but he was involved in some funny business."

"What's funnier than getting blown up in a crystal meth lab?"

"I'm not quite sure, but his wife thinks he wound up getting killed by the same guy who killed Elvis Presley."

"You stumbled across all this while visiting your ma, did you?"

"Yeah. She lives in a town right near Mesopotamia."

"Earl was killed in Mesopotamia," Gus said. "That's what Iraq is, you know."

"The cradle of civilization," I recalled.

"And we're the graveyard of civilization. That's what I feel with every new article I write, every fluff piece on Britney and Amy . . ."

"And Twinkle Toes McGillicutty," I kidded.

"Mess-up-o-tamia—that's where we live."

"True, but I don't really think tabloids are killing America."

"No, neither is bad government or corporate corruption or religious fanaticism—but altogether they are slowly bleeding us dry. And for our part, instead of pursuing real news stories like the fact that boys like my nephew Earl are dying for absolutely no reason, while companies like Halliburton grow richer and move to Dubai, we're hunting down supermarket fodder." He then lapsed back into silence.

After another thirty minutes, the rains started falling just as my cell phone picked up a signal. I made a call to my New York neighbor whose named rhymed with asshole to see if there had been any change on my homeless status. Upon getting Wanda's recording, I hung up, knowing she'd never call me back. Despite—or due to—the mix of drumming rain, an Eminem CD, and Gustavo's baritone snore, I found myself growing increasingly drowsy. If my cell hadn't chimed when it did, I might've driven off the curvy road. Checking the display, I saw that it was Vinetta, the merry widow. Wishing she'd just go away, I let the call go to voice mail then checked her message. She said she had made a *big* discovery. Perhaps she had remembered that *she* was her husband's killer.

In fairness, my entire time with her had not been in vain. Because of those poorly exposed photos in Loyd's cellar file, I had a possible confirmation on the hunch I was pursuing. As the wind and rain blasted, I kept speeding into the twenty-five feet of winding road that my headlights barely illuminated.

The further northeast I drove, the more runny red circular flashes of reflective mirrors replaced roadside lights. The outer rings of Hurricane Irene were moving upstate at an alarming rate. No high-speed windshield wipers could've improved the smudged view of dark swirls, which was all that was visible.

Finally conceding that I was driving blind, I pulled over and waited for the deluge to subside. Gustavo slept the entire time. After forty minutes I was beginning to worry that the road was going to get washed out from under us, so I slowly resumed driving.

Around midnight, in the face of a demonic wind, I spotted a sign that welcomed me to the submerged township of Daumland. Gustavo slept through the occasional broken branches whacking into the side of the car. He snored through a ferocious pelting of what must have been golf ball–sized hail on the windshield. It was the roar of a freight train that eventually awoke my colleague from his slumber. As I stared ahead in terror, the first thing he did was pull a Dixie cup out from thin air and carefully fill it with his silver flask. Little streams of water were trickling through the sealed doors.

"Did we drive into the Mississippi?" Gustavo shouted, holding his little cup in one hand and the flask in his other.

"I don't know!"

"What's that fucking sound?" He peered out into the dark netherworld. "We're not on any train tracks, are we?"

At that moment, we started moving, but it wasn't forward. We were slowly spinning counterclockwise.

"Oh shit!"

I had unwittingly driven us into a fucking tornado! As we spun once, twice, three times, I instinctively clung to the sides of my little car. Fearful that any moment might be my last, I glanced over at Gustavo. He was happily slurping from the top of his cup as though we were on a carnival ride.

When we finally stopped spinning, and the incredible deluge started tapering away, I assumed he was still preoccupied with his nephew's murder as he muttered, "I sure hope he didn't suffer."

"I'm really sorry," I said sincerely.

"Where the hell are we?" he asked, apparently hoping to change the subject.

"Near the Blue Suede, I suspect." My car didn't display any noticeable damage, so I slowly resumed driving.

"And what the hell is that?"

"The roadhouse where I saw the pink Cadillac."

"Why is it that every answer you give me only makes me more confused?" He was still clearly out of it.

Since we weren't making much headway, I again tried to bring him up to speed: "Remember the plumber's electrician?"

"Who you showed your tits to!" he exclaimed happily.

"Kind of. Anyway, he saw Missy Scrubbs—"

"The missing child bride!" he shouted out as though on a game show.

"He saw her in a mall near here kissing some guy in a car, and I believe I saw that very same vehicle out here." I spoke slowly as though to a child.

"So what now?"

"I thought if we could find the car and follow it, maybe we can find the child bride."

"Sounds like a great idea."

"Thank you," I said, still driving along through the dark rain.

As I recalled the pink Cadillac with the Elvis decal parked in the lot behind the Blue Suede, I also remembered something else. "Jesus."

"What?" Gustavo stirred.

"When I was in the woods behind that saloon, I saw a rectangular mound of freshly plowed dirt."

"You think it's a grave?"

"I hope not. But it looked like a strange place to put a flower garden."

"Tell me again about this saloon?" He was too tired to grasp all the other messy details.

"Just let me handle it."

"Wake me up when we get to this honky-tonk, cause I definitely need a drink."

CHAPTER NINE

When the blue sign finally caught the glare of my headlights—*The Blue Suede Shoes Tavern*—I turned into the lot, past a couple battered pickups, and drove toward the dilapidated garage in the far corner. Just as I remembered, a pink Cadillac was parked there; I pulled up behind it. In the headlights through the streams of rain I could make out the Elvis pompadour bumper sticker that the electrician had mentioned on the phone. The only problem was that the plumber's informant had described an old beat-up Caddy. This one was brand spanking new.

It was time to show where I excelled beyond all others. As I located a flashlight and took off everything that I didn't want drenched, Gustavo again woke up.

"We'ze low on der drinky. And I . . . I need to take a leaky," Gustavo tried to rhyme. He was grinning with his eyes closed. Even though he was slurring and his bladder was filled beyond capacity, he still wanted to squeeze more alcohol into his system. Since this was more characteristic of me than him, I knew he was still trying to blot out his profound grief.

"I'll be back in a flash and we'll get a new bottle together."

Opening the door was like popping the hatch of a submarine. I was grateful for the relatively mild winds as I walked over to the pink Cadillac and looked inside: two shiny, empty seats. There was nothing in there indicating an abduction, let alone a murder, had taken place. In fact, it looked like it had just been driven off a 1960s car dealer's lot. Still, I knew that if a crime-scene unit were able to dust and scour the vehicle, they'd turn up some print, fiber, or telling residue. So I didn't even try opening the door lest I should inadvertently wipe any of it away. I went over to the wooden garage and tried the warped door; it was padlocked shut. Walking around back I looked into one the cobwebbed windows. Again, no great secrets were yielded. It seemed plausible that the body might turn up under that fresh mound of dirt in the hillside. Taking a deep breath, I trudged up the same hill I had climbed a few days before. After getting hit by countless pelts of Spanish moss dangling from the many oaks like nature's own car wash, I was utterly soaked. In the muddy darkness, I eventually located that-rectangular plot of quicksand. While stomping around in it, my right foot sunk deep into the earth and rose up shoeless.

With no shovel in sight, I got on my knees in the warm mud and started slinging handfuls of black water downhill, looking both for my missing shoe and the possible remains of one Missy Scrubbs. Thanks to the driving rain, the mud from the sides of the hole kept rushing back in with every scoop. Five, ten, fifteen minutes later, having found neither my shoe nor her body, it felt as if I hadn't actually dug any deeper; I was merely diverting the slow flow of a mudslide. I would've kept digging, at least for my shoe, had the gun blast not brought me to my feet.

Scurrying down the hill, I could see a red light spinning through the trees. In the foreground a flashlight was pointing uphill in the woods toward me. A walkie-talkie broke through the pitter-patter of rain.

"Yeah, I need an ambulance pronto!"

Relieved to see that whatever was happening was nowhere near my car, I called out as I approached.

"Hands up!" I heard a sharp voice shout out. Two flashlights from different angles caught me coming down that dark hill.

"What's going on?" I asked, lifting my drenched hands above me. As I stepped closer I could see the body not far from where

I had seen the dead Elvis impersonator a few days ago. Moving closer, I made out Gustavo splayed out over the walkway, groaning. A large old man was bent over him trying to compress his wounds. It was Jeeves.

"NO!" I raced over and pulled his large wet head into my lap.

"Who the hell are you!" a cop shouted.

"His wife!" Only by saying that would they allow me to help him.

"Just hold on!" another cop said, trying to grab me.

"I can vouch for her," Jeeves kindly intervened.

"Oh dear," Gustavo mumbled, "I can't believe this."

"An ambulance is on its way," Jeeves said. He had tied a tourniquet around Gus's limbs trying to keep the blood concentrated in his torso. Yet it did no good. Blood was bubbling out of him. Sitting there, I pressed my hands down over the big hole in his chest, but it was useless.

"I'm going to die here," he smirked, "in the state that Gore lost to Bush, costing him the election."

"That's Florida."

"But Gore didn't serve Florida in Congress for sixteen years . . . He should've won this state hands down . . . And if he did, we wouldn't have invaded Iraq and Earl would still be alive . . . And I wouldn't've needed that drink."

"You can't blame all that on Tennessee," I replied, though I knew that he was half-joking. When he didn't respond, I whispered goodbye and just held him until Jeeves gave me a gentle nudge.

"Who the fuck shot him?"

"We'll ask the questions," said the first uniform who had spotted me. "What were you doing up there?"

"Whoever shot him is a *murderer*."

"You are trespassing," said the single African American cop in the group. "You have the right to—"

"I know my rights! How about arresting the racist son of a

bitch who shot Gustavo!" I yelled, searching around for those fat drunken losers I had seen in the bar who looked like they were just waiting for an opportunity to kill someone.

"Ma'am, you're under arrest for trespassing and disorderly conduct," said the black cop as he and another guy in a Smokey the Bear hat stepped forward. Out came the handcuffs. I was frisked and, still wearing only the one shoe, loaded into the back of his squad car.

When we arrived at the station house, I was led into a small interrogation room, where I was offered a towel and a cold cup of coffee. Then I was asked to take a blood test, which I consented to since I wasn't caught driving and really didn't think I was that intoxicated. A moment later, the inside of my forearm was swabbed and a hypodermic withdrew a small plunger of blood.

"Doesn't it seem odd to you, deputy, that they killed Gustavo in the same exact way they shot that phony Elvis just three days ago?" I asked the arresting officer, who I imagined would be more sympathetic since he was African American.

"I'll ask the questions," he responded without looking up at me.

"Do they know who shot Gustavo?" I asked, crossing my legs so my bare foot wouldn't touch the filthy floor.

"I'll tell you who shot your friend if you tell me what the hell you were doing up there."

"Taking a piss, or at least intending to. We decided to stop for a drink and found the place locked. So I went up to pee in the woods."

"Were you driving the vehicle?"

"Nope."

"What was your friend doing?"

"He wanted another drink, he probably tried pulling at the door just like—what's his name—Pappy East. It was probably one of those old bastards who always sit at the bar! Because I'll

tell you right now, that Snake son of a bitch and his sleazy buddies tried raping me the last time I was there and—"

"I shot him," the officer interrupted me.

"What!"

"I got a report that a suspicious car had pulled into the closed
lot. The Blue Suede closed early tonight because of the weather.
I went up to investigate and saw this strange man holding a rifle
over his shoulder. When I told him to put the weapon down, he
pumped it forward with both hands, like he was loading it, so I
shot him." He paused and added: "We didn't know until afterward that it was an umbrella."

"FUCK!" I remembered the goddamn novelty umbrella sitting on the floor of the car and would've taken it myself, but
the rain was coming from every direction at once. It would have
been pointless using it in a storm like this. He asked me a few
more questions, but I just couldn't talk. My personal effects were
removed, then I was fingerprinted, photographed, and a pair of
oversized flip-flops were located for me. Since I was permitted
one phone call, I dialed the boy editor. Expecting to get his voice
mail at that hour, I was surprised when he picked up. I told him
that someone had killed Gustavo Benoit and I had been arrested.
If he would call someone to try to post bail for me tomorrow
morning, I'd greatly appreciate it.

"Why were *you* arrested?"

"Drunk and disorderly and trespassing, I think, but that
doesn't excuse him."

"Who?"

"The cop who shot him."

"Are you okay?"

"I guess."

He asked for a variety of details, contact information and
such, then said: "I'll call our legal department."

"Thanks."

"Cassandra, I'm sure you're a fine reporter and I'm truly sorry about Gustavo, I really liked him, but in this business we'd rather find the news than make it. We're already regarded as one of the most hated professions, and stories like this don't help us—"

Without even waiting until I was out of jail or had mourned the death of my closest friend, the jerk was firing me. Instead of letting him get there, I hung up.

Led back to my lonely little cell—no other women were incarcerated on that stormy night—I laid down on the hard cot and thought about poor Gustavo and wondered how I would get by without him. I don't think either of us ever felt discriminated against in a major way, but we initially bonded because we felt like two outsiders in a white male profession. Perhaps because he was gay, I always thought of him as my best girlfriend, and felt painfully at fault for his death. I shouldn't have even gotten out of his car, but I certainly never envisioned anyone shooting him. Danger was where you least expected it. As I tried to keep my eyes dry, staring up at the ceiling of my smelly claustrophobic cell, I knew that this was undoubtedly the single worst day of my life.

Early the next morning, a paunchy, balding man introduced himself as Sheriff Nick politely through the bars. Fearful that he might already be suspicious of me, I decided not to let on that we had briefly spoken just a few days earlier regarding the Vinetta Compton Loyd case. He informed me that he had elected to drop the drunk and disorderly charge, but could not dismiss the trespassing charge. He asked if I wanted to call anyone before going before the judge at ten o'clock.

"For a misdemeanor, I imagine they'll ask if I'm guilty and if I say yes, it goes right to sentencing, right?"

"Usually it's pretty informal. He'll give you either a fine or a short stretch of jail time."

"What kind of fine?"

"Well, I'm not supposed to be advising you on account of the fact that our office is pressing the charges, but for a tresspassing charge with no priors that led to your friend's unfortunate death . . ."

"I didn't shoot anyone."

"But whatever hanky-pank you two were up to cost him his life, didn't it?" When tears came to my eyes, he softly asked, "What exactly were you doing up there anyhow?"

"It was cold, we were wet. We just figured we'd stop for a drink. I never imagined anyone would shoot us."

"If you don't piss off the judge, you'll probably get three hundred bucks or three days. Something like that."

"Shit." I had given the last of my cash to the plumber. I asked him if I could use a phone.

"How 'bout that one." He pointed to a public phone just outside the cell and started opening the door.

"I'm sort of broke, but it's only a local call," I replied. I had decided to try to reconcile with Rodmilla for the second time in three days.

He took out his own private cell phone and handed it to me. "Keep it short."

I dialed her number. The phone rang continuously for about two minutes before it turned into a busy signal. Either she wasn't home or she wasn't picking up.

"Is there any way I could get *my* cell phone."

"Not until you're released."

"Damn, I need a number on it."

"A local number?"

"Yeah."

"One sec." He came back five minutes later with a skinny White Pages covering the five towns and surrounding area that made up Murphy County. I looked up Vinetta Compton's number and dialed it.

After ten rings she picked up.

"Vinetta, this is Sandra Bloomgarten."

"Hallelujah! You got my message!"

"Yeah, but—"

"It's like Floyd saw you from heaven and sent me a telegram from beyond the grave."

"That's wonderful but—"

"Do you want to see it?"

"I do, but actually, and I know this is going to sound funny, I need *your* help."

"You? What on God's green earth can I do for *you*?"

"I got myself arrested and I'm going before a judge in about an hour. I was wondering if you could lend me three hundred dollars just for a few days to bail me out."

"You kidding?"

"I wish. I'm right near you."

"You going to the county courthouse?"

I checked with the sheriff who said I would indeed be there. She said she'd see me as soon as she got the older kids off to school. I thanked her, gave the cell phone back to the sheriff, thanked him for his kindness, and laid back on my hard cot for about an hour before a jailer finally opened my cell door. I was handcuffed and led me out to a van where six handcuffed and scary-looking men were waiting. Silently, we were all driven to the courthouse. There, I was singled out and led me into a small courtroom, a large cherry-paneled arena partitioned by waist-high wooden balusters. I was up first. Although a few men, women, and children were sitting in the back rows, presumably waiting for their unlucky loved ones, I didn't see any trace of Vinetta.

A bald, wrinkly, square-headed judge who looked like a giant shar-pei barely looked up during the entire proceedings. He seemed to be reading a magazine as he mumbled, "The People of Tennessee versus Cassandra Bloomgarten, for trespassing, how do you plea?"

"Guilty, your honor," I replied meekly.

"You and a Mr. Gustavo Benoit were frolicking around the Blue Suede Shoes Tavern intoxicated, which led to his accidental death. Is that right?"

"We weren't frolicking," I said softly.

"According to the results of your blood test," he held up a form, "you were twice the legal limit for driving."

"I wasn't driving, your honor."

"Well, either you or the deceased were," he said accusingly.

"We didn't start drinking until we had parked the car," I said emphatically. They couldn't prove otherwise.

"Well, what the hell were you doing up there?" He looked at me sternly.

If I said I was urinating, I'd be guilty of a crime; if I said I was searching for a shallow grave, I would sound just as crazy. I shrugged.

"Answer me!" he barked impatiently. "What were you doing while your friend was getting shot?"

"Regurgitating." I didn't think there was a law against that.

"We don't have a lot of murders up here, accidental or otherwise," he stated. I didn't correct him by mentioning the two recent dead Elvis impersonators.

"Five hundred dollars or five days," he said severely.

I let out a deep sigh. It was nearly twice the amount I had asked to borrow from Vinetta.

"Do you plan to pay?"

I thought mournfully about five more days in that cold tiny cell.

"She's paying," I heard a sharp voice ring out. The possible husband-murdering, would-be insurance cheat had entered the courtroom along with four of her clan.

"It's five hundred," I told her softly as she marched up the aisle.

"Got it," she said, and handed me a roll of twenty-dollar bills with a rubber band wrapped around them. The bailiff brought me to a cashier and I paid. I signed some document and was free. In the hallway, I saw the arresting officer who said he was truly sorry about Mr. Benoit's death. I asked how I could claim his body.

"He'll have to be checked out by the M.E. first," explained the cop. "Leave your number and we'll notify you when he's done."

CHAPTER TEN

Since my car had been towed to an impound lot, Vinetta drove me back to the sheriff's office and I claimed my personal effects. While the little mother went shopping, she left me at a small park where I checked my messages. Hearing an old one from Gustavo, it really hit home once again that he had been killed for nothing, for a bogus investigation that ended up costing me a job. Right then and there I thought life could get no worse. But then I suddenly knew what I had to do. I tracked down the phone number of Gustavo's only living sibling, his poor sister Clementina, who had just lost a son. As I timidly introduced myself, I heard the trepidation in her voice. When I broke the news that her beloved older brother was gone too, I listened to her scream, "NO!!!"

She wept so harshly I found myself shaking and had to hold the phone away from my ear. I quickly regretted not making sure someone was with her before I told her.

"I don't know how I'm going to endure this," she said through wails. "I've been leaning on Gus since I got the news of Earl's death. Now I'm alone." After another moment I explained that I could stay in Daumland until they released Gustavo's body.

"Oh God! I can't even afford to bury him . . ."

"I thought Gus has life insurance."

"He told me he canceled it to pay for cable TV."

"I suppose I can bury him down here," I heard myself saying.

"That would actually be a big help," she responded with obvious resignation.

We talked a bit longer and I promised I'd keep her notified of the funeral when plans were made. She started weeping again, and before I could say anything comforting, my cell phone lost its weak signal. I tried hitting redial a few times until Vinetta's truck pulled up.

"It's a miraculous gift from beyond the grave, and it fills in all the blanks. It's about the guy who owns the Blue Suede," the young mama said leaning out the window. "It even establishes Carpenter's motivation in killing Floyd." Before I could find some polite euphemism for *Shut the fuck up!* she added, "And I ain't letting Minister Beaucheete come by no more neither."

"That sounds very wise," I said.

"Why don't you get in here and I'll show you what Floyd left us."

I owed her that much for bailing me out and had absolutely nowhere to go, so I climbed in. She drove me to the county impound lot where I reclaimed my car and slowly followed her. Twenty minutes later we pulled into the Tornado Alley Trailer Park.

"After you left, I finally got around to fixing my septic tank and found out why it wasn't draining," Vinetta said as soon as I got out of my car. "And that's where I got my divine message. It was stuck in the catch basin."

"What kind of message?" I remembered the terrible smell of her front lawn.

"A small cardboard tube sealed in a heavy-duty plastic bag was blocking the intake valve."

"You don't say," I tried to act interested.

"Floyd musta dropped it in the tank thinking no one in their right mind would search there. He knew that if he didn't pull it out in a week or so, it'd start clogging the pipe and eventually the crap would rupture up through the earth. He also knew I'd be the one to have to fish it out. Course, I shoulda done it months ago."

"It would've been a lot easier if he just mailed it to you," I said as we entered her immobile home. "What was in this tube?"

She pointed to a bulging folder on her tabletop. Scrawled on the outside in black magic marker were the words: *IF ANYTHING SHOULD HAPPEN TO ME, READ CONTENTS.* I opened the folder and found an old leather wallet and read a carefully handwritten statement:

My Dear Vinny,

If you are reading this it probably means something awful happened to me & I'm so sorry if that's the case cause I know I acted a little nutsy for the past year or so, but there was a reason. I was trying to do right by you and the kids. See I stumbled on something awhile back, when I first started doing all the Elvis stuff. It was long after I kicked drugs and was clean and sober so I don't want you thinking I was tweaking again.

Last year, in August 2004, I got an assignment to check out a cheating husband who used to meet his girlfriend in the Blue Suede. I hung out in the woods just above the parking lot during a stakeout, watching the dude's car. Night after night, he left there drunk and alone, but she kept paying me, so I hung out up there for about a week. I passed the time leaning up against an old tree facing a big stump that I was kicking on. By the end of that week that damn stump broke free and tumbled down the hill. That's when I spotted something hard in the earth below. I got a stick and started digging and realized it was the sole of an old cowboy boot, and when I tried to pull it out, I realized there was a foot inside. So I kept digging. That's when I saw there was a body caked deep in there, an older male. It had gotten dark so I spent about two hours carefully excavating it out.

He must of been buried there years ago. Once out, I saw a large entrance wound in the back of his skull. I would of called the police, but being a PI myself, I went through his pockets and that's where I found the rotted wallet, along with the strands of hair and a ring. His driver's license had the man's name: Rod East. When I got home, I checked the name on the Internet and found out that he was the guy who along with his brother, Pappy East, wrote that book, "Elvis, Why?" Anyway, I discovered Pappy lived over in Knoxville, so I called him up and asked him if he had a brother named Rod.

"Sure do," he said. "The sonofabitch stole ten thousand bucks from me and disappeared a number of years back." I told him I knew where he was. When he asked where, I asked what it was worth to him.

"I'm broke since he robbed me dry, so it's worth me cutting off one of your nuts if you don't tell me."

So I slammed down the phone and was going to just call the police, but the next day, since I was heading down to the county courthouse working on another case, I ran Rod East's name thru their computer and guess what I came up with? Other than a Rodney H. East in Harrison County, I discovered that John Carpenter, the secretive owner of the Blue Suede, had legally changed his name to Rod East seven years back!

I initially thought the body was Rod East, but after reading that I was confused. I wondered if the dead guy had burgled the Daumland mansion and took Carpenter's (who changed his name to Rod East) wallet. Carpenter must of put the bullet in this guy's head instead of calling the police. I figured he probably buried the body out there himself. Then I did something kind of gross, Vinetta. Since he was dead anyways and I couldn't exactly store the whole rotting corpse, I went back the next night with a shovel and chopped off one of his hands. Doing a little more math here, I figured Carpenter is loaded. He must of stole ten grand years ago from his own brother, then partnered up with Snake Major and opened the Blue Suede Shoes. If that weren't enough, what kind of roadside tavern did he have? An Elvis bar. And who was he, the guy who wrote the big exposé on Elvis Presley, causing the King a lot of heartache during the last months of his life. So I added one plus one and thought, okay, there's no reason I can't cut myself a slice out of this little pie, but (here's the weird part) in Rod East's stolen wallet, I found this tiny envelope and written on it in faint pencil were the words "Elvis's Hair." This was the thing that got me going crazy into Elvis with the Sing the King and all. Inside that little envelope was a clump of hair, but it was white as snow! Yet Elvis never lived to see his hair turn white, did he? That means either this was someone else's hair (which seemed most likely), or someone robbed Elvis's grave and peroxided his hair white, or Elvis Presley, the King of Rock & Roll, is still alive somewhere. Now I don't believe in UFOs, Santa Claus, or Elvis being alive, and I was content to leave well enough alone, but that brings us to that crazy day earlier this year, when I saw that strand of Elvis's hair on eBay for eight hundred dollars. I figured it was worth the gamble and bought it. What you don't know is I spent another five hundred having it tested against the white hairs in the old wallet. Sure enough, there was a 97 percent match! So I figured this was the real reason why the burglar had broken into John Carpenter's house. Carpenter must know where the King is, right?

Anyway, I heard that Carpenter is only around during Sing the King, and even then, he only comes out to shake hands with the winner. There isn't even a photo of the guy. So that's why I was practicing on becoming an Elvis impersonator. But then we suddenly inherited two more kids when your poor sister passed, so I figured that instead of waiting three more months I'd speed things up a bit. So what I did was I anonymously contacted the coowner of the Blue Suede, Snake Major, and said I found Rod East's old wallet with gray strands of Elvis hair. (I didn't say anything about the burglar's body, let alone that I chopped off his hand for safe keeping.) I offered to give Major the wallet and hairs for a bargain price of fifty thousand dollars. Now if you're reading this, things didn't go exactly as I had hoped, but I want you to know I did this for us, Vinny, so we could get a big old place somewhere for the kids to get them out of this toy house we live in. Anyway, you're sleeping as I'm writing this. But tomorrow, if Major leaves the money, I'll tear this letter up and all you'll know is that life will be a whole lot easier. I'll give him the wallet fair and square.

If, however, you're reading this and something awful has happened to me, I wanted you to have some idea of what went on. But just to be on the safe side, I still left the burglar's hand in a box of frozen *vegetables in the back of the fridge for evidence. (I figure they've probably already disposed of the rest of his body.)*

So that's about it. If John Carpenter did turn out to be Rod East and he knows where Elvis is, and if it turns out he did something awful to the King, well then I'm glad I died trying to extort the old bastard. I figured this is our one big shot at getting out of the trailer park before the next big twister blows us all to kingdom come. Anyhow, if this whole thing turns up snake eyes, I don't want you doing nothing cause Carpenter has Sheriff Nick in his pocket and he could flip around and bite you like an old water moccasin. I just didn't want you spending your entire life wondering, and I know you know I love you & all our babes.

I'll be waiting for you on the softest cloud up in heaven,
Floyd

As I finished this sad yet moronic letter, I heard Vinetta silently weeping into a hanky. I opened the decayed leather wallet that accompanied it and looked inside. Other than thirty-two bucks laced with crud and algae, I saw only one rotten piece of ID—a driver's license. The photo was almost entirely blackened, only revealing the outline of a man's head. The name, however, read, *Rodney East.* His birthday was listed as May 2, 1943.

"Where exactly are these gray hairs that supposedly belong to Elvis Presley?" I asked Vin. Still weeping, she simply shook her head, then said she hadn't found any gray strands. This was unfortunate as that would probably have made the biggest story of the new century.

Recovered methhead Floyd Loyd had launched an interesting little investigation. His biggest flaw was getting himself killed while trying to extort John Carpenter (now Rod East?). The other mistake Floyd made had cost the life of the recent Elvis impersonator, Pappy East, who I witnessed when I first stumbled across this damn case. Pappy had probably star-sixty-nined Floyd's phone call inquiring about his brother Rod, and subsequently tracked him down to this area. From here, it was just a short hop over to the Elvis cover bar. Pappy must've come face-to-face with his elusive brother, the Cain to his Abel, who had run off with the money the two had made on their best-selling Elvis tell-all. I vaguely remembered the peaceful expression on the dead man's face. It did not convey the shock that most would've expected when getting a shotgun blast from one's own brother.

"Is there a severed hand in your fridge?" I asked Vin.

"I saw the top of a mysterious box of corn buried in the bottom of my icebox. For the life of me, I couldn't pry it out." Looking out the window at the dark silhouette of a small church missing its steeple, she added, "Shit, that must've been what he was looking for."

"What are you talking about?"

"One night after we . . . I saw Reverend Mo digging holes out back. When I asked what was up, he asked if Loyd had buried a cat or something cause its scent was driving his dog nuts. But I was suspicious cause the smell out there was so bad already."

"When did you first start sleeping with him?"

"If you're suggesting that I cheated on Floyd . . ."

"We know that he hangs out with those guys at the Blue Suede, and we know that *they* know that Floyd had that hand, and they want it back."

"We never did nothing while Floyd was alive."

"When did it start?"

"I guess we first . . . dated about two months after Floyd died." It appeared to finally be sinking in that the minister could be involved in her husband's murder. "Shit, he lived nearby and he'd always be helping me around the house with the children and all. How can I be so stupid!"

"So he did chores for you?"

"Yeah," she said with a quiet disdain.

I remembered that empty bottom drawer in the storm cellar

office and wondered if the minister or someone from the Blue Suede had removed the Elvis gray hairs? For the first time, I also wondered about that last rusting filing cabinet pushed all the way up against the wall, the one I never reached.

"If that bastard did anything to my Floyd, I mean, God!"

"Let me ask you something," I said tensely. "How much is the policy for?"

"What policy?"

"Floyd's life insurance policy."

"What insurance policy?" she shot back.

"Sheriff Nick said he had a policy."

"That's a bold-faced lie!"

"How about the crystal meth lab, is that also a lie?"

"Yes! He never had no lab!" she shouted back. I stared at her silently until she added, "I mean, he did once. Years ago, before I knew him. But he was done with all that when we hooked up. They knew all about it and decided to try to frame him with the explosion. But I was in that shed every day and I know for a fact that since we were together, Floyd never cooked up nothing. Never used nothing! Never sold nothing! And he coulda too. He kept saying that if he started manufacturing and selling narcotics again, he coulda got us outta this place in a flash, but he wasn't going to do that to us. You've gotta believe me."

"You could have told me this before."

"I swear on the lives of my little ones, Sandy. He didn't cook no drugs."

Although I initially doubted her, Floyd's letter looked credible. Still, cynic that I am, I would've probably wished her good luck, then paid her back the five hundred bucks with a generous gratuity as soon as I could. But Gustavo's big face rose in my mind like a full moon. He would've looked into this—particularly when he was self-righteously intoxicated.

Additionally, I recalled how suspicious and menacing Snake was about what I might've seen that very first day I stepped into the Blue Suede. I also recalled how delicately Sheriff Nick had questioned me before releasing me that morning. Something was definitely up.

They must have received the extortion letter from Floyd and dug up the corpse buried in the back. That would explain the large rectangle of tilled soil where I had fruitlessly searched for Missy's body. It was right below a large oak tree.

By now, they had probably incinerated the burglar's body. Though the hand in the freezer was evidence of possible foul play, it alone proved nothing.

"Can the Elvis connection help?" Vin added.

"Only if you can find Elvis's gray hairs that Floyd mentioned."

She looked helplessly around the unswept floor of the little kitchen.

"Let me ask you another question," I said, shifting back to my original mission. "You don't know if your husband worked for a man or woman named Scrubbs, do you?"

"You mean like Missy Scrubs, that child killed by that black guy down in Memphis?"

"Yeah, but there's no evidence he killed her." Suspicion was too frequently equated with guilt in the press.

"Floyd never mentioned her to me, but he rarely talked about his cases at all."

So I had a decomposed hand, a rotten wallet, two dead Elvis impersonators (actually, Pappy was only loosely dressed like the King), and an unsubstantiated claim of Elvis's gray hairs suggesting the King of Rock was still alive out there somewhere. I might be able to spin out a couple tabloid pieces, but as far as justice for Floyd—no way. It was difficult to believe Vinetta's husband tried extorting Carpenter with such scant evidence. The only thing that really gave credence to Floyd's story was the fact that he had been killed. That's when the answer came to me: "The only chance we have of seeing any money or, for that matter, getting any justice for Floyd is picking up where he left off. But we have to do it right this time."

"What are you talking about?"

"You got seven kids. You live on scraps, and as your husband said in his valediction, it's just a matter of time before another tornado hits. This Carpenter guy owns the biggest mansion and most successful bar in the county. Let's extort the son of a bitch!"

"Extort him with what?"

"That thing in your freezer," I explained. "We probably got it and they probably want it."

"How much do you think we can get for it?"

"Floyd asked for fifty thousand dollars. I think we should stick with that. That'll let them know that we're picking up where he left off and that if they try killing us, it'll just keep coming."

"Then what's our next move?"

"You live fifteen minutes away from the Blue Suede and have seven kids. The minister is probably keeping an eye on you for them. I don't think you should do anything. I, on the other hand, live in New York City. This is my last trip to this neck of the woods. I can do what Floyd *tried* to do, only this time I'm going to stick to his original plan."

"What plan?"

"Instead of approaching that bastard Snake, we go right to his recluse, this John Carpenter guy. I'll tell him that I know he killed this burglar and show him Polaroids of the man's hand."

"Are you going to mention Floyd's death?"

"No, we don't have adequate proof that they killed him. Let's just stick with what we can prove. There is probably a missing person's report on this guy somewhere. At the very least we can get the hand fingerprinted."

"Hardly anyone's ever seen this Carpenter fella," she said. "How're you going to find him?"

"The same way Floyd was going to do it. Have you ever gone to this Sing the King ding-a-ling?"

"Just once. But it's usually mobbed so now I stay away."

"Floyd's letter says Carpenter judges it himself. I heard they're going multicultural this year, so I'll sign up and hang out there."

"What if they grab you and torture you until you give them the hand?"

"They didn't shoot or beat Floyd. They planted a bomb along with incriminating evidence in the toolshed. It was a very careful and patient murder."

"So why won't they come after you?"

Violence against journalists was nothing new. Twice I had been attacked on the job. Once a ridiculously corrupt assembly-man whacked me with his cane, which left a red welt on my back. I was able to get him convicted for fourth-degree assault. The second time I was punched in the stomach by an old, fat-ass slumlord who I slugged right back, sending him to the curb with a broken hip. Both times only invigorated me. I sure as hell had never let fear govern my life.

"I'll just have to convince him that if he does that, the hand will go to the FBI along with a letter prompting an investigation into my death."

"They killed Floyd," she repeated.

"Cause he didn't scare the living shit out of them!" I replied, fueled by Gus's death. I had gone down this road before.

"Suppose Carpenter goes to the sheriff and *we* get arrested for extortion?" she wisely asked.

"It's your call, Vinetta. But nothing comes without a fight."

"Can I sleep on it?" she asked. I told her to go ahead.

She spent the afternoon outside with the kids while I took a nap in the storm cellar. When I awoke, I headed into the house in time to hear her playing her answering machine and murmuring, "Son of a bitch!"

"What's the matter?"

"Beaucheete just asked me if I wanted to join him for a drink at the B.S. Bastard! Using me like a fool and thinking I'll just merrily go with him and have a drink with those old farts who killed my Floyd." She snatched up the phone and said, "I'm going to give that son of a bitch a piece of my mind—"

"Hold on!" I stopped her. "You end things abruptly, they'll know something's up. I'm sure they're keeping tabs on you through him."

"Shin splints!" She slammed the phone down.

"You almost cursed!" chimed in Floyd Jr. from the living room, "You got to sing Elvis."

Vinetta ignored him.

"Do you know them?" I asked.

"Who?"

"Those barflies who hang out there."

"You mean that group who make up the band? I know a couple names, but I don't really know any of them personally."

"I just keep thinking that they must be Carpenter's little posse," I said. "They've got to be the ones behind his dirty little tricks."

"If it'll help, I can probably go to the bar with Mo and see what I can come up with. I mean, they've all seen me in there, so I'm sure I can blend in."

"If you can get their names I can check them out, but I don't want you taking any risks or doing anything crazy."

"It'll probably take a few nightcaps to casually get all their names. The only problem is I'll need someone to babysit."

The idea of handling seven kids at once filled me with a sudden dread I had never known while doing investigative reporting. "I don't know if I can babysit that many at once."

"They're a well-trained group, not nearly as bad as you think. Most of them are fast asleep by eight."

"All right, if you risk it, so will I," I said.

She clasped my hand and thanked me profusely for taking up her case. I could see she was touched that someone was finally listening to her.

I didn't tell her that I wasn't really doing it for her. I barely knew her, and normally no amount of money would compel me to take a risk like this. I was a reporter, not a private investigator. Although I was grateful for her bailing me out, the boundless guilt from losing Gus tormented me every waking moment. I knew myself well enough to suspect that if I just went back to my homeless, unemployed life, I would hit the bottle until I killed myself. At the very worst, this seemed like a relatively noble—if slightly clownish—way to die.

CHAPTER ELEVEN

For the next few nights, around eight o'clock, Floyd Jr. and his oldest sister would finish the dishes and help Ma put the younger ones to bed before jumping in themselves. Then Vinetta would tug on a nice dress and head out to the B.S. where she'd meet up with Minister Beaucheete and absorb as much information as she could over a few drinks. During the daylight hours, I drove over to the parking lot of the pub and would set up one of Gus's cameras with a long lens. Though I was hoping to find the mysterious Mr. Carpenter, I was only able to get photos of the five or so drunks who seemed permanently balanced on barstools inside. At the week's end, we went into the root cellar and put together a wall of real names and identities, replacing Floyd's fanciful artwork.

It wasn't so bad babysitting the kids at night. Slowly they grew on me. One night when I was putting Urleen to bed, she asked me about the shape of my eyes.

"If you want to know whether they hurt," I anticipated, "the answer is a little, but just along the edges."

"No, I was just wondering if you can see in small places, like through keyholes and stuff."

"Oh yeah, I can see through walls. Sometimes if I squint really hard I can see right into a person's heart."

"No, but . . . but do you see things like this." She pulled open her eyes really wide. "Or do you see like this?" She squeezed them so they were nearly shut.

"I guess I see things the same way you do."

"Then why are they like that?"

"It's strange," I said softly. "People from every part of the world are a little different—different colors, different shapes, different food and languages—and yet when you really get to know them, you find that they are all really pretty much the same."

She scratched her head and thoughtlessly gave me a kiss, which I happily returned, then closed her eyes.

Slowly the information started coming together. The first target of my investigation was Snake Major. We already knew everything we needed to know about him—a major snake. Next was a tall skeleton named Leo Jones, who farted frequently and referred to them as his "air babies." Vern Lawrence seemed to think that dogs were leashed to poles as a public service, so that they could be kicked. Irv Packer allegedly had a slew of kids—black, white, brown, and round children scattered all around the county. He didn't know exactly how many, or where they all were—he probably didn't even know where they all came from. Finally there was Ernie Dreysdale, who liked heavyset girls, the fatter the better. His supreme sexual fantasy he had confessed to all one night was to have a human she-hippo forklifted down upon his skinny, quivery midsection.

After four anxious evenings of babysitting and reconnaissance, Vinetta's little investigation came to an abrupt end when the minister drunkenly grabbed at her breasts. She smacked him across the mouth and said it was officially over between them. I was eternally grateful. They had publicly broken up so there would be no suspicions as to why, and my babysitting sentence was over.

The next afternoon I called Blue Suede and told them I wanted to enter their upcoming Sing the King contest.

"Then you best hightail it in here quick, sweet'em," said the rough male voice on the phone, "cause deadline's in three days."

"I'll do just that."

"And I hope you have somewhere to stay cause every hotel and motel in the county's been booked for months."

"I took care of that," I replied. "I just need to know exactly what I have to prepare for."

He explained that I had to pay a twenty-five-dollar entry fee that was nonrefundable. In addition to providing my own costume, the format involved singing one Elvis hit for the preliminaries. If I made it through that stage, I had to sing about fifteen minutes of Elvis for the finale—usually three songs. The odds that I was going to memorize and learn three Elvis tunes better than anyone else in the contest seemed highly unlikely. But I only had to be there long enough to get a lay of the land and find this Carpenter fellow. Additionally, I had the slight advantage that the judges this year were looking for multicultural Elvises.

"You're also permitted to make some ad hoc Elvis-like remarks," he added, "but you can't use profanities, or say anything controversial. That's an automatic disqualification."

"I wasn't planning on it."

"Well, we had an Extreme Elvis in the past who flashed the audience, and this year the contest is being filmed for several local TV channels," he said proudly.

"Which ones?" I had no desire for any more publicity than absolutely necessary.

"Channel 37 in Nashville, Channel 28 in Memphis, and Channel 22 in Chattanooga."

My call waiting pinged, so I thanked him and took it. It was the Murphy County morgue informing me that I could claim the body of Gustavo Benoit as well as his death certificate. I explained that I would not be able to collect the body for a few days. They explained that I had one week before he would be buried in a county field—very nice, considering they killed him.

His sister Clementina had specifically asked if I would handle burial. The only problem was, having started out broke, I was now *very* broke, living on new credit card debt paying off old credit card debt. Since I knew many of the upper-management people Gus had worked for as a journalist and I was not too proud, I spent the next day inviting them all down to the funeral, knowing full well that none of them would travel to a small town in the middle of nowhere. Fortunately, money alleviated their guilt. After calling and e-mailing about half a dozen of his more successful friends, I half-begged, half-borrowed more than enough—about five grand—for the Gustavo Funeral Fund.

Again Vinetta came to my rescue with ground support. In addition to poor Floyd, she had buried a slew of relatives, so she personally contacted a small funeral parlor run by a distant cousin. For thirty-three hundred, they organized a cheap, tasteful funeral, and the director knew of a bargain plot of land nearby. In fact, it was located in my mom's hometown of Mesopotamia. Apparently, a field that had once been the site of a minor civil war skirmish had recently been redesignated as Patriot Hills Cemetery, and bodies were just pouring in. After making the arrangements, I called Clementina and asked if she would be coming down for his funeral in two days.

"Tell me where and I'll be there," she said stoically.

Two mornings later, Clementina arrived on a Greyhound bus. When I picked her up at the station, I was surprised to see that she had brought along her two beautiful teenage daughters. She explained that though they could spend the night if necessary, there was a bus returning at seven. I assured her that I'd have them on it.

I put their bags in the trunk and drove them down to the funeral parlor, where the girls sat before his open coffin. Clementina took out a photograph of her son Earl, proud in his uniform, and slipped it alongside Gustavo's little pillow, then kissed him on the pancaked makeup covering his swollen cheeks. After a quick service from a local African American minister, they closed his lid forever. A group from the parlor carried his budget coffin to an awaiting hearse. Clementina and her girls joined me in my car and we began the small procession. Vinetta and her kids, all in their Sunday best, followed in her truck. Together we returned poor Gustavo to the earth from where we are all on loan. Clementina and I wept. Afterward Vinetta led us to Somerville's, the nicest little restaurant in the area, and we all got early-bird specials. Vinetta's children settled down and she politely asked Clementina about Gustavo, what made him the man he was. Clementina recounted a few ancient memories of growing up together in the turbulent 1960s when the old South was still casting off the last vestiges of its antebellum past.

"I firmly believe that seeing all those sit-ins and marches and freedom rides compelled him to serve as a witness for all injustices. And journalism was the best place to testify."

After I paid for the dinner, Vinetta and her kids went home. I brought Clementina and her two quiet girls back to the bus stop. Before leaving them, I offered Clementina her brother's belongings that he had left in my car. She only took a few personal effects.

"If you could donate his clothes to Goodwill I'd appreciate it." I handed her his expensive suitcase of photographic gear. "I'm sure Gus would want you to have that," she said, "to report the truth." I didn't have the heart to say that tabloid journalism was frequently the opposite of truth.

After some hugs, they said goodbye and stepped up onto the seven o'clock bus. That night, I fell asleep weeping.

I awoke early the next morning to the dull thuds of Vinetta chipping something from out of the bottom of her old fridge.

Flipping on my Dell, I dialed up and went online, surfing for images of Blue Suede's in-house band—the Evils. Nothing came up. It was only while typing in each of their names—Irv, Snake, Ernie, Vern, and Leo—that I had a mundane revelation. Rearranged, the first letter of each of their names spelled out E-L-V-I-S.

Later that morning, as I continued my research, Vinetta dropped a small box on the table next to me.

"You can do what you want with that," she informed me, "but I don't want it mixing with the food." It was Floyd's boxed hand that she had been excavating from her fridge all morning.

"Can we leave it somewhere to defrost?"

She put it in a bucket under the sink in the laundry room. I assured her not to worry. The ghoulish task of fingerprinting it would be done far from the children.

"I'm signing up for the Sing the King thing," I declared. "If you've got any pointers that Floyd might've shared with you . . ."

Vinetta directed me to Floyd's boxes of Elvis videos in the storm shelter. Tapes of the King's movies, live concerts, and interviews were all brought into the house. Upon selecting "Are You Lonesome Tonight?" as my feature song, my next three favorites were "Viva Las Vegas," "Suspicious Minds," and "In the Ghetto." I handcopied the lyrics to each song off an Elvis web site. Then I spent the afternoon repeating the words over and over, pressing them into the dry hard clay of my unretentive memory. As I watched the performance tapes, the twins and other youngins sang along, using the opportunity to fine-tune their own words of penance.

The next day, while all the kids were out, I chanted the four songs over and over as I secured an inkblotter, two sheets of white paper, and a pair of old dishwashing gloves. Using a pencil, I drew five little boxes on the two pieces of paper and in the top of each box I wrote, *Pinky, Ring, Middle, Index,* and *Thumb.* I also checked the defrosting box of corn. It was finally melted enough to relinquish its gory contents. I locked myself into the laundry room and emptied it. Along with hundreds of kernels of frozen corn, a small, withered, brownish, yellowish claw of a hand fell to the bottom of the deep sink. It looked gothic, like something from an Edgar Allan Poe nightmare. Floyd must've chopped it off with the blade of an old shovel as the bone was splintered just below the wrist and dark purple marrow oozed from it. Slipping on the rubber gloves, I picked up the monkey claw and searched carefully for any identifying marks or scars. It looked like a typical severed hand.

Using Gustavo's Polaroid camera, I snapped several photos of it, which I planned to use for extortion purposes.

Opening the inkblotter, I carefully rolled the ball of each of the prune-shriveled fingertips onto the blotter. Then I pressed the inky fingers from left to right, one by one, into each labeled box on the two sheets of paper. When all five fingers were fingerprinted twice, I washed the ink off the hand, dried it, then tucked it back into the box that still had some frozen corn stuck along the bottom. Although I should've asked Vinetta for permission, I didn't want it to decompose any further. Discreetly, I slid the container back into the icebox under a bag of frozen gizzards. Next I took one of Gustavo's largest cameras and took clear, well-lit snapshots of each fingerprint, creating ten jpegs.

That afternoon, Vinetta removed Floyd's old Elvis getups from his study and we picked one—his white Vegas outfit with huge lapels. In it, I resembled the backside of a swan. While I watched endless footage of the King, she made delicate chalk lines on the costumes, where she was going to make alterations.

When I began practicing the songs myself, Vinetta made an ugly face.

"What?"

"Have you ever sung a song before?"

"Not professionally."

That evening, Vinetta, who had a beautiful singing voice, coached me on the scales. Only after getting a basic grasp of my abilities did she give me pointers in mimicking the master.

Early the next morning, I made the calls and tracked down my old connection, Marcos, who worked as an underpaid file clerk for the Boston Police Department.

"I found a hand and I need to know who it belongs to," I explained.

"Got the prints?"

"Yeah." We had done this several times before. "Is it the same price?"

"Yep." Three hundred bucks via Western Union. "But I'll only be able to trace them if he already has a record."

"I remember."

Ever since the Patriot Act passed, Marcos believed, the government had been reading all his e-mails. Because he was actually taking advantage of his restricted post, he set up anonymous e-mail accounts for both of us. I was instructed not to use any names or details that could be tracked back to me. I gave him my cell number so he could call to give me the results.

The next day, I misappropriated three hundred dollars from the Gustavo Funeral Fund and converted it into a Western Union money order and I sent it over to him. Then I slipped the flash-card from the camera into the USB port on my laptop. Moments later, I sent the ten jpegs to Marcos's anonymous account.

Last stop was the Blue Suede. Today was the deadline for the contest registration. When I stepped through the door of that dark, beer-stenched cesspool, I heard someone holler: "What the fuck you doing here?"

As my eyes adjusted I realized it was proprietor Snake Major sitting at the bar.

"I decided to take up your offer," I announced as I walked toward him.

"Oh, then you're not here for . . ." He seemed flustered.

"Why else would I be here?"

"We had another parking lot mishap." His euphemism for Gustavo's murder.

When I said I just wanted to pay tribute to the King, Snake instantly grew friendly and led me to the sign-up table in the rear. In addition to filling out the Sing the King registration form and paying the nonrefundable fee, I was told that my performance would be graded by a set of judges for originality, vocal ability, general appearance, and delivery.

"Who are the judges?" I asked nonchalantly.

"The best in the world." He pointed to the inebriated inbreds parked at the bar behind him.

"And why exactly are they the best in the world?"

"Well, I won't say who, but some of those boys worked with Elvis himself back in the day."

"Really?"

I wanted to ask him if coowner John Carpenter was going to be among them, but I didn't want to set anyone on edge. Before I left, the old bastard who I recognized as Irv staggered out of the john and slurred, "Who's this cutie-pie?"

"Just someone trying to do right by the King," Snake replied.

"Then you shoulda been here twenty-six years ago when he was looking for a little Chinese Ginnie." Both men let out big guffaws. But it was as though Gustavo had shouted out from the great beyond. Ginnie Ginnalian was living somewhere down in New Orleans. If anyone knew who these guys were, it would likely be his final girlfriend.

On the drive back to the defunct trailer camp, I called New Orleans information and discovered that although no individual named Ginnalian was listed, there was a Ginnalian Rugs in the Yellow Pages. When I called, some woman answered.

"My mother's thinking of buying an Oriental rug, but she gets disorientated easily." I couldn't resist the wordplay. "I heard there was someone there named Ginnie who would treat her right."

"That's me. You tell her to ask for me, and I'll take care of her personally."

I thanked her and hung up. It would have been absurd to try to conduct a surprise phone interview, but I wanted to establish that she was down there before I took the long drive south. Grabbing a few things, including all the photos of the Evils band, I abruptly informed Vinetta I would be away for a few days.

"Back up to New York?"

"The other way. New Orleans."

"Mardi Gras isn't in August, darling."

"It's a bit of a long shot, but I might have a break."

"Don't drink and drive," she warned. Although I hadn't touched the bottle in the past several days, she knew me well enough, an old drunk just waiting to fall off the wagon.

On the six-hour drive down to New Orleans (speeding the whole way), I practiced singing my four Elvis songs over and over. Caterwauling those tunes decently was like tiptoeing over the Grand Canyon on a tightrope, one wobbly note at a time until I was done. Then I'd turn right around and sing them all over again just a little stronger and faster.

Arriving in the Big Easy after business hours, I was too late to meet Ginnie, but I was just in time for an early-bird special at Pot o' Gumbo, a local diner. Nearby I found a cheap motel called Jazzing Around, where I was able to flip through a Yellow Pages to get the exact location of Ginnalian Rugs.

Once my head touched the strange, lumpy pillow, despite rhythmic banging and distant screams, I fell right to sleep.

After a quick breakfast of eggs, grits, and biscuits the next morning, I marched over to the rug palace. The place was a funky old showroom just starving for a makeover.

Through the unwashed front window, I saw an attractive middle-aged woman hunched over a desk, with a coffee in one hand and a phone in the other. A moment later, a teenage girl rushed into the store and a frantic conversation ensued. It was obvious upon first sight that Elvis had a particular type of girl he pursued. Ginnie looked uncannily similar to Priscilla. Watching her yell at the girl—who looked like a younger version of herself—I realized this had to be her daughter. She looked a little younger than Ginnie had when she started dating Elvis back in early 1977.

Though I didn't want to spend a second night at the motel, I knew better than to approach Ginnie at work where every prospective buyer and phone call would interrupt us. I waited in my car for her to take a lunch break. Unfortunately, business seemed slow and she worked right through the day. When she finally stepped out around four, she just stood in the doorway and lit a cigarette, so I approached.

"I was wondering if you might help me."

"Sure," she said, probably expecting to be asked for directions to a local Starbucks.

I took out my small stack of photos and handed them to her. "Do you by chance recognize any of these men?"

She inspected me carefully. Then, taking the photos, she flipped through them and asked, "What's all this about?"

"I know this sounds crazy, but I'm investigating a possible murder."

"A murder?"

"Well, I'm not sure."

"Oh my God." She stared at one of the photos. "This looks like . . . both these guys look like . . ." Slipping on her glasses, she said, "I haven't see him in eons."

"Who are they?"

Peering back at me, she asked, "What are you, some kind of reporter?"

"Not today; today I'm a private investigator."

"This isn't about no murder," she said. "How'd you find me?"

"A friend of mine said you were down here."

"Who's your friend?"

"A black guy who helped you a few years back."

"Who?"

"You won't know his name. But he said someone tried to snatch your purse outside a Dunkin' Donuts."

"I remember," she said introspectively.

"Gustavo was a truly decent human being."

"But how did he know . . ."

"He was a tabloid reporter and he'd been following you all day. He was supposed to write a piece on the twenty-fifth anniversary of Elvis's death. He had been taking photos of you, but when he saw your purse get snatched, he couldn't take advantage of you. He was just that kind of guy."

"I'll bite. Where is he?"

"He was killed . . . and indirectly, some of these men played a role," I said. "So I'm here trying to get him justice."

"These guys?!" she asked, looking down at the photos.

"I think so. That's why I'm here now. I thought maybe you could help me figure if any of them are dangerous."

"How do I know you're not lying about all this?"

"Well, I can't prove everything, but . . ." I took Gustavo's press card out of my wallet and showed it to her. "Was this the guy who helped you?"

She sadly nodded. "Tell you what. I'll look over your photos provided you promise me that you'll never see or call me ever again. For any reason whatsoever."

"I promise I won't," I said earnestly. "I can also promise you that everything you tell me will be kept confidential."

She reviewed the photos carefully, comparing a few of the Blue Suede men in one photo with other pictures of them.

"Okay," she finally said, pointing out the two Evils I knew as Vern and Irv. "It's been awhile, but these two look like Stan Persnip and Mike Hollenbroke. They were part of Elvis's day-to-day business association. I don't think Elvis completely trusted them." This confirmed that they were using pseudonyms. Looking at Snake, she added, "Oh, I remember this little shit. He was a regular Hitler, he was."

Inspecting the last two grisly men in the photos, Ginnie told me they looked familiar, but she wasn't sure. They might have been part of his security staff.

Last I showed her a fuzzy photo of Jeeves.

"I have no idea who this poor devil is," she said, staring intently, "though he does look vaguely familiar."

"Do you think there's any chance that Elvis Presley was killed?" I asked earnestly.

"When John Lennon got shot four times in the chest, *he* was killed. When I found one of the saddest and loneliest men I ever met dead in a pool of his own vomit and they traced over ten different pharmaceuticals in his system—pills everyone saw him taking for years—that's slow suicide." As she returned the pictures I thought I saw tears forming in her eyes. "Everyone stood by and no one did anything. I was just young enough to believe that somehow it'd all be okay. Thinking back, it was like selling tickets to someone's drowning. You carry that guilt to your grave."

As I thanked her for all her troubles, my cell phone's beep reminded me that my battery was low. It also reminded me of something else: "There's another photograph I want to show you, but it might be a little disturbing. It's of a dead body."

"This is enough to make me quit smoking," Ginnie said, snubbing out another cigarette.

I took out my cell and found the photo I had taken on it.

"Oh shit," she muttered after staring at it for a full minute, "it looks like it might be one of the . . . Asshole Brothers."

"Who?"

"That's what Elvis used to call them. The East brothers who wrote that damn book."

"Oh, you mean . . . ?"

"*Elvis, Why?* It brought Elvis so much pain and grief."

I could see his pain reflected on her face from all those years ago.

"That black fella, what's his name?"

"Gustavo Benoit."

"Well, he did me a big favor that day which he didn't even know about."

"What was that?"

"In that purse was a bracelet Elvis gave me for my birthday. It's really the last thing I have of his other than a lot of bittersweet memories. It actually meant a lot to me."

When a prospective customer walked into her shop, Ginnie went to assist the woman. Checking my watch, I realized that if I drove like hell I could save the cost of another night at Jazzing Around and get back up to Vinetta's in Daumland just before she put the older kids to bed. As I took Interstate 55 out of the city, it occurred to me that Elvis's last girlfriend had revealed a new possible motive for murder—even while opening up a new mystery. Pappy East had betrayed the King, but so had his brother Rod—now named John Carpenter. Why would one brother kill another? Ten thousand was a lot, but was it enough to prompt a murder?

The further north I drove the more questions I had. Why would John Carpenter open an Elvis cover bar? It didn't make sense. On the long drive back up to Tennessee, I only stopped once, at a convenience store. I got a large cup of coffee and a bag of bananas.

CHAPTER TWELVE

Though I made record time, it was dark when I finally parked and walked up the unweeded path toward Vinetta's trailer singing "Are You Lonesome Tonight?"

As I opened the door, Floyd Jr. started applauding me. Vinetta and the other kids joined in.

"My God, your singing's really gotten good," Vinetta said. She was trimming the hair of one of the restless girls. "You really do sound lonesome tonight."

"Well, I don't know if I'll win any contests, but I'm going to give it the old college try."

"On top of the costume and performance, you got to get his look down."

"I plan to."

"Then you better step on it," said Floyd Jr., "cause you only got a week."

"I know."

"Floyd Jr. had me buy you some glue-on sideburns," Vin said, and surprised me by holding them up for me—two thick strips of fur.

"Thank you. Oh, I got some sweet bananas." None of them were interested.

"Why don't you put your fanny in this chair and let me Elvisize you," Vin said to gloss over the fruit rejection.

"You think you can do it?"

"I always got compliments with Floyd's pompadour."

When the little blond girl hopped off the stool, I removed

several thick elevating books from it and sat down. Vinetta wrapped a checkered tablecloth around my neck, and to a cassette of Elvis's "Don't Be Cruel," she wet my hair back and began snipping away.

There was no mirror, so it was a leap of faith as clumps of my hair feathered down onto the floor.

"Did you know I am a quarter Apache?" Vinetta said. "My grandfather on my mother's side."

"Really?"

"Yep, and I've just been dying to scalp your wonderful head of black hair."

For half an hour, as her kids yelped for dinner and got into scuffles, Vinetta kept cutting, sometimes pausing and comparing my head with photos of Elvis. When she was done, she yanked the red checkered cloth away and said, "There you are—Elvis on a great hair day."

"Really?" I nervously glimpsed at myself in the reflection of a shiny pot.

"Well, you still need about a gallon of bear grease to lube it back, but you are Elvis from the forehead up."

In the bathroom mirror, I saw that she had actually done it. I donned Elvis's combed-back dorsal fin.

Unsurprisingly, the more I looked the part, the more energized I felt. I launched myself further into Elvis mania. Online, I saw that there was an industry of books about him. There were books on his flamboyant clothes, on his retro cars, on his fat-filled recipes. There were tomes on how to impersonate him, how to walk, talk, and sing like him. There were stories about the day he died, and volumes on his relationship with everyone who ever brushed up against him. Eventually I even found a book about the books of Elvis.

At Floyd Jr.'s suggestion, I watched one of the King's movies, *Kid Creole*, on their home VCR. Carefully I tried mimicking his gestures and voice.

"Elvis had about half a dozen signature expressions," Vin said, having sized him up and whittled him down with Floyd. "One of his sexiest was when he was trying to hold back a smile."

Soon she suggested just staring at myself in a pocket mirror practicing facial expressions. Gradually I surprised even myself as I belted out his songs, hit the various notes, and slowly it all started coming together. I tried to pair up different parts of three songs with his key expressions.

Three days before the contest, after nonstop practice, I woke up not feeling my usual self. My breasts were strangely tender and my stomach had cramped up. I had this dreaded fear of cancer, so I was grateful when the feeling passed. As I left the bathroom Vinetta was up in her nightgown preparing bagged lunches and breakfast for her food-slinging crew.

As she woke, washed, dressed, and fed the older members of her brood, I tried to help. Tossing a laundry load in the machine before marching them off to the bus stop, she returned to break up a fight and clean the play area. Then she washed the breakfast dishes. Her thankless day went on like that incessantly.

"Christ!" she exclaimed, sitting down winded for the first time around one. "How'm I gonna make it to the store before three?"

Grateful for a reason to get out of the trailer park, I drove down Makataka Road out to the Murphy County Mall. There I started filling up a cart with everything on her list, replacing some of her items with nutritionally superior products that cost a bit more, picking up exotic food like tofu and cinnamon rice cakes to broaden their culinary vocabulary. I also bought two extra-large containers of suntan lotion. En route I rang my neighbor, Miss Basall, to see whether our landlord had corrected the structural damage that had left us both temporarily homeless.

"Nope," she said dopily, "but I got an adorable sublet in Williamsburg."

While returning to the homestead, I noticed recurrent posters on utility poles announcing, COUNTY FAIR. I stopped and read that it was going to be held that weekend on "the old Daumland airstrip." Back at Vinetta's, I showed her some of the things I'd picked up. She looked confused at the tofu.

"D'ya stew that in the suntan lotion?" she kidded.

I offered to cook the tofu and informed her of the dangers of the sun on children and the risk of skin cancer later in life; I also pointed out that rice cakes were better than all the sugary crap she bought and mentioned the dramatic rise of childhood diabetes. While helping her put some of the items away, I noticed that she had food with partially hydrogenated oils, and warned her about the dangers of trans fats on her kids' systems.

Fearing that I was beginning to sound like some sanctimonious know-it-all—like my mother—I quickly changed the subject and mentioned that the fair was going to open the next day.

"That's great. It rarely comes to this part of the county, but we still can't go."

"Why the heck not?"

"The secret to raising seven kids," she explained, "is you don't take them off the farm. At least until puberty. That's when they escape on their own."

"Come on, Ma!" the eight-year-old yelled.

"Yeah, we never get out," the seven-year-old added.

"We want to go to the fair!" others chimed in.

"Oh, look what you've started," Vinetta said to me. "Keeping an eye on seven kids is just way too hard."

"We can do it together. That's only three and a half kids apiece."

"Another thing is it costs too much. I'm on a tight budget."

"It'll be my treat."

"Please, Ma! Please, Mama! Please!" chirped the many little mouths.

"We just can't!" she hollered back. "Now I don't want to hear nothing more about it."

There was a somber mood in the house the rest of the day. I let her have her space while she prepared dinner. Glancing over at some point, I noticed she was slicing up and steaming the tofu.

"I thought you never cooked tofu before."

"That's cause you think I'm some country bumpkin, so I end up playing the role."

"If that's true, I'm sorry."

"If I told you the real reason we can't go to the fair, you'd think, yep, she's just a dumb hick."

"I swear I will not be judgmental."

"All right. After Floyd died, I realized I was in deep over my head. No money, seven kids, I was in a real bad place. So I made a deal with . . ." she lowered her voice, "with my Lord. It was very simple: I would devote myself to just staying here and living the simple life and in return he'd keep an eye on us."

"Look, your relationship with your god is entirely your business, and no person should interfere with that. But this is just the county fair across town. And it's not even about entertainment as much as education. Someday soon your children are going to be leaving Daumland and they're going to have to draw on what little they know of the world beyond this trailer park."

She didn't respond. Without intending to, I was indeed getting into her business. I returned to my Elvis recitals. Maybe it was how quiet everyone was, but about midway through dinner Vinetta suddenly announced, "We're going to the country fair tomorrow!"

"Ye-e-e-eeh!!!" the kids screamed. Ecstatically, Floyd Jr. and Urleen started marching around the room like they had just won a battle. It was such a strange experience being with them because it had been so long since I felt excited, or had even looked forward to anything. Now it was impossible not to get swept up in that maelstrom of infantile joy. It also saddened me to remember all the innocence I had lost so long ago.

That Saturday, after the sloppy feeding ritual and the excruciating process of washing and dressing all seven kids, Vinetta gathered everyone outside and she read them the riot act: "Y'all have to hold hands in public. And if any one of ya wander off, look for an official and tell him my name, so they can say it over the P.A. Also, if anyone of y'all get out of hand or has a tantrum—that's it! I'll have you all back in the truck and we'll be back home in a wink."

After an unsynchronized chorus of agreement, they loaded into the back of the pickup. Vinetta kept her eyes on the highway while I craned my neck around to watch the kids. We bounced along the mile or so of Makataka Road until we came to the interstate.

Half an hour later we pulled into a large gravel-strewn parking lot half-filled with old and dented cars, some of which had decals of the Confederate flag or bumper stickers with slogans against gun control, gay marriage, and abortion. We unloaded the seven kids and carefully corralled them to the entrance.

There everyone paid a one-dollar admission fee and we walked down the busy lanes of hastily erected booths and strange vehicles that had been transformed into small carnival rides.

I converted a twenty-dollar bill into two rolls of quarters. One by one, we let each of the kids take a turn at various events: bumper car rides for the three boys, who couldn't resist smashing into other children; cup and saucer rides for the two older girls, who screamed and cried the entire time, then immediately asked to go again. I felt vertigo just watching it all.

At the very end of the walkway, a group of massive tents had been pitched. A series of contests and exhibitions were scheduled there throughout the day. The world's largest squash and pumpkin were allegedly on display with big blue ribbons. There were pie making, pie eating, and pie throwing contests.

We watched light rodeo competitions. Children were lassoing and bronco-busting sheep and goats. Charity auctions were being held throughout the afternoon for homemade or homegrown items. And there were endless rides: hay wagon rides, camel rides, balloon rides, and looming behind it all was a huge Ferris wheel.

All wanted to go up on the big red wheel. When we got in line, Vinetta bumped into her cousin Edwina. They had been best friends growing up. The two immediately regressed into a pair of schoolgirls, chatting and giggling nonstop. I bought them all tickets, and cherished my five childfree minutes alone on the ground.

Able to calmly take in some of my surroundings for the first time that day, I spotted old Snake Major. Near him were the others from the B.S. It turned out they were peddling beer from a booth that was advertising the upcoming Elvis contest. To win a free Elvis lamp or T-shirt—or whatever merchandise they could press Elvis's face onto—a string of contenders turned up their collars, slipped on a plastic Elvis pompadour, and, with the help of a karaoke prompter, belted out an Elvis hit.

For an instant, I had this urge to go right up to Snake and just lay it on the line: the dead burglar's hand for fifty grand. But then I remembered that Floyd may have given in to that same impulse, and if so, it had cost him his life.

I watched to see if I could learn anything from these spontaneous improvisers. One woman attempted to sing "Blue Suede Shoes," but she didn't have her glasses and couldn't read the teleprompter, so she just made up her own lyrics: *"You can steal my iPod, wreck my car, hit me over the head with a mason jar . . . Just don't step on my blue suede shoes . . ."*

"Too bad Elvis didn't have a teleprompter, he was always blowing his lines," I heard behind me. To my surprise, standing there was the last man I had been intimate with—Jeeves, the human train wreck. He looked even older and more grizzled in the naked light of day, but I liked him all the more for it.

"I'm truly sorry about the situation the last time we met," I said, referring to Gustavo's tragic death.

"And I'm real sorry for your painful loss. It was just an awful mishap."

"I never had to watch a friend die." I sighed heavily just thinking about it.

"Over the past seventy years, I've watched everything die, including myself once."

"Wow! I figured you were at least ten years younger." I was astonished by the notion that I had been bedded by a septuagenarian.

"It's the bounce factor. Few years ago I hit bottom. After that I bounced back up. Keep fit. Eat right. Long walks every morning."

"When I hit bottom, I just landed flat," I replied. "What's your sign?"

"My birthday is in early January."

"That makes you a Capricorn. I would have taken you for a Sag." I had picked up astrology while writing for the tabloids, another dirty habit.

Tilting my head toward the Blue Suede booth, I mentioned that I had just registered for the Sing the King contest, so I was looking for tips on impersonating Elvis.

"Really?" he asked, amused. "Why?"

"I love Elvis, and since I'm here anyway I could sure use ten grand."

"God," he said, "I wish I could just give it to you."

"Well, I appreciate it, but I wouldn't take it." Then I innocently asked him, "Do you work at Blue Suede?"

"Not really, I just kind of watch the mansion and the grounds above it."

"Do you know this guy John Carpenter?"

"Seen him around, why?"

"Isn't he the lord of the manor you work for?"

"Kinda. Major is really the big boss."

"I heard Carpenter was judging the contest."

"He used to be one of the judges," Jeeves replied, "but he doesn't come around much anymore. He leaves Snake to taking care of business nowadays."

"Snake seems like a shady character."

"We all live in the shade down here," he said with a smile, then added, "Hey, I can probably give you a few tips on singing the King."

"Really?"

"Sure, I saw him perform a few times. Hell, I've impersonated him a few times too."

"When?"

"Oh gee, when he first started out in the early '50s. Before he was the King. That's the thing, most people focus on his Vegas years, but he had different looks at different times in his life. I remember when he was clean at the start—and he was much more awkward. Then he got better, but he grew too comfortable, got lazy."

"Did you ever see him perform when he was high?"

"He was always high. Toward the end he was just plain flying. But I really don't remember much."

"Ca-saan-draaaaaa!" came Vinetta's voice from over near the big wheel. She was headed in my direction with her wayward little cavalry.

"I'm a little short on time, so if there's any one single magical Elvis lesson you can impart . . ."

"If I learned any one thing from watching him, it was simply this: be mindful of his moves and voice, but ultimately make the performance all your own."

Suddenly the seven little ones descended upon me like pygmies attacking a missionary.

"Oh God, are these all yours?" asked Jeeves.

"I'm their drunken aunt," I answered, producing a big lopsided grin on the wrecked man's face.

One of the girls thoughtlessly jumped up on Jeeves, who grabbed her under the shoulders and swung her high to the blue skies. She shrieked in horror and dashed away as soon as he set her down.

"What a beautiful little lady!" he remarked. As the children started pulling me away, I thanked Jeeves for his pearl of wisdom. Vinetta and I were promptly dragged off to the petting farm, where each kid paid a quarter to get spat upon by a llama and butted by a baby goat; and finally they got to molest the world's smallest pony.

We soon wandered back to the gaming section of the fair, where Vinetta vetoed anything she felt was potentially dangerous, like throwing darts at balloons and the automatic BB gun game. She reluctantly allowed the boys to shoot streams from waterguns into the mouths of plastic clowns to see which balloons popped first. Five minutes didn't pass that afternoon without someone stopping her with a "Howdy, Vin."

"You should run for office," I commented. "Everyone in this town knows you."

"That comes with being in a rut."

"Mama, Mama!" Floyd Jr. barked. On behalf of all the kids, he said they wanted to see the rodeo. We collected the full crew and got in another line, where we were charged another dollar per child. All pushed through a shiny turnstile and into the gated corridors behind open stalls that bordered the large rodeo.

As we filed slowly past the tight pens with kicking bulls and snorting horses, I spotted Minister Beaucheete in an open-collar shirt. He was moving up the stairs with his family to watch the upcoming sheep-lassoing contest. Two skinny blond kids were walking before him, presumably his own. That was when I saw his own private burden. About five feet behind him, led by a third child, was the minister's wife, easily the heaviest woman I had ever seen. Children in the area were pointing and snickering as embarrassed parents tried to get them to stop.

Her sad eyes appeared to be drowning in her ever-expand-ing face. She walked with her arms extended, as if physically unable to fold them inward. Vinetta noticed me staring and explained that diabetes was slowly robbing the wife of her sight.

"Shame that only celebrities can afford stomach staplings," I commented, not mentioning that this poor woman was the real victim of Vin's storm-cellar liaison.

"When I first met Thelma she was the prettiest gal in high school," Vin said.

"Sad."

"Hey, maybe you can use your literary gifts to write to one of those shows where they do surgical makeovers and they could—"

A loud metallic gong, and Vinetta hit the earth like a ton of bricks. Blood immediately began running from the back of her skull. I thought she had been shot until I saw the old metal pail rolling in a circle nearby.

Screaming, then bursting into tears, the seven children raced around, grabbing their fallen leader.

"Someone get a doctor!" I hollered.

An old cowboy rushed over apologizing profusely as he checked her wound. "I'm so sorry, ma'am, my bull kicked the bucket from his stall." He pointed a short distance away.

"You asshole!" I screamed. "When we're done suing your ass, you won't have any buckets left!"

Slowly Vinetta started coming to. Though blood was still trickling from her crown, nothing was coming from her ears or her mouth, a good sign. Still, she was unable to fully get her bearings. In another moment the ambulance that had been parked out front came around and a gurney was wheeled over. The children started screaming again, some of them hysterically. Floyd Jr. tried comforting them, but it was obvious that even he was having difficulty coping.

"Oh God," she said dizzily. "I can't leave my babies." The seven blubbering kids grabbed on to her like a flotilla in the stormy seas.

"You need stitches and you should get X-rayed," said the paramedic. "Just to make sure you don't have internal bleeding or a concussion."

"But my kids!" she groaned.

"I'll take care of them," I said nervously.

"No! Don't leave us!" shrieked one of the little girls.

"It'll be okay."

"You go on, Ma," the eight-year-old said, strengthening up. "We'll be just fine."

"Call Edwina if you need any help . . ." she hollered out as they wheeled her into the back of the ambulance and slammed the door. I didn't know Edwina's phone number.

All her poor babes wept as the ambulance sped off. Floyd Jr. and I gathered the kids, and I assured them their mother would be okay. They cried almost in tune while I led them back to the banged-up truck. All I could think was: I had interfered in her covenant, and God had exacted His toll.

CHAPTER THIRTEEN

On the drive back to the trailer park, I pulled out my cell phone and called information trying to locate a charitable babysitting service somewhere in the county.

The nearest one I could find was in Memphis, Nannies & Mammies. After relaying all the details to a receptionist, she wanted a hundred dollars an hour to send two high school dropouts to watch seven kids for seven hours—the minimum time, which included the three-hour drive there and back. Since I didn't have seven hundred dollars, I declined.

When we arrived home, where all the kids and the two dogs howled, yelled, cried, and fought, it hit me with full force that I was seriously screwed. Until she was well, I was food provider, diaper changer, and all-around prison guard for seven psychotic, unfinished convicts. That first night was sheer hell. I checked out the food pantry and put together a menu for our collective dinner. It really came down to two diets: one for the one-to-three-year-olds, who I had to spoonfeed, and a second meal for the five-to-eight-year-olds, who ate under supervision. I really couldn't have done it without Floyd Jr. Not only was he surprisingly well organized at making dishes, he also knew how to handle the other kids. Still, I was the substitute teacher and they knew that meant they could get away with anything. After wearily cleaning up, it was all I could do to push them all in the direction of the bedroom.

"Nighty night," I called out as I fell back onto the sofa, exhausted. The sounds of shouts and cries did not diminish. Twenty minutes later Floyd Jr. came out and explained that civil war had again broken out.

"You can't just dump six kids into a room and expect them to go to bed!"

"I can't?"

"No, you have to go back in there, make them put their pj's on, watch them as they brush their teeth, have them all say their prayers, and finish them off with a bedtime story."

So I pulled myself back up and tiredly did so. By the time they were all properly back in bed, I was barely able to kick off my shoes.

That morning I slept right until seven, when the two-year-olds started bawling their eyes out again for Mommy. It was the first night most of them had ever been away from her. With the help of Floyd Jr., meals were prepared and children were comforted.

Vinetta called that afternoon. Before I could say that I didn't think I could do this much longer, she explained that the X-rays had revealed a hairline fracture in her cranium. The good news was that she had received a CAT scan and MRI, and though there was mild swelling, the prognosis seemed generally fine. Still, they wanted to keep her for a few days just in case.

"To be honest with you, Vinetta, this is not really something I have an aptitude in, and I—"

Floyd Jr. suddenly snatched the phone out of my hand. "Ma! How's your head! You okay?" he shouted desperately, "Yes'm, Ma, sorry." He handed the phone back to me. "Sorry, ma'am."

"Listen, Sandra, good parenting comes down to balancing power with compassion. Focus on meals, laundry, and getting them out of and into bed. In terms of their behavior, they are all little rebels. And they are constantly testing your borders. You have to give it to them twice as hard, single them out for praise and punishment. No one hits my kids, but humiliate them with the Elvis songs. They work. There's a lot of shame in Elvis's music, a lot of remorse."

"What do I—"

"Assign them specific chores, specific times when things begin and end, otherwise they'll completely overwhelm you. Just remember, if they fear you they love you."

"I guess I can try—"

"Try hell," she shot back. "You'll *do*! You're all I got and you have to hold down the fort till I get back. The good news is you'll find strength you never thought you had. And I'll be home tomorrow night, the day before your big Elvis contest."

Her gung-ho talk invigorated me. This was one mission that would be accomplished. At my best, I had been an anal-retentive, fault-finding bitch. It never occurred to me I could use that as a weapon. Since the other six kids were swarming around me to say hi to their mom, I made them form a line and handed the phone to the first one.

"You got one minute, then hand the phone behind you." I stared at my wristwatch.

"Yes, ma'am."

"Don't call me that."

"What should we call you?" asked one of the half-pints.

"Mother Bloomgarten," I replied.

"Yes, Mama Bloomgarten," their adorable Southern-accented voices said in chorus. I had to struggle to keep from smiling.

The next day, in addition to my maternal duties, I was able to make some phone calls. They were precautionary, in the event our little extortion backfired again and turned into a murder case with me as the corpse. Intermittently I shouted out orders and the kids jumped. I used them to guide me through the chores, but wasn't timid about modifying what didn't work. The hardest part was formulating activities: telling the kids exactly how many minutes they could play on the collapsed swing set, or ride their tricycles with flat tires. At the same time I didn't want to push them too far. I knew that if my demands became too arbitrary, the eight-year-old—despite his helpfulness—was just waiting to revolt.

Vinetta called that night with good news: the doctors were waiting for final results, but if all went well, she should be back at the trailer the next night.

"Do me a favor and don't tell them," she added. "I want it to be a surprise."

My maternal stint would soon be over. This got me thinking about my own mother. Even though I didn't believe it was my fault, I felt bad about parting with her on such bad terms. At noon the next day I called her. She answered, but her voice sounded strangely free of all that stressful bitterness. It took me a moment to realize it wasn't her at all, but my sister Ludmilla.

"Cassie," she said upon recognizing my voice, "I can't believe it's you. Sweetie, I have awful news: Mama passed away in her sleep two days ago. We just buried her, and we're all here sitting shiva today and tomorrow."

"Oh my God!" It was exactly as Rodmilla had said. She had probably just been waiting to see me one last time. "Why didn't you call me?"

"I was going to, but I knew you were on bad terms," Ludmilla responded. "I figured you were on assignment somewhere and I didn't want to bother you."

"Bother me? She was my mom too!"

"Please don't be cross," she said. "I just meant that we all have our kids here, so it's a little tight and I know you and her didn't really see eye to eye."

The hidden message, as I inferred it, was, *She's not your real mother. You were just another liberal, well-intentioned project she took up years ago.*

"Well clear a place at the table," I fired back. "Cause not only am I coming, but I'm bringing *my* kids."

"*Your* kids?" I had hardly spoken with my sisters in the past ten years so it was at least somewhat plausible.

"Don't worry, we'll just stay for the day."

"You're coming all the way from New York City just for one day?"

"I like driving."

"At least stay for dinner!"

"Fine, see you in six hours."

"You're coming tonight?"

I turned off my cell phone. Mom's house was only about twenty minutes away. I figured I could load all the kids in the truck when the older ones returned from school, rush them to Mesopotamia for a visit and a dinner, then get them back home for Vinetta's return that night.

I hardly knew my sisters anymore. How many questions would they ask the kids? If my sisters did discover I wasn't the mother, no harm done. If I pulled it off, though, I knew they'd feel crappy for treating me like this. Besides, not having to cook dinner and clean up afterward, for even one night—that alone would make the trip worth it.

I spent the next hour trying to pull together decent clothes for the kids. When the two oldest ones returned from school, I had just finished dressing the younger ones, so I began coaxing them out to the pickup.

"Okay, kids, Mama Bloomgarten's got a little game for you all."

"I'm hungry, where's food?" seven kids said in seven different voices, volumes, and tones.

"That's the game!"

"What's the game?" one of them growled—I think it was Rufus.

"Escape to Witch Mountain."

"Why would we want to escape *to* something?" asked one mouth of the seven-headed monster.

"Play it right and you'll win food."

"Sounds scary!"

"See, we're going to go visit some witches pretending to be ladies. If we do that, we get to eat the magic food, then we'll get back into the truck and go home."

"What happens if they catch us?"

"Then you all have to stay and talk and get kissed and hugged and stuff."

"Eww!" a chorus returned.

"Why don't you just make us food?" one snotty little head suggested.

"Because we're all out, so let's not screw this up."

"Why don't you go shopping?" the eight-year-old piped up.

"All out of money. Now let's—"

"You ain't out of money, you're just being lazy!" the seven-year-old shouted.

"I beg your pardon!"

"We're tired," said the eight-year-old rebel leader.

"Yeah, we don't want to go nowheres!" said his second-in-command.

"That's it, I want some Evil Elvises!"

"Fine, but we ain't leaving," said the eight-year-old.

"Yeah, no one's leaving," one of the younger kids echoed him, and I realized that my authority was evaporating.

"Make us some food, why don't you. That's what you're supposed to do!" another little screamer joined in, chirping orders at me.

Right then I had a flashback; I recalled a fight, almost exactly like this one, over thirty years earlier, with Rodmilla. With horror I realized I had been the insurgent in our family. I suddenly had the urge to apologize to that older woman who I had spent my entire life fighting with. That's when it really hit me that she was dead. There was no one left to fight. I sat down on the ground, and as the kids kept yelling at me, I envisioned her face thirty years ago. Tears came to my eyes.

"Hey," the eight-year-old suddenly said to his crew, "that's enough. Let's get dressed."

"No, it's okay. I guess we have some food around."

"No, Mama Bloomgarten," he said softly. And I realized they had seen the tears. "It's no trouble."

"We'd only be going about twenty minutes away," I told him.

"Then let's shake a leg," he said to the others. "Maybe they'll have some pizza!"

In a few minutes they were pulling clothes from their wardrobe. I helped them, checking their progress.

About twenty minutes later we were all outside in the truck. It was there I explained, "If you can all do me one small favor, I want you to pretend while we're at this place that I'm your real mama. Can you all do that?"

"*You're* our real mama?" asked Urleen.

"Yeah, and that we're all here visiting from New York," I added.

"New York, the city?" the eight-year-old replied in awe.

"Yeah, and if one of the little kids accidentally slips, I'm hoping one of you will cover for him," I said to Floyd Jr. and Urleen.

"What do we get if we do this?" asked Kayla or Eugenia.

"I told you, magic food."

"Mars bars!" Cotton or Kayla swiftly demanded. Clearly they had already given this matter some thought.

"Tell you what, I'll give you a Mars bar for every time you pull me out of a rut," I proposed.

The youngest ones got in the front next to me. All the others piled into the rear of the truck. Before we backed out, Floyd Jr. hollered, "Stop!"

"What?" I feared a child had tumbled out the back.

"You want us to pretend we're from New York?"

"Yes!" I resumed backing down the driveway.

"Stop!" he shouted again.

"What?"

"This pickup has Tennessee license plates. How you going to explain that?"

The eight-year-old had a point, so we all somehow packed into my crappy little compact with the New York plates. Little arms and legs were sausaged every which way. As we drove, I called out, "Who wants to play a little game?"

"We're already playing a game," one of the smarter heads reminded.

"The game thing is wearing thin," said the eight-year-old.

"This is a better game. It's called pretend. Are you ready to play pretend?"

"Yeah, that we're from New York," one kid tiredly replied.

"Yeah, but we're also on this secret mission. Now, who's your mommy?"

"You're our mommy!" some shouted back.

"And where d'we *pretend* live?"

"Here," yelped some without hesitation.

"No, New York City," the oldest boy corrected, and all repeated.

"And where's your daddy?"

"With God in heaven," one of the kids shouted back.

"No, in the game of pretend, Daddy's alive but he left us. So let's repeat that, ready? Where's Daddy?"

"He left us!" the kids yelled out.

"This game sucks," the eight-year-old muttered.

For the remaining twenty or so minutes, as I drove, we kept up the pretend game quiz. Every few miles we'd pass a billboard that announced the upcoming Elvis contest and some of the kids would scream out or sing. I kept returning to the "game," drilling the same facts over and over into their seven little attention-deficit heads.

Finally, we pulled into Ludmilla's house of horrors. I parked between two new white Mercedes-Benz SUVs, cigarettes to the lungs of our dying planet. One had a bumper sticker that read, *My Daughter Is an Honor Student at South Lane High School.* The other car had a Jesus fish—so much for five thousand years of Judaism. By the time I pulled the seven little bodies out of my vehicle, they were hungry, whiny, and the youngest needed to be changed. Linking hands we all headed up the walkway.

"Oh my God!" cried a gold-highlighted, stallion-haired lady who turned out to be my sister Ludmilla. She hugged me, making me feel self-conscious about wrinkling her expensive clothing. Looking at my Elvis cut, she paused and said, "I . . . um . . . like what you did with your . . ."

"Thanks."

Squatting low, Ludmilla grabbed some of Vinetta's kids and started indiscriminately kissing them, something that would never have occurred to me. As they wiped off her tacky lipstick, she squealed, "Look at all these beautiful, beautiful children! Do you know me, I'm your Aunt Ludmilla!"

"Aunt Umbrella?" asked one.

"No, Lud-mil-la," she sounded it out for them.

"Lump-milla?" said the cunning eight-year-old.

"Call me Aunt Luddy."

"What kinda crazy name is that?" his partner in crime asked.

"Russian," she responded politely. Then, looking up at me, she revealed that she knew something about recessive genes: "How come two of your babies are blond?"

"Oh, they were Paul's from a prior marriage."

"Mom said you were going through a d-i-v-o-r-c-e," she said.

"Yeah, but please don't mention it in front of the k-i-d-s."

As Ludmilla stared into their cute white faces, another inconsistency suddenly occurred to me. "Paul's eyes are extraordinarily round—"

"I was just wondering about that," she cut me off.

"Their doctor said their eyes will grow more a-l-m-o-n-d-i-n-e as they get older."

"Mama said that when folks spell things out," Floyd Jr. blurted, "they're usually talking about sex."

"That's true," I chuckled awkwardly. "I did say that."

"Well, come on in and meet your cousins," Luddy said. Snatching the two-year-old out of my arms, she led us inside.

"Oh my God, just look at this brood!" said my other sister, nasal-voiced Bella, who also turned into a frenetic kissing machine.

In the living room before the burning fireplace, seated politely on sofa sectionals and recliners, were Ludmilla's three well-behaved, impeccably groomed boys, Yale, Downer, and Swan—they sounded like some Madison Avenue firm. Bella's two girls, Curtis and Micah, sat quietly next to their two brothers, Seven and Theobald.

"This is Clinton," I began.

"Cotton," the five-year-old corrected in a surly tone.

I pointed to each child as they chirped out their names.

"Urleen."

"Kay."

"Eugenia."

"Ruffy."

"Sterling."

"And lastly—Floyd Jr."

"Wait a second," Bella asked, "isn't Paul your husband?"

"Yeah, but Floyd Jr. is the boy's full name. It's a long story."

"Very original!" Luddy said. Even Floyd Jr. smiled at that one.

Ludmilla's scientifically engineered offspring, sitting side by side with Vinetta's ragtag litter, really brought out their trailer trashiness. It wasn't just their irregular hand-me-down clothes and homecut hair, but their lack of conduct and animal mannerisms. Still, I refused to feel any maternal shame. They were the marvelous harvest of my loins, the best things that had *ever* happened to me, and I loved each of them a little more every day. I watched with a frozen smile as the youngins carefully emptied bowls of raw almonds and raisins into their small pockets. Ludmilla's liberal guilt appeared to make her doubly receptive to the poorly reared waifs and less questioning of my parenting skills.

Upon excusing myself to use the upstairs bathroom, passing by Ludmilla's bedroom, I noticed her brand-new, miniature, state-of-the-art Apple laptop. It was wafer thin. The screen was on some recipe from the Food.com site. Attached to it was a beautiful, tiny laser-jet printer. Unable to pass up the opportunity, I checked my e-mail. I could hear the children screaming, but I went on Google and, since I was about to go into this contest to find Rod East—formerly John Carpenter—I typed in his name and hit *Images*. Up came a single photo of a shady thirty-year-old man with muttonchop sideburns and a wifebeater T-shirt—classic 1970s.

"Stop it, you witch!" I heard a child scream at one of my stepsisters. I pushed the print button and dashed out to grab one of the little girls who was battling Ludmilla's attempt to wipe off her sticky face.

Another little girl suddenly yanked an American pilgrim action-figure out of Yale's manicured hands. He looked completely baffled by her bold aggression.

"Shame on you, Kayla," I shouted out.

"Do an Elvira," the eight-year-old tyrant said.

"*Ainnotin buttahunda, cryin allda-tine, aintnotin buttahunda, cryin alldatine* . . ."

Both my sisters and their well-behaved offspring stared at the little girl in jaw-dropped awe.

"What's she doing?" Luddy finally asked.

"It's like a timeout," I explained. "I make them sing Elvis songs."

"Oh my God, did you get that from *Psychology Today*?" Bella inquired.

"No, I just thought of it myself."

"That is so cleverly adorable!" said Bella. "You know, there's an Elvis Presley contest tomorrow in Daumland just a few miles down."

It chilled me that she knew this, but considering all the billboards and local coverage, it shouldn't have been a surprise.

"Cassandra, you are truly the most amazing woman I've ever met," said Ludmilla with a wide, warm smile.

"If we're good for nothing else," I replied, "God gave us the mitzvahs of children."

"You sound like you're making fun of Mom now," Bella said.

"Hey, why's the mirror covered up like that?" asked one kid.

"Cause they're vampires," whispered the eight-year-old, just loud enough to be heard.

"No, silly," Bella said. "It's one of the things we do when we mourn someone's passing."

"Where's the pizza!" demanded another.

"They've been driving all day and are just starved," I explained as the doorbell chimed.

"There are some hors d'œuvres in the dining room," Bella said.

"The real food's in the kitchen," Luddy amended, "we just haven't had time to bring it out."

"I'll take care of it," I offered, allowing them both to go to the front door.

I followed the rampaging urchins into the kitchen just in time to hear one of them ask, "What's this shit?"

The kitchen table was packed with Jewish delicacies: gefilte fish, horseradish, chopped chicken liver, beet and cucumber salad, various olives and pickles, lox and cream cheese, and a mountain of freshly imported bagels.

"*Fear Factor* food!" said one of the twins, poking up a rolled-up grape leaf.

"That's enough of that."

Cured meats were steaming on the stovetop. I quickly assembled seven little pastrami and brisket sandwiches, all on rye, for the Loyd kids, adding a dollop of potato salad and coleslaw—food they recognized. When the neighbor finished paying his respects at the front door, Ludmilla and Bella gathered the kids at the long table in the screened-in veranda and brought sodas out for everyone.

I returned to the kitchen to get a cream soda and came back just in time to hear Ludmilla saying to Floyd Jr., "In just five years you'll be practicing for your Bar Mitzvah."

"You mean Mars Bar Mitzvahs," he countered, not missing a beat.

"What is this?" asked Rufus, lifting the rye off his sandwich.

"Northern ham," I assured him, figuring the word pastrami might scare him.

After they had eaten, the kids scattered around the house, probably searching for more things to steal. At least my sisters and I were able to talk.

"I can't believe you balance such a glamorous and busy life with all these fabulous kids!" said Ludmilla.

"Huh?"

To my surprise, my sisters had been following my tawdry features in the various supermarket tabloids over the years. Like Vinetta, they seemed to think I hobnobbed with the rich and famous.

"Tabloid reporting is trash, but it pays well and it's flexible."

"I'm just amazed that you were able to pile everyone in that little car and zoom all the way down here so fast."

"Speaking of which," I said, looking at my wristwatch, "I've got to get them back home. Tomorrow's a school day."

"But you just arrived," said Ludmilla.

"You have to spend the night, at least," Bella added.

"Yes!" insisted Luddy, grabbing my arm. "It'll be so much

fun—we're getting a babysitter to help with our kids. We can get a second sitter to help with the rest—"

"—and we can have a slumber party," Bella completed her thought. They looked at me searchingly, and I sensed they were eager to repair the huge rift of sisterly neglect. But Vinetta was getting out of the hospital in just a few hours. And the longer I was there, the greater the risk of being revealed as the fraud I was.

"Two of the children have dental appointments and a third has to see an eye doctor," I invented. So, to the relief of their well-mannered cousins, I had the jackals put on their hand-me-down jackets.

"The headstone won't be unveiled until the first week of December, but would you like to pay a visit to Mom's grave now?" Luddy asked. "She's in a brand-new cemetery nearby."

"Absolutely."

Bella kissed everyone goodbye and stayed with the uptown kids. We all squeezed into my compact as Luddy got into into her seventy-five-thousand-dollar luxury SUV and led us three miles away to the kosher section of Patriot Hills—the same cemetery where I had just laid Gustavo to rest. My sister joined me as I put a flat pebble near the fresh mound of earth that covered Rodmilla's plot.

"She really did love you a lot," Ludmilla said softly. "And because she did, she expected so much from you."

The idea of being adopted, or, more specifically, the selfless generosity of a complete stranger named Rodmilla Bloomgarten, swelled up and smacked me like a tsunami. I was standing above a dead woman who had arbitrarily snatched me from a destitute life in an orphanage halfway around the world—long before Angelina, Madonna, or even Mia had made it popular—and brought me to this land of excess, where everyone was given more than enough rope to hang themselves. She had nourished my self-esteem and sense of fairness, provided me with ample opportunities to use my intellect, and always encouraged my ambition.

I wasn't sure at exactly what point one had to stopping blaming the parents and take responsibility for oneself, but at that moment I realized that it was *I* who had turned myself into an alcoholic almost-divorced tabloid reporter, not she. And I also felt like I was finally on some long, freaky road to recovery.

Barely was I able to sniffle before the shrill cacophony of another woman's children alerted me to the fact that the Loyd goblins were defacing the graves of other dead parents, knocking mournfully placed pebbles off neighboring headstones.

"Back in the goddamn car!!!" I screamed.

By the time Ludmilla and I had squeezed all those little sardines back into my dented can on wheels, I could see that there were tears in her eyes too.

"It's okay," I said, hugging her.

"I'm not crying cause of her, I'm crying cause of you!"

"Me?"

"You're our sister, but you were always different and we were always sort of scared of you."

"Why were you scared of me?"

"Because you were most like *her*!"

"Like who?"

"Mom, you ninny!"

"Give me a break."

"You were the only one who stood up to her, and she hated that. We remember those awful fights. We should've stood up with you. And now we're all grown up and you're not a part of the family and it *shouldn't* be this way, Cass! Life passes so quickly and—" She broke down completely and, hard as I tried to fight it, so did I.

"Look, I promise I'll be back soon . . . I'll come back for the unveiling."

"Really?"

"My hand to God," I said, raising it high. She knew that though I was being playful, I was also serious, and gave me a hug that nearly cracked my spine. I would've stayed awhile longer but I had already put the kids through enough, and their real mother was probably waiting for them. Also, tomorrow was my big Elvis impersonation day and any chance of success depended on some frantic final rehearsals. So we hugged and kissed, and Luddy made me promise to bring them all back down soon.

"I swear I will," I repeated, wondering if Vinetta would mind renting out her swarm for another day.

No sooner had I started driving away than Floyd Jr. yelled, "Ten Mars bars. You owe me ten Mars bars!"

"Me too!" cried another.

"Those women touched me all over!"

"That food was totally icky . . ." Slowly and in their own white-trash illiterate preadolescent way, all pitched in their complaints.

"Fine, fine," I said, feeling too good to let their nagging bother me. Not only was I now a confirmed pro-lifer, I firmly believed that every drip of homeless sperm should be indiscriminately paired up with each forcibly harvested egg—regardless of how deformed or inbred or genetically challenged the donors were. The great pageantry of Mankind needed to literally burst off the globe, so that from space our planet would look like a giant black-brown-red-yellow-pink flower of human skin. I didn't care if oceans needed to be drained, mountains had to be flattened, or polar caps required melting—every inch of the planet had to be converted to living space. (Love would save the earth from global warming and whatever else.) If panda bears, blue whales, and condors had to undergo extinction to make room for more nurseries and playgrounds, so be it. If great paintings from the Louvre and the Hermitage had to be recycled into diapers, so much the better.

All parents were absolutely right—it was a bottomless well of ceaseless joy. Cancer researchers, dilettante poets, great world leaders, and busy philanthropists—all jobs were a very distant second to that most important job in all the world: being a mommy.

CHAPTER FOURTEEN

When we screeched into their dirt driveway, Vinetta immediately rushed out of the trailer with a bandage around her head. The kids raced to her from all sides, each one kissing, grabbing, and loving a different huggable clutch of her. Seeing that mosh pit of love, I sensed why Vinetta didn't mind sacrificing her life for those little screamers. But it was all just a fleeting emotion. For love-camels like myself, such a sacrifice was a bit much. In the way most hungered for love, I usually longed for solitude.

"Where the hell were you?" she finally let me have it.

"We went out for a little dinner."

"She made us lie," tattled the seven-year-old from hell.

"My mother just died, so we went to pay our respects," I explained.

"You shoulda left a note or something. I thought you done stole the lot of them."

"I'm sorry, I thought we were going to be back sooner. My sisters were holding a wake, and I hadn't seen them in ten years."

"She had us all pretend *she* was our mommy," one of the twins ratted me out. "But you're our real mommy."

"How's your head?" asked the eight-year-old.

"Healing," she said, hugging them harder to keep them from grabbing at her wound. "I just missed you all so terribly much."

I finally interrupted all the gushy stuff: "Tomorrow evening is the contest. I was hoping we could get a little more rehearsal in before the big show."

"That's fine. Why don't you suit up," she suggested.

Twenty minutes later, as I carefully pulled on the starchy white jumper with eagle embroidery in the front, she and the kids positioned the clip-on lamps around the room to spotlight me. Upon her cue, I introduced myself and began my little repertoire of songs. While I sang, Vinetta barked out directions: "Pick up the pace . . . More Southern drawl . . . Don't forget those expressions!"

As I found myself struggling to simultaneously sing in Elvis's voice and make his key faces, she advised me to limit myself to Elvis's two main expressions, the restrained grin and sultry stare. Upon taking it all in, I sang "Are You Lonesome Tonight?"

"Why do I feel that you're just trying to get through it?" Vinetta lamented, sounding her most Simon Cowell.

"I *am* just trying to get through it!"

"At his best, Elvis loved the stage! He would stay as long as he could. The stage is where Elvis was his *most* Elvis."

"Well, it scares me." I had been feeling shaky during the past few days, and considered getting a drink, but I knew that if I did, I'd either forget important details or get nervous that I was forgetting important details.

"Aren't there some pills that'll calm you down?" Vinetta asked.

"Isn't that what got Elvis in trouble?" I joked, but she was right. I remembered Gustavo's diet supplements, which I suspected were Xanax, that he'd left in my car. I decided to bring one with me just in case I had stage fright at the big gig. After a couple more run-throughs, we called it a night. I needed sleep.

Early on the morning of the big Sing the King contest, I jumped out of bed and rushed into the bathroom and vomited. Breathing slowly, I felt flush. I had missed my period by two days, and my body usually functioned like clockwork. I didn't need to dip a two-tone swizzle stick into a fresh cup of pee to know it wasn't cancer. I had a little blessing in my own microwave. It only took me a minute to do the math and figure out that the crippled geriatric groundskeeper I'd slept with on that drunken night two weeks ago was my baby's daddy. He was in fact the only man I had coupled with since breaking up with Paul.

After trying so hard and for so long, I was finally pregnant again—at the worst possible time. I was amazed that I hadn't miscarried, particularly given all the drama of the past week. I tried to go back to sleep, but I could hear Vinetta stirring in the tiny kitchen. I got up and went out to see her staring into the gray distance over her chipped mug of coffee. She had put a scarf up over her head bandage so it wouldn't look quite so horrible.

Electing not to mention my newfound condition, I said to her, "I guess you were right."

"About what?"

"Your deal with God not to leave the house. You went to the county fair and almost got killed."

"No, that was just an accident, and if it wasn't, then God's either wrong or just plain mean."

"I feel so guilty."

"Well don't, I didn't go there for you. I did it because you were right. The kids need some exposure. Someday they're going to leave this dung heap and they're going to have to interact with the world at large."

"Did you enjoy your hospital hiatus?"

"Worst few days of my life," she muttered. "When I wasn't worrying about the kids, I was thinking how empty my life is and wondering how I got myself in this damn mess."

"It isn't all that bad."

"Easy for you to say, you're a successful reporter dealing with exciting celebrities, breaking big stories and such."

"I've never met a celebrity who couldn't be replaced by another one. As for success, yesterday I borrowed your accomplishments to make myself look better."

The first howls from the youngest child woke the others, breaking up our little pity fest. In all the towns and villages around Daumland, Elvis impersonators were popping amphetamines, forcing their congested hearts to beat a little faster. They were greasing up their tar-black pompadours and selecting the loudest, gaudiest costumes they'd ever wear—all getting ready for that great croon-a-thon that would establish their Elvis bona fides, so they could launch successful careers as wedding singers and novelty acts.

I spent the morning practicing my songs and trying to pretend that I didn't know I was pregnant. I needed one more day to not worry about anyone else's life. In the middle of practicing "Viva Las Vegas," my cell phone chimed for the first time in over a day. It was a rising young tabloid star, Hailey Page.

"I heard the awful news about Gustavo Benoit and just wanted to express my condolences." It turned out one of the funeral fund donors had posted his obituary on a journalist web site.

"Thanks."

"What exactly happened?"

"We went to this dive for a drink but it was closed. While we briefly separated, a cop drove by and thought Gus was trying to break in."

"Why ever would he think that?"

"It was pouring rain and Gus had this novelty umbrella that looked like a shotgun. When he drunkenly pulled it, they shot him."

"Poor Gus." She paused. "You guys were working on the Scrubbs case, weren't you?"

"Everybody is. Why?"

"I just thought maybe he'd been killed while discovering something." There it was—Hailey had left her tasteful little gardening column in some Midwestern paper for a lot more cash in the tabloid compost heap. She must've smelled a story in our direction.

"We didn't find anything. What's going on down on Beale Street?"

"It's overrun with reporters in search of news, and there just isn't any. So are you upstate?"

"No. Why do you ask?"

"I just heard that Missy Scrubbs's family was from upstate somewhere, but no one seems to know exactly where. And I thought Gus said you were from around these parts."

"I'm at a seismographic center in Purdue University."

"Oh my! Whatever for?"

"Well, keep this to yourself, but they're finishing a secret study for the U.S. Geological Survey on the New Madrid fault line," I misinformed her.

"Why is it a secret?" she asked softly.

I explained that in 1811, a major earthquake that was estimated to have been above 8 on the Richter scale had struck Memphis, Tennessee, killing an unknown number of people.

"Wow!"

"The real story now is whether we're prepared to handle it." Before I could say anything else, pandemonium broke out. Two of the children had gotten into a donnybrook and others were joining in. Vinetta was outside, so I told Hailey I had to run, then broke up the fight myself. An Elvis competition was waiting.

As I began final preparations for my performance, I thought about the new life inside of me. This was going to be an awful day to miscarry. Nothing stayed alive in me very long. I knew I should just stay home and take it easy, as I had those other times when I tried to have a kid with Paul. But they had all come to nothing. At least this time I'd miscarry with my boots on.

Vinetta offered to fix me eggs and grits. Though I was hungry, I declined as I didn't want to increase the likelihood of vomiting. Nervously, I rehearsed onward.

After feeding the brood, Vinetta said that this was the only time left—between lunch and dinner, while the laundry was in its longest cycle—when she'd be able to help me get ready for my performance. Fine. She spent half an hour working on my hair, gluing on my sideburns, then fixing my cosmetics. Once we were done, she tended to her laundry while I pulled the Elvis Vegas wear back on.

"Look, Ma, it's Dad!" said Eugenia, vaguely remembering her father dressed like me.

"My God, you're a regular Elvira Presley," Vinetta said as I slipped on my official orange-tinted Elvis sunglasses.

"*Thankya very mush.* Now here's what's going to happen. I'm going to go to the Blue Suede, meet this Carpenter character, and tell him he can have the hand for fifty thousand dollars. I'll show him the photos and—"

"What do I do?"

"Do you have any kind of weapons around here?"

"I have Floyd's old possum gun stored away and I'm a pretty good shot."

"Actually, I was hoping you might have a pistol that I could borrow. I thought maybe you could take the kids and spend the night at your cousin Edwina's."

"Guess I can do that."

"If you don't hear from me by midnight, don't go home." I scribbled a number on a piece of paper. "Call here and ask for Special Agent Ron Wallace at the Memphis field office of the FBI. I left a message for him yesterday. Tell him you're in immediate danger and give him this letter." I placed it on the table in front of her. "You tell him I'm missing and give him the hand. The letter explains everything."

She solemnly nodded.

"Also," I took out another letter, "if anything should happen, I want you to mail this to my sisters. Can you do that?" In this letter I explained that I didn't actually have seven kids, I was only the babysitter, but I was still grateful for their kindness and sorry we had grown apart and that I behaved so childishly.

"Sandra, don't do this." The gravity of the situation seemed to suddenly hit Vinetta. "You're taking an unnecessary risk."

"Before coming here, I was drinking myself to death, avoiding so many things, and just feeling worthless. I probably would've finished myself off if I had left here after Gustavo died. Instead, I haven't touched the bottle in a week. I might've broken a multiple murder case. I got to briefly say goodbye to my mother and reconcile with my sisters. I even got a big helping of motherhood. Not to mention I learned to sing Elvis like a pro. Everything I've done turned out to be a necessary risk. I'm not stopping now."

CHAPTER FIFTEEN

If I can get the kids to bed early and Edwina feels comfortable, I'll go over and see you. How's that?" Vinetta asked.

"Don't worry about it."

"I'm still gonna try to come by later," she swore.

After I packed what I needed, she gave me a hug, the children all wished me good luck, and I left. Roughly a mile shy of the Blue Suede, traffic started slowing down. It was bumper-to-bumper for the last ten minutes before I finally reached the tavern and saw what was up. On the crabgrass in front of the Blue Suede a makeshift stage had been hastily erected. Would-be Elvises were lining up and performing their audition songs. A series of beer booths had been tossed up around the grounds. Shiny kegs were sitting in large tubs of ice. When I drove past I could see that the parking lot had been closed and converted into a second stage. Traffic cops were waving people through into town. I was lucky to find a tight spot just a couple of blocks away.

Considering we were in a small town equidistant from Memphis and Nashville, the crowd of two to three hundred folks milling outside the bar was a regular Lollapalooza. Elvis had died and come back as merchandise: Elvis shirts, Elvis lamps, Elvis statues, Elvis hats, Elvis books, Elvis crap of all variety was packed onto tables, going for top dollar.

As I walked from my car to the check-in wearing my Elvis costume—the only Asian she-Elvis around—I found myself being targeted by amatuer photographers. Initially I tried dodging them, but desperate shutterbugs dashed around and got me from ugly angles, so I finally just posed for them. It was the first time I had ever gotten a taste of my own tabloid medicine.

At the registration table, I was given the number twenty-eight on stage two. I had to perform my best song—"Are You Lonesome Tonight?"—at the stage on the parking lot. I thoughtlessly bought a sudsy beer, but remembering that there was an outside chance I might actually have a baby, I left it on a table and found a caffeine-free soda instead. Taking out my printed photo of Rod East I tried to imagine him years older and looked for the man in the crowd—to no avail.

In all shapes and styles the Elvises strutted forth: there was an Elvis wearing a dark green uniform complete with a duffel bag over his shoulder, harking back to when he was discharged from the army; a bearded Hawaiian Elvis was ringed with a variety of colorful leis; the multiculti Elvises included several black and Latino variations. Soon I spotted a few other Asian and a couple Native American Elvises. Among the white-caped and gold-laméd standouts was a nervous, overweight Elvis covered in pimples, a twitchy Elvis tweaker, who kept running his fingers along his lips. I also counted five surgically enhanced Elvises. To my comfort, I spotted one other female Elvis, a voluptuous blonde who someone said was named Thelma Presley. Locating a small bottle of cranberry juice at a concession stand, I just stood in the back of the crowd and watched the back-to-back auditions while waiting for my name to be called.

After an hour, most of the Kings blended into one another. Rubbing elbows with these pretenders to His throne, I soon got a sense of two key psychological profiles. Most were raven-haired, benign guys who never got very far on their own music careers and through Elvis they tried to find a way to pay their mounting credit card bills. The other type of Elvis impersonators were just plain nuts. These were lonely, functionally insane guys who had completely transferred their egos to the romantic ideal of the King. Their height, weight, hair color, and body shape didn't matter. In fact, nothing else mattered but their pathological fixation on Elvis or, more particularly, their wish to blur into him until there was a fused Elvis identity.

After one 1950s Elvis finished his hackneyed "Hound Dog," one of the three preliminary judges, a tall, beef-jerky guy who looked nothing like Rod East took the stage holding a clipboard and called out my name. When I went up the wooden steps, I got an unusual blast of applause. Apparently, my sex and race worked to my advantage. Down before me was a table with three lecherous-looking older men. One of them, the barfly who I thought was named Irv, winked at me.

Taking the mike, I introduced myself as the illegitimate daughter of Elvis and Don Ho, which got a polite laugh, and then I executed a fairly smooth "Are You Lonesome Tonight?" By the end of the song, staring into each of the judges' eyes, I softly performed my best impersonation of the King: "The stage is bare, I'm standing there, with emptiness all around, and if you don't come back to me, they'll bring the curtain down . . ." An explosion of applause and even some sniffles followed.

"Thank you—next!"

Over the next twenty minutes another six auditions followed, then the preliminaries were complete. The other stage had also wrapped up its auditions. It took an hour for our judges to make and break so many dreams, by posting their results on the door of the pub. Emotions ran high as some Elvises shouted joyously while others grew mournfully silent. Of the fifty-two contestants, ten from each of the two stages were picked to perform inside the Elvis palace for the final round. One older Elvis tributer who had supposedly made it into the finals every year since the Sing the King contest first began, was cut this time. I watched him weep inconsolably, sitting in his customized van out back.

I was amazed to see that I had made the cut, though I was the second from the bottom. Another Elvis impersonator explained that the list was compiled in the order of appearance, so the Elvis at the bottom had simply been the last to perform.

"There's the best damn Elvis I've seen all day!" I heard a hoarse voice call out. Turning around, I saw Jeeves—who was the right age, but looked nothing even remotely like Rod East/John Carpenter. Yet there was still something about that broken-down old geezer that made me blush and giggle like a schoolgirl.

"Did you see me sing?"

"Sure did, and I'll tell you right now, Elvis shoulda been imitating *you.*"

"If I can only convince everyone else here."

"*Girl, are you lonesome tonight?*" he sang to me softy, imitating me imitating the King. I wanted to tell him I wasn't lonesome tonight because he had impregnated me, but I didn't want to scare him off. I still refused to believe that I could possibly bring a fetus to full-term, but I couldn't bring myself to end the pregnancy either. Only God could abort this particular life.

"You gonna watch the finals?"

"Don't have a choice," he said. "I'm tying an apron on and clearing tables."

"Let me ask you something." I figured that he might be able to help me with my investigation. "Do you know Rod East?"

"Sure do," he said, "you're looking right at him."

"Come on."

"If you want to know God's honest truth, that's his car right over there." He pointed across the parking lot to an old pink Cadillac that was in the process of backing out onto the road.

"You kidding?"

"Swear on my mother's grave I'm not." He crossed himself.

Bumping into people as I traversed the lot, I raced over to the vehicle just as it swung out onto the street. Though I didn't get there in time, I managed to spot the decal of Elvis's pompadour on the back window, confirming it was the car that the electrician had seen Missy Scrubbs leaning out of in the Murphy County Mall. All roads pointed to Rod East.

When I returned to where I had left Jeeves, he was gone. The Quasimodo of Daumland had returned to his bell tower—or the kitchen.

With some time to kill, I walked away from the crowds to a relatively empty lawn across the road where a big-top tent had been erected. Inside they were holding an Elvis epic: a three-hour movie montage consisting of most of Elvis's movies had begun at noon. In chronological order it showed the best parts of *Love Me Tender, Loving You, Jailhouse Rock, King Creole, GI Blues, Flaming Star, Wild in the Country, Blue Hawaii, Follow that Dream, Kid Galahad, Girls! Girls! Girls!, It Happened at the World's Fair, Fun in Acapulco, Kissin' Cousins, Viva Las Vegas, Roustabout, Girl Happy, Tickle Me, Harum Scarum, Frankie and Johnny, Paradise, Hawaiian Style, Spinout, Easy Come, Easy Go, Double Trouble, Clambake, Stay Away, Joe, Speedway, Live a Little, Love a Little, The Trouble with Girls,* and, finally, *Change of Habit.*

I once read that if all of Christ's words were calmly spoken aloud, they'd only come to about one hour of play time. The King had made over forty hours of motion pictures. Though they weren't exactly *Citizen Kane*, it was still an impressive body of work considering the short span he had lived, only nine years longer than Jesus.

In his first flick, *Jailhouse Rock*, young Elvis played an ex-con who learned to sing in the clink. Presley played an impressive bad boy. For a moment I actually forgot I was watching the future King of Rock and Roll. Soon, though, I drifted off to sleep. When I opened my eyes, Elvis was a few years older, in some other film, crooning to a new beautiful girl on his arm. A moment later he was racing with some bad guy. Then I closed my eyes again and pondered whether—if I couldn't find Rod East—I dare approach Snake Major, as Floyd probably had, or just leave?

Watching Elvis at some 1960s luau, I decided that I had already invested far too much. If I didn't find this chimerical man tonight, I was going to risk a confrontation with the venomous Major.

Feeling strangely disconnected from my former life, I had this sudden urge to speak to someone from back home in New York. Gustavo was dead, so I decided to try calling my soon-to-be-ex-husband, Paul. Even though I dreaded the conversation, I simply didn't make friends easily and there was no one else left.

I dialed his cell, only to have my call go straight to voice mail. I boldly called him at work. Unfortunately, it was too close to the news hour so I was trapped in his voice mail there too. I left a message saying that if he wanted to talk, now would be a great time, and hung up.

Then, in the distance, I saw mass movement and realized that the Blue Suede was finally opening. It was my time to shine.

CHAPTER SIXTEEN

Several news vans were parked outside with large satellite dishes on long retractable poles that plugged the Blue Suede into the rest of the world. Unlike the outdoor stages where standing space was free and limitless, inside the numbered seats had all been sold in advance. Even the standing room was sold out.

My performance slot was second from the last; number nineteen of the twenty performers who had made it into the finals. All of us clones were ushered into the rear entrance, then led to a large rectangular dressing room that had two long benches in front of two lines of mirrors. Elvises sat in both directions as if it were the galley of a Las Vegas slave ship. With the two rows of mirrors facing each other, it looked like an endless room with hundreds of Elvises fading in the eternal distance. I seemed to be one of only two she-Elvises, though there were three other Asians and four African Americans (or perhaps they were just two who had been reflected). Most of them seemed to know each other. I listened as they talked, exchanging jokes, gossip, and other Elvis-related news. Some of them spoke with a kind of indelible Elvis twang that made me wonder if they had lost traces of themselves in their commitment to their role.

A short, red-faced man with a gin blossom nose let out an incredibly loud whistle, compelling everyone to listen up.

"Okay Elvises, here's what's going to happen. I'm the emcee and y'all'll go in the order that you got picked." This meant I was second from the last. "When all the patrons are seated and the judges are ready, I'll come back here and call out your number and you'll go onstage. You'll do your three songs, take a bow, and come on back inside quickly. No dedications, no speeches, no shenanigans. We have to be quick about this as we're figuring about four or so performances per hour in order to be done by eleven-thirty and ordain this year's King by midnight.

"Now, the good news is, no one will go home empty-handed. So if you'll just follow the rules, there are concession prizes for everyone based on how you place. And all of them are worth more than the entry fee, so you're already all winners."

Everyone clapped for the little Elvis wrangler. He exited and a few minutes later we could hear him saying, "The Elvises have entered the building," then spectators wildly applauding. After some cursory remarks and a few jokes, the little man rushed back in and shouted out, "Number one, you're on!"

A slightly overweight Elvis in a leather bodysuit arose elastically like a S-and-M Gumby doll and strode forward. The quivery rolls of his tightly corseted fat gently bounced as he strutted out the little doorway. He had the clear advantage of being the first in a room full of imitators. All of us listened through a small amplifier that was wired into the changing room as he sang an electrifying "Jailhouse Rock." As soon as the applause tapered, he burst into "It's Now or Never," then wrapped it up with "Mystery Train." To thunderous cheers, the leather Gumby came dashing back, sopped in sweat, closely tailed by the little emcee who shouted, "Number two, pronto!"

When Elvis number two, who was in the bathroom, didn't respond, the man shouted, "I want the next fucking Elvis to be waiting for me here when I come out this door or you'll lose your turn! You got to shit, piss, vomit, or jerk off, do it now!"

When number two dashed onto the stage and opened with "Mystery Train," it was déjà vu all over again.

"This is going to be a long fucking night," said the guy next to me. Some of the more experienced Elvises quickly took charge. They checked the songs of the younger imitators to make sure there were no more back-to-back performances of the same numbers.

Over the course of the next two and a half hours, watching that chain of Elvi slowly jump onto the dark cliff of the stage, I had some clue of what the real King must have had to go through trying to remain sober year after year in the face of so much pressure. Almost everyone smoked cigarettes and a single busboy kept shuttling back and forth bringing full trays of drinks as the slowly diminishing group of Elvises got liquored up. This sing-along was as competitive as any blood sport, and you had to pay your dues to move up the ranks.

"Did I see you at the Branson regionals?" a Native American performer who went under the moniker Big Chief Elvis asked me with a lascivious grin.

"Not unless it was a testicle-twisting contest," I shot back.

"I don't like the white man either," he countered. Throughout the evening he kept looking over, catching me in the mirror and winking.

Finally, I decided to go out for some air. While outside, I canvassed the nearby parking lots to see if I could spot the dirty pink Caddy belonging to the enigmatic owner. Though I saw a couple of Cadillacs, I didn't find the one with the decals. Turning on my cell phone and checking my messages, I discovered that I had received a call from my friend at the Boston PD, who said the fingerprints from the hand I had sent him belonged to one Rodney East, previously arrested for drunk-and-disorderly.

Holy shit! The man I was looking for—who I had gone through this entire charade to meet—was none other than the dead burglar. Then who the hell was John Carpenter? Was he the dead man? Before I could decide what to do next, my cell chimed. It was Vinetta.

"Most of the kids are asleep. Edwina, Floyd, and I are watching the contest here on TV," she said excitedly. I could hear some of the kids screaming in the background. "You haven't seen the East guy, have you?"

"Uh . . . no." I didn't have the heart to tell her all that remained of the man I was looking for was the shriveled hand in her fridge.

"Isn't he one of the judges?"

"I guess, but I'm the second from the last to perform so I haven't seen him yet."

"Well," she said nervously, "I just wanted you to know that we're all rooting and praying for you."

"Me too," I said, and feeling demoralized I told her I had to go. For a moment I considered just walking to my car and driving north, all the way back to New York. Then it occurred to me that even if Rod East was dead, there was still someone else who previously went by the name of John Carpenter. I strolled over to the hill behind the tavern and began a slow ascent.

The key thing that really compelled me to stay there was all the time and effort I had already invested. I decided to press on in my search for the man pretending to be John Carpenter. And if he didn't exist, there was still Snake. Feeling increasingly anxious, I dialed Angela Basall, my old New York neighbor.

"Hello?" she answered.

"Hi, Angela, how you doing?"

"My name's Wanda," she corrected. "Is this a telemarketer?"

"No, it's me, your old neighbor Cassandra."

"Do I have to get a restraining order?" Wanda asked before I could get the charm going.

"I was wondering if you have any updates on our building."

"Yeah, they're tearing it down," she said. "Now will you please stop calling me?"

"Are they really tearing it down?"

"They declared the damage too extensive." After pausing a moment she added, "Hey, it's not so bad. The insurance company is paying a lump sum check to everyone, and Hell's Kitchen is dead anyway. Brooklyn is the new Manhattan. I got a place on the fourth stop out on the L train and it's actually kind of cute."

"Well, I'm not going to be pushed out of Manhattan!" I shouted from a hilltop in Tennessee.

"Good for you," she replied, "but do me a favor. In the future, tell someone who gives a damn." She hung up, thus ending my relationship with the New York neighbor who I only really became acquainted with when I left the city.

I walked down the hillside, past the spot where Floyd had found the burglar's body, setting my entire plight in motion. When I entered the side door of the Blue Suede, someone greeted me. It was the beautiful Thelma Presley, the other female Elvis.

"You still got a ways to go," she said, seeing me check the posted roster. They were about three-quarters of the way down the list.

Even though she was older than me, she said she liked to think of herself as a younger Elvis when he was still androgynous looking. Since she had suddenly decided to be chatty, I asked her a variety of questions about the Blue Suede.

"This is honestly the first time I've had the confidence to go into competition here. If you want the voice of experience, ask Sir Elmo Presley," she said, pointing to the dealer at a table full of poker-playing Elvises. "He been singing in sideburns since the beginning."

By this point most of them were fairly boozed up and relaxed. Pulling up a chair, I watched their card game. Pictures of Elvis at different stages of his fame were imprinted on the face of different cards. A boyhood photo of Elvis was on the 2s, and the Vegas Elvis appeared on the kings.

"You did that wedding down in Knoxville, did you?" I heard Sir Elmo mutter to another.

"You mean in June?" answered another. Both men were clearly older than Elvis had been when he died.

"Yeah, the Gunthers."

"The Gustlers," Sir Elmo corrected. "They approached me first and I told them I wouldn't do it for a penny less than five."

"I told them four," another Elvis said, issuing his asymmetrical grin. The man no longer even knew he was imitating Elvis—he had become the King.

"Well believe me, when I was done," said the Elvis impersonator who got the Gustler job, "I wish I passed on it cause there was about a thousand guests and that bride was nothing but a bitch in satin. She didn't like my 'Hound Dog.' Said I wasn't moving my pelvis fast enough, and on and on."

"I wouldn't mind moving her pelvis," joked Sir Elmo. In a moment, another younger Elvis dropped some chips in the pot and called. All showed—Sir Elmo won with a two pair, king high.

"Any of you fellas know this John Carpenter guy?" I spoke up as they were throwing in antes for the next hand.

"Carpenter? You mean the owner here?" asked one African American Elvis with a pencil-thin mustache.

"Yeah."

"I knewed him," a raspy voice grunted.

"Me too." The others slowly nodded as the dealing began.

"Does he judge this shindig?"

"He's one of the judges, I think," said a decrepit-looking Elvis who probably most resembled the King in his grave. "Snake Major is the main judge. He was one of the original Memphis Mafia. Sits right in the middle."

"What does this Carpenter guy look like anyhow?" I asked one and all.

"A nice, quiet, older gentleman," said Sir.

"Does he have any identifying marks or features?" I asked.

"I don't rightly remember. It's been a few years since I saw him naked." Everyone chuckled as he started replacing cards that had been cast away.

"Do any of you fellas remember seeing him?" I asked.

"I believe I once saw him when the place first opened," said the lecherous chief Elvis. "He was all messed up, in a wheelchair—I think he was Elvis Knievel." A couple others laughed. Sensing he was just trying to get into my jumpsuit, I ignored him.

"I thought he was the short, fat guy who looked like a mobster," said one Italian Elvis puffing a cigar. In that room, Elvis almost seemed to be a recessive gene.

"No, that guy's one of the locals who works here. I think he's a manager."

"Isn't he that fella with the busty mermaid tattooed on his arm?" asked another.

"No, that was old Sylvester. He was the manager here back in the '90s, but he died of lung cancer a few years ago."

Though everyone was reluctant to say it, they were confirming my worst fears. No one knew of this phantom partner, let alone what had led him to turn this place into an Elvis-themed establishment. One by one, as the minutes ticked away, the remaining Elvi fell like grains of sand into that great hourglass of the stage.

Many rested or dozed before their big moment. Most were able to instantly get buzzed up when their numbers came up.

While tiredly watching the card game and listening over the speakers to some young tense Elvis screwing up the lyrics to "Viva Las Vegas," I started getting queasy. That was when I felt a big hand grab my ass. Big Chief Elvis was standing behind me with a giant smile.

"You dumb . . . fucking . . . Elvis impersonator!!"

"What'd you say?" Everyone in the room went silent.

"You heard me!" I might as well have screamed out the N word at the Apollo Theater up in Harlem.

"Elvis was a great man!" he returned, and rose to his feet. "And I'm proud to honor that."

"Elvis was a bloated, pill-popping hack, but at least he didn't have to imitate anyone!"

"Lady," warned Sir Elmo, "I don't know who or where you

think you are, but this is a hallowed shrine of worship, and you just took our Lord's name in vain." All veiny eyes were upon me.

"Number nineteen!" the Elvis wrangler dashed in and shouted. It was the number I had spent my entire night waiting for.

"Wish me luck," I said to my colleagues, then dashed out.

CHAPTER SEVENTEEN

The spotlights, the cameras, the petals of the audience faces—all sucked the air right out of my lungs. *Do it for Gustavo*, I thought. I took a deep breath and started singing "Viva Las Vegas," which was actually a fun tune, even if it was a bit of a tongue twister. By the time the applause hit, I was winded but felt a lot calmer. I wiped my brow and began song number two. "Suspicious Minds" flowed from my lips quicker than I could ever remember practicing it. Though I thought I had done my best vocalization to date, I completely forgot to employ any of my well-practiced Elvis expressions.

Before singing the last song, I had the wherewithal to break the first rule of the contest by shouting out, "On behalf of all the Elvises here, I'd like to dedicate this song to the man that made this all possible, the owner of the establishment—Mr. John Carpenter. Please take a bow, sir."

Since no one was supposed to do this, it seemed truly innovative and I earned a huge cheer from the audience. Shielding my eyes, I looked at the three noble figures seated at the judges' table before me. None of them rose, let alone bowed.

"Well, I'd like to give Mr. Carpenter a big hand, even if it feels severed at the wrist," I said and clapped. Even though the audience must've thought the remark strange, they cheered again, and I felt that if he was out there, I was sure as hell getting his attention. I quickly commenced my last song, "In the Ghetto." Then I took my best little-girl curtsy, thanked everyone, and stepped back into the void.

"Just what the fuck do you think you're pulling?" the Elvis wrangler yelled at me as he followed me down the corridor echoing with applause. "If I didn't know you lost, I'd have you disqualified right then and there. And fuck if you're getting a consolation gift!"

"I don't want any bullshit gifts!"

"Fine, you head on back now. Some of them boys want a word with you." That was when I remembered that I had parted with my fellow tribute singers rather abruptly.

Rather than pass through the gauntlet of angry Elvises, I turned left and exited through the kitchen. Heading out to my car, I tugged off the sideburns and caught my breath. I knew I had lost, but I also knew I couldn't just leave. I had to go back inside that bar and still try to locate that goddamn phantom Carpenter. The only problem was, I was truly exhausted. Not only was my mojo low, I now doubted that the man actually existed. And I was certain Snake was a killer. I felt bad for Vinetta and the kids, but I had a strong urge to drive back to New York, even if it meant moving to goddamn Brooklyn.

I decided to turn around and pay my final respects to Gustavo at that spot where he had been shot. Instead of stopping there, though, I kept walking up to the little clearing at the top of the hill. With the old mansion behind me and the Blue Suede before me, I looked down over its roof and could see one of the two narrow rivers that defined distant Mesopotamia. Five minutes turned to ten before my cell phone rang.

"Cassandra, is that you?"

It was Paul, my soon-to-be-ex-husband, returning my call. Feeling incredibly isolated, I took a deep breath and said, "Yeah, how are you?"

"Where are you?"

"About an hour and a half northeast of Memphis, stuck on a dead-end story."

He said he had heard Gustavo died and that he was very sorry.

We talked awhile, tiptoeing awkwardly around a minefield of sensitive topics, until a big cheer went up from the old roadhouse. They had undoubtedly announced the King of the Sing. Paul mentioned how his new job was sapping up all his time. He was now sleeping, shaving, and eating in the studio.

"I tried to get some coverage for your FEMA story," he said, "but you know how the news works. It's only news after a disaster happens."

While we talked for several more minutes, I watched waves of people getting in their cars and zooming off.

"So what are you covering down there anyway?" he asked.

"The Scrubbs case," I explained. I mentioned that I would've been home by now but my building had been condemned and I was temporarily homeless. As our conversation unraveled, the last of the dented jalopies that had created such an acute traffic jam finally broke up and drove off. That year's Sing the King festival was officially over.

"So are you seeing anyone?" he asked.

"No. Are you still sleeping with your interns?"

"It was just once, and believe me, I wish I didn't—" *Wham!*

An instant later, when I came to, I was on the ground. My skull hurt and my cell phone was nowhere to be found. Snake Major was standing over me with three other assholes.

"Where the fuck is it?" he hissed.

"Where is Carpenter?" I replied. Despite my throbbing head, I rose to my feet.

"You don't know shit, now give me the hand!"

"I know that Rod East and his brother Pappy wrote that book about Elvis and you killed them."

He grabbed me by the throat and pinned me back to the ground. "I will fucking kill you quick if I don't get that hand back."

"Special Agent Ron Wallace of the Memphis field office of the FBI has possession of the hand."

Snake smacked me across my mouth, then shouted back behind him, "Instead of fucking that half-wit widow, you were supposed to get it."

"Sorry," I heard, and realized he was talking to Minister Beaucheete. I also saw that the other two of his beer-bellied scumbags were holding rifles. Snake suddenly pulled a hatchet out from his belt.

"Hold on there." The minister began backing away.

"I need a hand," Snake said to me, "and if you don't have it, I'll take yours—and throw the rest of you away." He dramatically lifted the small axe above his head.

"There's three of you here," I warned. "One of you will talk and the others will spend the rest of your lives in jail. It always works out that way."

"She's right," Beaucheete affirmed.

"That's a risk we'll just have to take." Snake grinned at me.

"I sure as hell ain't taking part in this," the minister said, and started walking down the hill.

Ignoring him, Snake barked, "This is your last chance, where's the fucking hand!"

"I don't think so, you son of a bitch!" came a shrill female voice in the distance. Vinetta dashed forward, pointing Floyd's old hunting rifle before her.

Snake calmly set the axe on the ground. While turning to look her square in the eyes, he pulled a pistol from a shoulder holster. She shot him squarely in the chest, knocking him down with a load of buckshot in his lungs. In terror she dropped the rifle.

"Fuckin' hell! Shoot that bitch!" Snake groaned. One of the other barflies let loose a shot in her direction.

"I've got seven children and no father thanks to you!" she shrieked, cowering to her knees.

Two rifles were now trained on her. Each man seemed to be waiting for the other to pull the trigger.

I jumped forward, grabbing at the nearest rifle, but was

knocked to the ground by its barrel. A weapon was now trained at me. The second prick still held Vinetta in his sites.

"Stay away from my mom!" It was Floyd Jr.'s squeaky little voice coming from behind a tree. The guy pointing his rifle at me suddenly took a shot at the eight-year-old. Vinetta screeched and, ignoring the guns, raced over to him.

"I told you to stay in the truck, damnit!" she yelled as she grabbed him.

"What are you waiting for!" Snake called out again, considerably weaker. He wasn't exsanguinating quickly enough.

"That's enough," a deep, stern voice somewhere above us rang out.

One of the assholes dashed over to the Snake, who had finally passed into unconsciousness.

"He did this to protect you," the other one said to the mangled groundskeeper, not putting down his rifle.

"I can goddamn well protect *myself*," Jeeves growled back angrily. "I sure as hell never asked anyone to do anything, particularly kill on my behalf!"

"He murdered my husband!" Vinetta shouted out, pointing at Snake. Floyd Jr. grabbed her hand.

"All I know is that your husband tried to extort me. And you shot Snake, who might've been behind his killing, so at best we're all even." When Vinetta reached down to pick up her gun, the barfly who was still holding his weapon aimed it back at her.

"You take your mama down to the parking lot, son," Jeeves said calmly to Floyd Jr.

"No sir, we ain't leaving without Miss Bloomgarten," the eight-year-old said boldly.

"Well, she's free to go, but I think we still have things to discuss."

"We certainly do."

"Then we'll stick around too," Vinetta said.

"You guys go ahead," I said. "I'm okay. I'll meet you at home."

"She's quite safe," Jeeves assured them.

Vinetta and her son turned and started down the dark, wooded slope.

"You sure you want to handle it this way?" one of the old bastards quietly asked Jeeves.

"You guys call Nick and get him back over here. Tell him there's been a terrible accident." It sounded like Nick was more of an employee than a law officer. "Oh, and do it from the bar. Keep me out of it."

"Will do," one of them mumbled.

The two old alcoholics trudged downhill and I followed Carpenter the other way, toward the old mansion.

CHAPTER EIGHTEEN

Vinetta is now the sole provider for seven kids living in a broken-down trailer," I explained as I caught up.

"I'm sorry for her woes," he said, "but contrary to popular belief, I'm not a rich man. And as a matter of principle, I refuse to pay off blackmailers or their survivors. Her husband shouldn't've gone around extorting people."

"True, but he shouldn't've had his shack booby-trapped either."

"Let me tell you something about Snake. If you say he shot this husband, I might believe you, but no one around here can so much as plug in a waffle iron without getting shocked. There's no way he could've trip-wired someone's house."

"How about Rod East?"

"Who?" he said, snickering a bit.

"The first Elvis impersonator who was killed outside the Blue Suede."

"I have no idea who you are talking about."

I wasn't sure if he was just feigning ignorance, but I gave him the benefit of the doubt and filled him in as we walked up to his mansion: About thirty years ago, two guys, Rod East and his brother Pappy, cowrote a book called *Elvis, Why?* about the King's unknown drug problem. The book sold well, and a number of years ago Rod turned up here and tried to extort the owner of the Blue Suede. He was killed and buried on the hill. Then, more recently, a local private investigator named Floyd Loyd accidentally discovered the body. Shortly afterward, he tried to extort the owner of the Blue Suede and he was blown up along with his toolshed, allegedly the result of him making crystal meth, only there was no real evidence of this. Then, about two weeks ago, a guy was shot while allegedly trying to break into the Blue Suede. That was Pappy East, the brother of the first extortionist.

"And that young mama was married to one of those brothers?"

"No, she was married to Floyd, the investigator whose shack blew up, but she swears he had nothing to do with drugs. He was killed by someone here."

"How do you like that," he said.

"Well, I'm a little confused by something that I was hoping you could help me with."

"What's that?"

"First, why would you assume the name of someone you killed?"

Jeeves stared and smiled. "For starters, I never killed anyone."

"Okay, but you can't say you didn't know who Rod East was. Why would you take the name of someone Elvis had despised?"

"See, I was using the name Carpenter, but it wasn't my legal name and I desperately needed a new identity—ideally someone real with a past, but no friends or family. Snake said no one even asked about the guy once he vanished. He was the one who suggested I take the name."

"So you knew the burglar?"

"He woke me up one night, trying to kill me. Snake grabbed him, but I didn't see what he did with the guy."

"But if you took his name . . ."

"Yeah, I figured they killed him."

"So why would you take the name of a murder victim?"

"I needed a legal nomenclature to establish ownership. People here usually just call me John. And I know it sounds odd, but I guess taking the name of the man who the King of Rock and Roll hated seemed like the best way to distance myself from Elvis."

"Wouldn't taking his name make you the number one suspect?"

"Yes, but a lot of time had passed without so much as a missing-person's report. I mean, Snake described it best when he said it was like he was never born."

"Ever think that maybe Snake was trying to set you up?"

"Wouldn't put it past him," he replied tensely. "Snake likes having his hooks in everyone. It makes them much more controllable, don't it?"

"So what exactly are you hiding from?" I asked meekly.

"I guarantee I never killed or hurt anyone," he said as he opened the door to the old mansion, wiping his feet on the doormat. "Also, there are no warrants out for my arrest, and that's all I'll say about that."

"Well, why did Rod East attack you in the first place?" I followed him in.

"First, I just thought he was a burglar, but then I figured he was trying to extort me."

"Extort you with what?"

"The same thing your friend Loyd was trying to extort from me."

"And do you know what that was?"

"Just being who I am," Jeeves said, then pursed his lips and sadly looked dead ahead.

"And who are you?" He didn't respond. Since I was more preoccupied with getting some settlement for Vinetta, I asked, "Snake and you own this place, right?"

"Along with the liquor store and gas station. Why?"

"Cause I can't stop Vinetta from filing a wrongful-death suit against Snake's estate."

"She'd have a hell of a time trying to convince a jury of all this."

"True, but considering the fact that you're hiding your true identity, wouldn't her naming you in a suit throw up a lot of unwanted publicity?"

"That is true. On the other hand, I'd be very curious if she could even spell my name."

"Look, if you'd consider making an anonymous contribution," I said, "I can probably get her down to thirty thousand—"

"See, now, if I *was* in the business of killing extortionists, I'd shoot you right now," he interrupted as he led me into the luxurious bathroom on the ground floor. "I suppose you're doing all this for goodwill."

"I'm doing this now because my friend was just shot outside here a few weeks ago."

"I was here. And neither of you were supposed to be here."

"We were investigating the Missy Scrubbs kidnapping."

"Shit! That idiot son of his now gets all Snake's property."

"Snake has a little snake?"

"He sure does, and now I'm partnered up with his drugged-out, tattooed gangster ass." Jeeves rolled his eyes and looked off, exasperated.

"Where is he?"

"He took off with your little piece of jailbait."

"What jailbait?"

He turned on the lights around the bathroom mirror and poked through his medicine chest. "You just said you were investigating her." He was referring to missing Missy Scrubbs!

"Yeah, that's why we came up here," I said, not letting on that I didn't know this crucial detail until he just spilled it—Snake's son was Missy Scrubbs's abductor.

Silently, the older man spread some bacitracin on a cotton swab.

"How about this," he said softly as he dabbed my wounded scalp with the swab. "I'll tell you where you can find Roscoe Major and Missy, which should pay you a pretty penny in your line of work, and we'll forget all about this talk of lawsuits and anonymous donations."

The man wasn't dumb: viced in by two annoying forces—me and the prospect of partnering up with Roscoe Major—he knew how to use one against the other. "Let me get this straight, you're going to tell me where Missy Scrubbs is?" Dollar signs suddenly lit up in my eyes.

"I hate ratting folks out," Jeeves continued, "but he didn't have the good sense to run, even after I gave him my car, *my own car!* And there's just no way I'm going to be able to work with someone that stupid."

"You gave him your pink Cadillac?"

"I had just bought a new one." That explained the two different pink Cadillacs.

There was an awkward pause, so it seemed like a good moment to explain why I was giving him preferential treatment.

"There's something I should tell you."

"I'm listening."

"Remember that strange night when we slept together?"

"If I didn't, you wouldn't be here now."

"I'm presently carrying your baby."

He stared hard at me, then gasped for air. "Oh shit! You're not going to say I raped you or file for child support, are you?"

"Hell no. I'm a forty-five-year-old burn-out. In my position, if you're childless and pregnant, you have to keep the kid."

"Nothing quite like a mother's love," he replied, then abruptly changed the subject and said that he was starving. When I confessed that I hadn't eaten all day and was hungry as well, he led me into his large kitchen.

"You don't have to worry about anything," I assured him while he prepared snacks. "I've got resources. Hell, I'm even married."

"Won't your husband mind you carrying another man's seed?"

"He spent four years trying to impregnate me. We're in the process of getting divorced."

"Well, I sure ain't marrying again," He took a large cast-iron pot out of the fridge and put it on the stove.

"In the event that I do have this baby, can I ask you a question?"

"Shoot."

"Who can I say is the father?"

He halted his food preparations and just smiled.

"I guess I can say it was someone I met one drunken night in the parking lot of a backwoods bar, but I'd rather give him a name."

"See now, this is why I let old Snake run the front of the house all these years. This is why I want my name kept out of things . . ." This was also why Rod East tried extorting him in the first place, unleashing a massive tangle of murders, extortions, and retributions—all to keep his identity secret.

"You're secret's safe with me . . . Mr. Presley."

"I thought I read somewhere that Elvis Presley died."

"Then why does your DNA match his?" According to the tubular letter Floyd had left Vinetta in the septic tank, he had taken the tuft of white hair from Rod East's pocket and matched it against a single strand of Elvis's hair that he had purchased on eBay, thus launching his failed career as a blackmailer.

"My DNA matches his, huh?"

"There were gray hairs in Rod East's wallet." I bluffed since I never actually saw them.

Jeeves started laughing. "That explains why the son of a bitch yanked out a handful of my hair before Snake got to him. Holy shit! So that guy wasn't after *me* at all—he thought I was Elvis!"

"He's not the only one."

"Come on, quit kidding."

"At the state fair, you let slip that you were born around the same time as Elvis."

"A child is born every six seconds . . ."

"And someone dies every thirteen seconds," I completed.

"Do you think Elvis was the only kid born in Tupelo, Mississippi, that day?" he asked as he filled two big bowls of soup. He took out a thick loaf of multigrain bread and sawed off several slices.

"I guess the only thing left for me to do is poison you," he said, leading me to his beautiful mosaic dining room table.

"So if you're not the King, what's with the identity theft? Are you wanted by the law?"

"No, just a small syndicate of very large Italian American men. I had a major gambling debt that I could never hope to repay. When my face and body got scrambled in the car crash, I knew they couldn't ID me, so I took on the name Carpenter. But it wasn't permanent; I needed to slip into someone else's identity."

"You know, there isn't a law against being Elvis Presley."

"That's true. Hell, I know a bunch of people who want to be him. Look, if I was Elvis do you think I'd let my daughter marry that pedophile?" I guessed he was referring to Michael Jackson.

"Maybe you still secretly see her," I countered. "Don't worry, I won't tell anyone you stole his DNA."

"I'll admit it, we do have a few things in common. I was born on his birthday."

"And you have his *same* DNA," I kept pushing.

"Maybe so."

"Cause you're him."

"That's where it stops."

"How can you have the same DNA and not be him?"

"You have to be monozygotic."

It took me a moment to realize what he was saying. "You're his twin!"

"On January 8, 1935, Gladys Love Presley gave birth to two boys at a free clinic in Tupelo, Mississippi. What she didn't know was that just minutes earlier, another woman named Caroline Lee had just given birth to her third stillborn before passing out. Caroline was suicidal about having that boy. Her younger sister, Enid, just happened to be the birthing nurse—the only one on duty that day.

"After sedating her beloved sister, she came in and handled Gladys's labor all by her lonesome. When she saw my mother punch two healthy boys out of her belly, she grabbed me and rushed into Caroline's room, tossing me into her bassinet. Then she rushed back into Gladys's room with Caroline's stillborn and claimed it was me. All babies look alike, don't they?"

"Is this a joke?" My soup spoon no longer worked.

"I wish it was," said the man I called Jeeves. "In fairness, I really don't think my aunt intended it to be a permanent crime. I think she expected that when her sister calmed down, she'd return me or something, but that's not what happened."

"I never heard that Elvis had a twin."

"Then you didn't do your homework, cause Elvis's twin is public record. Instead of me, though, my biological ma unwittingly named that poor stillborn Jesse Garon and planted it in the ground."

"You're kidding me, aren't you?" There was one simple way to determine this: locate the twin's seventy-year-old grave, exhume the fetus, and perform a DNA test. But that was simply too gruesome.

"Look, people snatch babies all the time. And if you check, you'll see many of them are women who repeatedly try and fail to have their own kids. Your tabloids are always writing about it. There's even a word for someone like me: a changeling. But this time Caroline Lee's sister just didn't know she was stealing the twin of the great Elvis Presley."

I thought about it a moment. As someone who had lost a child after going to full-term, I was easily able to identify with Enid. A spare baby at that moment when Paul was about to walk into my hospital room would've saved my life.

"What was your adopted mother like?"

"Caroline Lee was a loving, capable mom, but I always knew something was wrong. She used to cry at night, hugging me close to her. I remember her saying things like, 'I did an awful thing, but I ain't never giving you back.'"

"You must resent what happened to you."

"At first I did, but the more I learned about Elvis's upbringing, the luckier I felt. This was near the end of the Great Depression and the woman who stole me had a much nicer house. Her husband made a decent salary."

"So what was your given name?" I pressed.

"None of your business," he answered with a smile. "But if your son or daughter asks who their daddy is, you can say he started out as Jesse but was renamed Langford Lee. And because I looked and sounded like Elvis Presley, once I got out of college back in the '50s, I immediately got a gig to sing the King when he was still in his twenties. Hell, I honestly think I was the very first Elvis impersonator back then."

"All those years and you didn't think it was odd that he looked like you and was born in the same time and place as you?"

"Course I did, I even wrote him a letter. But if even I didn't even believe it, why the hell should he?" Pausing a moment, he added, "I didn't learn the truth till after my parents died. My aunt told me in 1968, just before she passed away."

"So how'd you hook up with Snake?"

"Well, by the winter of '75 I owed a hundred grand."

"That's some debt."

"Oh yeah, it was a fortune back then. Hell, I had a hit put on me," he said with a swell of pride. "My wife took our little girl and left me."

"So what happened?"

"I went on the run is what happened. Then one night I was passing through Vegas and saw that Elvis was supposed to perform at the Sands. I had lost my last fifty bucks at the blackjack table, when some guy comes up to me and says, 'Whatchu doing here, boss?' That was the first time I met Snake Major. He said, 'Shit, anyone ever tell you you look like Elvis?' I told him what I had learned, that he was my identical twin brother. After I told him the whole story, he said, 'How'd you like to tell Elvis that yourself?' When I said I'd love to, he led me upstairs. Five minutes later I'm walking into a hotel room and shaking hands with the King of Rock and Roll."

"Wow!"

"By that time, the poor man was a total mess—bloated, sweaty, lying on his bed having difficulty breathing."

"Did you tell him you were his twin?"

"I took out my driver's license and showed him my date of birth. We talked and just compared notes. He was impressed about all the details, but . . ."

"Didn't you offer to submit to a test?"

"They didn't really have DNA tests back then. I mean, we looked alike, but so what? I couldn't exactly sue him for twin support. People were always trying to scam him. For my part, in addition to being grateful that he'd even meet with me, I was just amazed by all our similarities."

"Like what?"

"My wife had divorced me. I had a little girl. I wasn't doing great, being on the lam and all. I even had a substance abuse problem, but nothing like his."

"Then what?"

"Well, he still had some time left on his tour, which wasn't going very well, in terms of his health. Supposedly he got so tired he laid down on the stage during his previous show. So when Snake asked me if I could carry a tune, I belted out a couple bars of "Don't Be Cruel" and even the King thought it was good. It was funny cause he actually stood alongside me giving directions about how to hold the mic and other little secrets about singing."

"Wow, you got notes from the King himself."

"About an hour later Colonel Parker came into the room and auditioned me. I actually thought I did a crappy job, but he was just tickled pink. I was probably about fifty pounds lighter than Elvis. Even he said I looked and sounded better. I mean the poor son of a bitch had just been used up."

"So you toured in his place?"

"You heard of lip syncing, well I did body syncing. Ended up doing two of his shows."

"Then what?"

"Then I got two grand, which was the most I ever got paid per hour. Unfortunately, it wasn't nearly enough to get me out of debt, but it was a real blast. Elvis thanked me and said he'd call if he ever needed me again, but you could see he didn't like it. He loved his public and he wasn't trying to con anyone. He was stuck in a jam and I helped him out. I wish I had given him his cash back."

"And that's it."

"That's everything. Two years later, in August, I was working at an auto plant in Detroit when it came over the radio that he had died."

"How did you wind up looking like . . . you do now?" If Elvis Presley had looked into a mirror that was shattered into a million pieces and reglued upside down and backward—that's how Jeeves looked.

"On August 29, 1979, about two years after the King's death, I was speeding drunk as a skunk when I slammed my Chrysler LeBaron into a retaining wall. I was going about a hundred miles an hour. The accident burned over 90 percent of my body, and shattered many of my bones including my lower spine and skull. I died on the operating table and was brought back. That's when I realized there really is a God."

"I guess something like that would make a believer out of anyone," I replied, not meaning to sound disparaging.

"It was more than that. While lying in recovery, I was told that my heart had also stopped. The doctors worked and worked, and I came back at the last moment. See, that's what I realized. God took the both of us, my twin and me, but for some reason he returned only me. God gave *me* the second chance."

"Sounds like Elvis died for your sins."

"In a way he did, and since I got out of that hospital, I pray to God and my brother by taking care of myself—no drink, no drugs, no fatty foods. I walk thirty-three minutes a day."

"You still have drunken sex with strangers," I pointed out.

"Hey, darling, every Christian is a hypocrite. Besides, womanizing was never an affliction for me. I just didn't get any."

"How'd you get involved with Snake again and open the Blue Suede?"

"I bumped into him just after I got out of the hospital. He had a small bar in Memphis. When I told him that we met once, years ago in Vegas, he just said he didn't know me. Then when I said I was Elvis's twin, his jaw dropped. He said he didn't believe me. I looked . . . well, like I do now. But he saw that I was down on my luck, and apparently not many people knew about that event, so he gave me a mop and bucket and told me if I wanted to clean up the bathrooms at night, no one else would touch them. I did that for a few months, and then he let me clean up the bar. I couldn't work behind the counter cause no one would order drinks from this face. Gradually, though, it became clear that he believed me. I think it was my voice. That didn't change and I still did the best Elvis covers." In perfect Elvis pitch to the tune of "Suspicious Minds," he sang, "*I'm Elvis's twin, I can't change that, I was born with his baby . . .*"

"Wow."

"Anyway, after about five years, he took me aside one day and handed me a check and a proposal. It was for twenty grand. He said that he knew Elvis would want me to have it. Elvis was always about family."

"Amazing that he believed you."

"I think the fact that I didn't go to the tabloids with the story and try exploiting him for every possible cent made me credible."

"He's right," I said. "That would've been a million-dollar story."

"Truth is, I would've tried doing that, considering all the circumstantial evidence and whatnot, but I still had a contract on my head. Before handing over the check, Snake made a generous offer. He said he wanted to get out of Memphis, go back to good country living, and he'd found this old barnhouse up here. If I wanted, he'd keep the twenty grand and I could partner up with him. I think he wanted the Elvis imprimatur that only a twin could provide."

"How'd you get the mansion?"

"It's his mansion, I really am just the groundskeeper," he said. "Snake bought a newer house so he let me live here. He was always quite generous if you played ball with him."

I chuckled and confessed that I still didn't fully believe any of this.

"Hey, I hope you don't believe me."

"Okay," I countered, "let's just say hypothetically that Elvis did discover a twin or someone who kind of looked like him, but this was in the mid-'70s when his drug-addled lifestyle had spun out of control. And he desperately wanted a way out . . ."

"Please don't suggest something stupid, like Elvis killed his own twin just so he could—"

"I was going to suggest that the twin actually overdosed. I mean, what proof do you have that you're the copy and not the original?"

"Being Elvis's twin is like being the very small moon to a very large planet. Every day I feel his gravitational pull. And my pulling back is all I have to make me *me*."

"Have you ever considered how much money you can get just telling your story?"

"Didn't you say the story you came down here for was that little piece of tail from Memphis who ran off with Snake's son?"

"Who?"

"You know: the girl from Memphis who all you reporters are writing about . . ."

Despite all he was saying, I strongly sensed that I was looking at the living, breathing King of Rock and Roll. He was only bringing up Missy Scrubbs because he wanted me to overlook a much bigger story that would be far harder to prove.

Revealing this small-town bar owner as Elvis Presley—or even his twin—would make me an easy million. It would get me endless assignments and thrust me permanently into the limelight of tabloid writing. At the end of my life, it would be the lasting detail emblazoned on my obituary. Every bone in my body said, *Go for it*, but the little squiggly tadpole still inside my womb said otherwise. If this pregnancy did actually go to full-term, how would I tell my child that I sold out his daddy?

"So where's Missy Scrubbs?" I asked to bring it all to an end.

"Hiding out with Roscoe Major, living off the ransom money they took from that poor accountant husband of hers down in Memphis."

"And where exactly are they hiding?"

Jeeves said he'd find out first thing tomorrow. When I drowsily plunked down into a recliner, he offered to let me spend the night. It was around three in the morning and I could never get a full night's sleep at Vinetta's, so I agreed.

Several hours later I awoke to the sound of a police walkie-talkie. Sheriff Nick was moving up over the hill with one of the Evils, inspecting the site of poor Snake's recent hunting accident. When I peeked out, I could see one of the barflies handing over Vinetta's gun as his own. I returned to sleep only to be awakened about an hour later when my cell rang. It turned out to be Vinetta asking why the heck I hadn't returned home yet.

"All is fine," I told her, still too tired to elaborate. She let me return to sleep, but I didn't. All I could think about was what I could do for her and those seven needy little children. They were looking for some miracle and I was supposed to provide it.

The phone interrupted my worries. This time it was Ludmilla. Before I could ask to call back, she said that last night she and Bella had been watching a local variety show, which this week was the Sing the King contest, and to their shock they saw me performing onstage.

"You're supposed to be in New York raising seven kids!" she reminded me. "What the hell is going on?"

When I asked her where she was, she said she was still at Rodmilla's house.

"We're waiting for the agents," she explained.

"What agents?"

"Real estate agents, about selling the home and store."

I told her to drip some hazelnut decaf, I'd be there within the hour to explain everything. As I headed out, Elvis's alleged twin walked me out near my car and said, "Give me your cell number?"

I scribbled it down for him.

"I'm having a bit of trouble finding Roscoe's whereabouts, but I'm heading down to Memphis to get it for you."

"You're not going to vanish on me, are you?"

"You know I'll always be with you, darling," he said in perfect Elvis pitch, then he was gone.

CHAPTER NINETEEN

Forty-five minutes later, hastily dressed and still groggy, I was pulling into the gravel-crunchy driveway of Rodmilla's house in Mesopotamia.

Bella greeted me at the door and led me inside where I could see the place had been cleared out and cleaned impeccably. Many of the little personal flourishes acquired over a lifetime had been thrown out or packed in boxes. Most of the furniture was piled in the rear, close to the driveway.

"We're donating it all to whichever organization sends a truck soonest," Bella explained. "An agent came by yesterday and made an assessment."

"ZigRat's too?"

"We're closing it next week to sell off whatever stock we can. Poor Pete's taking it the hardest."

"What the heck's going on with you?" Ludmilla came flying down the stairs. "Why were you on that show, and where are your kids?"

"Would you like something to drink?" Bella said, a little more relaxed. "I just mixed a mint julep."

"Oh, I can't," I said. "I'm pregnant."

"You're kidding! An eighth baby?"

"I have a slight confession," I said. "Those weren't my kids. I was babysitting when you called, so I told them to say they were mine." The two sisters exchanged glances.

"We kinda figured as much," Ludmilla replied, chuckling.

"Really?"

"Sweety, you're of Asian extraction and you show up with

seven of the blondest Aryan children I ever saw outside of Germany. We might be dumb, but we're not stupid."

I started giggling with embarrassment.

"What we really want to know is why you pulled a stunt like that."

"I know it was dumb, but I just felt so inadequate with you both, and the fact that Mom died and neither of you even called me—I felt you were trying to squeeze me out."

"That doesn't explain what you're doing in an Elvis Presley look-alike contest," Ludmilla responded.

"Actually, I was working on a story regarding several murders down here—"

"Who's their real mother?" Luddy interrupted. "Where does she live?"

It was then the flash strobed across the wide synapses of my pickled brain, sparking the great idea: *this* big old home would be perfect for Vinetta. Not only would her kids have a great space where they could grow up, but she could run the old store out front, which always earned Mom a decent income.

"How much did the agent think this place could go for?"

"She thought that a small successful store and a big house out here could fetch somewhere between two-fifty and three hundred thousand."

"She said the local real estate market hasn't been too strong since the mine went under."

"Cassandra, if you're worried that we're going to cut you out," Ludmilla said, "I guarantee you'll get your third."

"No, I just think I might have a prospective buyer, but she's not exactly rich. She's the mother of all those kids."

"Where do they live?" Ludmilla asked with her typical maternal concern.

"In a broken-down trailer in Daumland," I said. "If I could get two-forty—that's eighty thousand dollars apiece—would you guys consider it?"

"I'd need some time to think about it," Ludmilla responded.

"Me too," Bella said, but then added, "I'd be more inclined to say yes if they agreed to keep Pete on."

"Absolutely," Ludmilla said, giving me a spark of hope. My sisters were both genuinely concerned about the man who had spent his entire life helping mom.

"Do me a favor and don't donate any of the furniture until you decide," I said. "In fact, hold onto everything except for Mom's personal effects."

"Why?"

"Vinetta will probably need them."

"Okay." Both had to make some calls in order to undo plans to scatter possessions, but they were willing to help.

I used the time to go to the store, which had about half a dozen people inside purchasing heavily discounted items.

"I'm so sorry about your mother's passing," Pete said when I greeted him.

I heard an annoyed cough behind me. One of the locals was holding a bag of nearly brown apples and a dusty carton of spaghetti. I stepped to one side and let Pete tally up and bag the purchase.

"How are you fixed for cash?" I asked.

"Between my disability, my savings, and Social Security, I'm okay," he said. "But what will I do with my days other than just sit in my room?"

"Well, I know a young woman who might take over the store. She has a bunch of kids and could use someone of your expertise, though she doesn't have much money."

"We can work that out." Pete was always kind and patient with us when we were growing up.

"She really doesn't know anything about the business."

"Well, I don't know anything else *but* this business, so we'd be a pretty good match."

I spent the afternoon chatting with my sisters, resisting the temptation to drink and smoke. For the baby's sake, I had to be good. Around four o'clock my cell phone chirped.

"Okay, write this down," Elvis Presley's twin said. "Snake's son Roscoe is staying at a private bungalow on a beach in Puerto Vallarta, Mexico."

"Go on."

"I don't know if he's still there or how much longer he'll be there for, so if you hope to do this, you had better move it."

"I'll leave at once."

"A serious word of warning: Roscoe's a horny nitwit, but he's as fierce as his daddy. If he finds you, he's going to try to figure out who told you he was there before he kills you."

"I've done this a bunch of times and haven't gotten killed yet," I assured him. He gave me an address on some street called Costera a Barra de Navidad, then wished me Godspeed. I thanked him and said I'd call him when I returned.

"Careful, and good luck."

I called United Airlines and made reservations for a flight leaving that evening from Nashville to Mexico City with a one-hour wait for a connecting flight on Mexicana Airlines to sunny Puerto Vallarta. My sisters were staying at Ma's house till the middle of next week, so I told them I'd see them in a few days.

In addition to my laptop, I packed a couple articles of clothing including a bathing suit. In the trunk of my car, I looked through Gustavo's suitcase of high-tech photographic gear— some dramatic shots of Missy the runaway bride would be vital. I took his longest zoom lens and his tiny digital camera. Then I sped over to Nashville International Airport and made it through security just as they announced that my gate was open. As I dashed through the long accordion-like passage to the airplane, my phone chirped.

"What's going on?" Vin asked frantically. "Are you okay? Did he give you any cash?"

"He feels that Floyd was trying to extort him and he's sorry

Floyd was killed but an extortionist is an extortionist." The air-line stewardess grabbed my ticket and pointed me to a seat. "So the bad news is he's not paying us."

"Do we take the hand to the FBI?"

"We could go that way," I said, as I loaded my carry-ons over-head, "but even with the hand we'd have a hard time proving anything. He's claiming Snake did all the murders without his consent or knowledge and, frankly, I believe him." People seated along the aisle were glancing at me nervously.

"Shit!"

"The good news is he kind of made a counteroffer, and I think it's pretty fair, but it's a little complicated." I squeezed past two people to a window seat.

"What is it?"

"Well, it all depends on a few things. I'd rather explain it to you in person."

"Where are you? Can you come out here now?"

"I'm in Nashville and I'm about to go down to Mexico."

"Mexico?" After a long pause, her tone grew clearly suspicious and she said, "I hope you guys aren't . . . I mean, I've got seven kids, Cassandra, and I just hope their daddy didn't die for nothing."

They announced that all cell phones and other electrical equipment had to be turned off.

"Look, I don't want to get ahead of myself, but I'm pursuing something that might get the money you're looking for."

The stewardess was walking up the aisle to make sure every-one's seats were positioned upright and their belts buckled.

"What is going on!" Vin sounded like she was losing it.

It was impossible to explain everything in a matter of sec-onds, so I simply said, "Vinetta, do you trust me?"

"I guess, but—"

"Then I'm begging you: give me a little while and I'll explain everything."

"But—"

"At this point I have nothing, and there's no point in talking when you got nothing. All I'm asking for is a few more days."

"But . . ."

"What?"

"Just tell me that he didn't give you a suitcase stuffed with hundred-dollar bills and you're running off with it."

"I give you my word." The stewardess was gesturing for me to hang up.

"Cause I've had a lifetime of that."

"Trust me."

Hesitantly, she said she did, then hung up.

I buckled up and dozed off almost immediately. I awoke to severe turbulence—we were passing over the dark, bumpy terrain of northern Mexico—and I felt nauseous. Fortunately, we soon landed in the mountainous megalopolis of Mexico City. Since the flight had taken longer than planned, I made it just in time to my connecting flight.

The tropical paradise of Puerto Vallarta was so touristed up that all the locals spoke a spicy English. When I got out of the airport I could see minibuses lined up waiting to distribute the arriving passengers to the beachfront luxury resorts. Piranha-like cabbies fought over the few wide-eyed tourists who were left over. I watched as three of them actually had a tug-of-war over some scared young girl's suitcase, not even permitting her to choose. When this frenzied school of gypsy drivers tried for my bags, I told them I was waiting for the next flight out. Over the next few minutes, several different guys asked me if I wanted to buy an oceanfront timeshare. I simply shook my head until they went away.

"You gotta be from New York," said a savvy female voice seated behind me. I turned to see a tough young Latina smoking a cigarette.

"Why, are most tourists here New Yorkers?"

"About half. They always look more like terrorists than tourists." She laughed at her own joke. "Actually, I used to live there myself."

"Where?"

"El Bronx, East Tremont," she said. "Hey, I know this is a dangerous question, but you're not pregnant, are you?"

"Yeah," I said after a pause of amazement, "and I suspect the father of my child is out here with his teenage yoga instructor. I want to catch them so I can get a nice settlement."

"Then you picked the right person," she said, getting up. "Cause I've been standing where you are more than once. Only I didn't want no stinking settlement, I wanted his balls hanging on my cab's rearview mirror."

She led me to her dented cherry Nova, and though there were no sets of testicles hanging from her mirror, she did have photos of two cute kids glued to her glove compartment. I sensed she put them there as a message to possible robbers: *Don't kill me, I got kids*. The backseat was littered with empty bottles and crumpled wax papers that looked like they once held greasy sandwiches.

"Sit up front with me, Mama," she said, opening the passenger door. "The name's Magdalena."

"Do you know how to get to this place?" I unfolded the address that Presley gave me. "Costera a Barra de Navidad, number 778."

"Yes I do," she replied as I put the address back in my bag.

She hummed "Feliz Navidad" as we drove, until she suddenly had an epiphany. "Oh boy! Your husband's smart. He's a good cheater."

"Why do you say that?"

"See, his place is on a private beach with a narrow roadway that connects it to the mainland. And if it's where I think it is, we probably can't get there by land. Here's what you can do, though: my cousin fishes tuna up the coast. If you want to throw him a couple bucks, he might be able to take you out for the day."

"You're not just saying this to get more money out of me, are you?"

"I'd be dumb if I didn't try to get as much out of you as I can, but I also happen to be telling the truth. If you think I'm lying, I can take you as far as we can go."

"I'd appreciate that."

She turned on a ranchera radio station, Mexican country music. With the windows rolled down, we drove in the dry heat until we reached the Pacific Ocean, where a cool breeze was welcome relief. Then we headed north up a narrow, winding road. It descended until we were just above the beach, at which point I started getting drowsy.

"Okay, we're coming up on the address," she said, slowing down. Then she veered toward the ocean on an even smaller road. "This is it."

Sure enough, we came to a locked hurricane gate; the road continued behind it.

I got out and looked around for some street sign or numbers, something to check the address with, but found nothing. Walking up to the gate, I saw that it extended right into the waves, blocking both sides of the narrow isthmus. I peered out and could see a fishing boat bobbing off in the waves.

"If you want, you can try swimming around the gate and back to shore, but I wouldn't recommend it in your condition."

"Let's visit your cousin."

She turned the car around and we drove further north.

It was like being blind. I essentially felt at the mercy of this stranger. Even if she were honest, I wasn't sure how sharp she was, and since I didn't know the lay of the land or the people, I couldn't judge the intelligence of her decisions.

Half an hour later, she pulled into a small driveway and stopped along a rickety pier crowded with old rowboats loaded with tackle, bait, nets, and traps. Of the few that were coming or going, all had one- or two-man crews. I grabbed my purse and we carefully angled our way along the narrow, congested pier, trying not to get shat on by seagulls.

"*Dónde está Cesar*?" she asked various fishermen, who mostly just shrugged.

"He ain't coming back for a couple hours," one boy finally said to her in English. We headed on to a small shack up the road where they sold fish tacos and cold beer. We sat at one of the sticky outdoor picnic tables. When a waiter came over, Magdalena ordered a sea bass stew and two Tecates. Very native. Though I only got a bottled water, I picked up the tab.

After she finished her meal, she fidgeted around in her chair and said, "Damn, he shoulda been back by now!"

"Where do you think he is?"

"Occasionally tourists rent his boat to watch the whales."

Magdalena excused herself and circulated among the latest group of incoming fishermen eagerly hunting for her missing cousin. I sat there tiredly trying to make sense of the Spanish chatter amid the tinny music of some mariachi band playing over a distant radio. After the long day of flying and driving, I felt increasingly drowsy in the hot sun and soon fell fast asleep.

I awoke not long afterward, when some scary-looking guy asked me if I was interested in purchasing a time-share. Immediately I realized that my purse was missing. I sprang to my feet and looked around for Magdalena, but there was no sign of her. I dashed back to her car. A red van was parked in its space. Frantically I returned to the pier, where I approached several fishermen asking if they knew a guy named Cesar. I also searched for the boy who had spoken to us in English.

One very sunburned man named Cesar was finally located, but he didn't seem to know Magdalena. I had been severely duped. That bitch had stolen everything. I didn't mind that she got my clothes and Gustavo's expensive camera equipment. I didn't even mind the fact that she got my purse which held my passport, my cash, and my credit cards. But the vital scrap of paper with Roscoe's beach address was also gone. I was seriously fucked.

CHAPTER TWENTY

It wasn't like I had to rebuild my life, only reaccess the identity of it. Fortunately, there was an American consulate in Puerto Vallarta. Once I was able to hitch a ride with a truck driver back downtown within walking distance of the consulate, I knew I wouldn't starve to death in a foreign land. I patiently explained my problem to the local receptionist who had me wait for a consular agent, some woman named Johanna Carlyle. I drifted to sleep while sitting in the line of chairs until this skinny blonde delicately woke me up asking me if I was Cassandra Bloomgarten.

"A cabby stole all my bags," I said simply.

"I don't suppose you got his name or number?"

"Her named was Magdalena and she had pictures of her kids on her glove compartment." I then gave her a complete physical description.

Johanna turned out to be my hero as she carefully went down a comprehensive to-do list. One of the first things she did was Google my name. She seemed to become even more helpful when she saw that I was a working journalist. She had a friend at the police station and said that they actually had a decent rate of recovering stolen goods here, and she explained it would be wise to tip the cops for their efforts. It sounded a lot like the police crew in Daumland.

"If you can lend me the money, fine."

She had me fill out a receipt and advanced me two hundred American dollars for pocket cash.

Next I filled out a DS-64 Statement Regarding a Lost or Stolen Passport. Johanna also dialed an 800 number to report my stolen Visa card.

She even coached me on what to say to get them to return my card immediately and told me to have them send the card directly to the consulate. After going through half a dozen questions and being kept on hold for the mandatory ten minutes, I was told by the Visa operator that Magdalena had managed to put two hundred dollars of charges on my card in the last thirty minutes. The card was officially canceled and she put in an order for a new card.

"We'll send you an affidavit to fill out to expunge her charges from your account," she said with professional courtesy.

When I was done, Johanna asked where I was staying. I explained that I hadn't gotten a room yet. She suggested a thrifty motel just a short walk from the consulate and called them to make a reservation. The consulate would put me up until my credit card arrived, then I could pay them back. Soon a Mexican police officer showed up. I calmly handed him a twenty that Johanna had advanced me. He silently slipped it into his shirt pocket and asked me exactly what had happened. I walked him through it, trying to remember as many details about Magdalena as I could.

"I know most of the crooks who work here in P.V., but she's not ringing any bells," he said in perfect English. "But come by the precinct tomorrow, we'll show you some pictures. Maybe you can ID her."

I thanked him and he left. Then I thanked Johanna for all her help. She confessed that this was her specialty. She routinely helped American tourists who had been ripped off.

"The consulate is glad to assist you, but of course we expect you to pay us back once you get your Visa card tomorrow."

It was the second time she had reminded me. I assured her I would, and she had me sign some more forms. But I didn't tell her that I was intent on staying in Puerto Vallarta until I hunted down Roscoe and Missy and snapped some sellable pictures.

She recommended an inexpensive local restaurant where I went and ordered a small taco salad and white wine. As soon as the waiter brought it, though, I remembered that I was still technically pregnant and asked if he could switch it for a mango shake. But it didn't matter, I was too angry about being duped to consume more than a few lettuce leaves to feed my wiggling fetus.

Next I went to the cheap motel and asked for a quiet room. I got one in the back: no audible neighbors but no ocean view either. I took a cold shower and tried to sleep. Unable, I found myself watching crappy Mexican soap operas. I played a little game of trying to figure out the melodramas based on the characters' expressions. In the universal language of daytime soaps, everything was either shocking, lusty, violent, patronizing, or shameful. I found myself starving for subtle irony.

The next morning, after an egg-white omelet and herbal tea at a nearby American-style diner, I headed off to the consulate for my credit card. Of course it hadn't arrived. Johanna let me use her phone again—for more wasted time on hold while my call was outsourced halfway around the world. I was finally told to be patient and wait a little longer.

I took a long walk around downtown Puerto Vallarta, wishing and willing that when I returned to the consulate my card would magically be there waiting for me. Unfortunately, upon return it still hadn't arrived.

Back outside, more sitting around reading trashy magazines. Shallow sleep. Telenovelas at the motel. Shallower sleep. Calling Visa again.

"It should be there first thing tomorrow" was their stock response.

By the end of the third day, I officially looked like the classic pushy American. Sadly, I was growing accustomed to the expressions of receptionists who dreaded seeing me.

Day four, stranded in Mexico, Johanna let me use her phone to call Visa yet again. I asked another faceless operator, from who knows where, what was keeping my fucking replacement card. She explained that for some technical reason my application for a new card still hadn't gone through. They had tried getting ahold of me but were unable. Even though no one in their right mind should have given me a credit card, I knew I wasn't being denied. Banks would issue a credit card to a gorilla with a gambling problem if he just applied. Patiently, I went through the entire application process yet again. This time, I gave them Johanna's office number and the woman promised to leave a message if anything went wrong. I also took the liberty of the free phone to dial Vinetta.

"Oh my God!" she freaked, having last heard from me when I hastily boarded the plane in Nashville. I filled her in on everything, detailing how Jeeves had given me priceless tabloid information. When she asked why I had waited four days to call, I told her that I had gotten ripped off and was waiting for a new credit card. But I also desperately needed her help.

"Go on." She had a lot riding on my success.

"I need an address from John Carpenter at Blue Suede."

"John Carpenter? How will I find him?"

"Remember that bent-up old guy who saved our asses outside the Blue Suede? If you could just go up to the mansion and ask him for the address he gave me, he'll know all about it."

"I really hate going by there," she protested in her twangiest Southern accent, "and two of the kids are sick."

"I know you have your hands full, but unless I get that address, there's no chance of recovering any money. Floyd's death, the Elvis contest—all this will be in vain. Do you understand?"

"Okay," she acquiesced.

I gave her Johanna's phone number at the consulate as well as my room number at the motel. I explained that it should be easy. A no-risk assignment. She simply had to call me once Carpenter gave her Roscoe's address.

She promised she would. When I got off the phone Johanna remembered that an Officer Lopez had left a message asking me to stop by the precinct. He had photos of the possible thief. With nothing else to do, I walked over to the police station where I discovered that computer technology still hadn't made its flashy debut. I examined several photo albums filled with mugshots to hopefully identify Magdalena, the kindly cabby. After flipping through four books, I finally spotted a photo that might've been her. The suspect's name was Elena Gonzalez and though she had never been arrested for stealing, she had worked as a prostitute in Mexico City. The officer promised he'd check her out and would notify Johanna if he learned anything. I tipped him two bucks, which was all I had on me, then returned to the consulate to find that the Visa card still hadn't arrived.

Dejected, I headed back to my motel room and watched some more crappy Mexican soap operas until I started going stir-crazy. I could even feel my fetus growing bored. Everyone kept telling me how wonderful the beaches are, so I took a tiny hand towel from my room and headed out there. I laid down in the sizzling sun and tried to relax. Some kindly older couple offered me a squirt of their suntan lotion. I would've preferred a sip of their gin and tonics. This was the exact situation booze was perfect for, but I couldn't touch it. The idea of no booze for roughly two hundred and sixty more days—if, God willing (God forbid!), the pregnancy really went to full-term—made me incredibly antsy. Then I realized that I was down to my last twenty dollars. I knew that if I didn't get that goddamn card by tonight, Johanna would have to loan me yet more money.

When I returned there around four, for the first time the secretary greeted me with a big smile: the orange-and-purple FedEx envelope had finally arrived. Inside was the little plastic card—I was reconnected to the power source that electrified us human machinery. The first thing I did was take it to the bank and withdraw the maximum amount of money—six hundred dollars. Rushing back over to the consulate, I paid Johanna all the money I owed and offered her an equivalent amount as a gift.

"We aren't allowed to take gifts," she said, "but I got something else for you—welcome to America." She handed me my new passport as if it were a high school diploma.

I then called Vinetta. She said she had hiked up the hill and knocked at the door of the mansion until her knuckles were raw and the kids were crying. No answer. Then she headed back to her pickup in the parking lot with all seven kids and sat there "for two goddamn hours and didn't see that old gimp nowhere."

Eventually she "gutsied up" and went inside the Blue Suede. There was a big memorial photo of Snake on the wall along with a brief obituary in the *Memphis Daily News*. She said it stated that he had been accidentally killed after he and a group of companions went to the hilltop and shot off some rounds to celebrate the end of their annual Elvis contest. So much for the bogus hunting accident.

Soon after she entered, Minister Mo Beaucheete tapped her on the shoulder and nervously warned her that she should skedaddle before someone accidentally shot her.

"You didn't ask him where Mr. Carpenter went off to?"

"Yeah, he said Carpenter was lying low until the sheriff finished up investigating Snake's death."

"Just keep looking for him," I said.

"Please don't ask me to do that."

"If you don't get that address, it's all over," I said for the second time. "Simple as that."

"Oh fudgsicle!" she blurted, and hung up.

The next day, my fifth in Mexico, although I was able to buy some basic comforts and decent grub, my life was still on hold.

Without any recourse, I took a cab to the airport, hoping that I might be able to locate the taxi thief myself. One by one, I asked all the drivers about my dear friend Magdalena. No one knew who I was talking about. It appeared she was a one-time scam artist and with me she had found the perfect mark. Late in the afternoon I returned to the hotel.

The next morning Vinetta happened to catch me by phone at the motel and she said she was sorry. A beautiful home, Floyd's death, none of it mattered. She just couldn't hike up that hill, knock on that door, or sit in her truck with seven kids a minute longer. It wasn't fair to them. She was going batty, and was afraid she might start whacking them.

I was about to yell at her about my own sacrifices and how we had come so close, but I knew I'd just be whipping a dead horse. As I contemplated leaving Mexico right then and there, I thought about how it was moments like this that divided exceptional people—who were rich—from the mediocre masses with their sad, steady pittance. I was once a good goddamn reporter. That ditsy couple were somewhere in this *ciudad* and, goddamn it, I was going to find them!

The first thing I did was go to a local bookstore for the most detailed map I could find of the city of Puerto Vallarta. Carefully I scanned the names of the swirling lanes and byways around the oceanfront streets. Taking a break and feeling relaxed for a moment, I suddenly remembered the con woman humming "Feliz Navidad." The phrase was in the street name!

I asked the clerk on duty if he knew a street near the ocean with the words "Feliz Navidad" in it.

"Not quite," he said, and opened my map. He pointed to a broad street that ran along the ocean toward the south end of town—Costera a Barra de Navidad. Bingo! It was only around ten a.m. I was about to grab a cab when I realized that I might actually bump into the kid and kidnapper. God usually gives you only one chance, if that, to get things right.

I needed to be prepared, and that meant having a good camera, something I now lacked. After spending the past four days bumming around town, I knew where to find a good photo shop.

I could've bought a digital camera for as little as eighty bucks, but since I was hoping to take pictures that would fetch a six-figure fee, I asked about their top-of-the-line model—a Canon 20D was going for fifteen hundred American dollars. I also grabbed a lens that ranged from seventeen to eighty-five millimeters for an additional two grand and a four-gigabyte compact flashcard along with some accessories. Putting the entire purchase on my shiny new credit card, it came to nearly four thousand dollars I didn't have.

"What exactly is your return policy?" I asked as an afterthought.

"You have one week to return any item, provided you have the receipt and it's in the same excellent condition as when you bought it," the clerk said, handing me the merchandise in a bag. "Also, your money is usually mailed back to you within several months."

The store closed at seven-thirty.

I stopped at a small café called Rosa's Bakery and bought a late breakfast to go and a sandwich for later. Bringing it all back to my hotel room, I carefully opened the boxes and delicately removed the Styrofoam shapes that secured the camera and lens. While eating an egg, potato, and jalapeño burrito, I studied the instruction manual and honed my skills as a photographer.

At about two-thirty, I dumped everything into a knapsack and hailed a cab. I was off to hunt for big tabloid game. Before getting in, I showed the driver my map of the city, pointing to the stretch of road far away from the annoying *turistas* and ubiquitous time-shares. Indeed, by all accounts it was where a loving couple might find optimum privacy. He nodded yes, and I got in. His radio blared as we drove along. It was only about three miles away, a rural isolated stretch of road, nowhere near the place Magdalena had brought me. Soon he started looking up at street signs trying to figure out where the hell we were. Twice he stopped and asked to see my map.

After roughly thirty minutes of driving, though—*nada*. Soon we spotted a sign for another town, Aguacate. We had gone too far. I told him to turn around. He sped back north for about ten minutes before we spotted the first home in a while. In the middle of nowhere, on the edge of a cliff overlooking the ocean, was a small yet attractive bungalow. As he sped by it, I saw a red light from an old tail-fin car sticking out of a narrow driveway. A moment later, my driver suddenly hit the brakes and his horn. A skinny blonde in tight blue jeans was dashing across the road with a rugged tattooed guy in tow.

"Fuck you!" the guy who looked like a trashier Tommy Lee shouted as we sped past.

Turning back in my seat, I saw them heading toward the cozy little house. The best image I had seen of her was from a tiny high school yearbook photo that had run in all the papers. It might've been her, I wasn't sure. Still, it was my best bet. I told the driver to pull over.

"You want me to turn around?" he asked.

"No."

If it was them and they were smart, they might have actually posted a video camera on the highway. Surveillance equipment was now cheap and easy to install. If they saw the same car coming back down that empty road, it'd tip them off. I had to go on foot and stay out of view. Still, I wasn't sure and didn't want to be stranded, so I told the driver to wait for fifteen minutes. If I wasn't back then, he should leave.

"Señorita, you don't want those people to see you, *sí*?"

"Yes, but I'll need a ride later, so if I pay you now, can you pick me up later?"

"Where?"

"Down here. But don't go anywhere near that house."

"When should I come back?"

"Around six p.m.," I said, figuring that if I made it that long without miscarrying, I'd have just enough time to return to the photography store and fill out the refund form.

"So I will wait fifteen minutes first and then leave if you don't come and I return later?"

I confirmed this as I counted out twice the fare as well as a sizable tip. Then I got out and headed back, walking along the very edge of the road. If it wasn't them, I had only fifteen minutes to confirm it and get back to the car, or I'd be stuck out here all afternoon. As I approached the bungalow, I remained vigilant for anything that might look even remotely like a video camera. What I finally did see compelled me toward silent ecstasy. A dusty pink land yacht was moored in their driveway—Carpenter's old Cadillac.

Looking through the powerful lens of my camera, I surveyed the house for any signs of bodyguards or security devices—nothing. All I could see were that the drapes had been carefully pulled. There was no stirring, nor sound nor lights, from within. The isolated structure was positioned between a remote highway and a steep incline—landscaped in indigenous foliage to reduce erosion. The vast and yawning Pacific Ocean was just waiting for all to topple right in. It was a smart location for Roscoe as it was on a bluff with windows on all sides, a clear panoramic view.

As I edged toward the ocean side of the house, I realized it had a back door that gave direct access to a beach about a hundred feet down. There was adequate shrubbery around, but it all came down a single question: on which side of the house should I position myself, the front facing the road or the back of the house near the sultry blue waters?

Seeing them several minutes earlier returning from their midday constitutional—probably after a feverish morning of fucking—I hoped that their next appearance would be out the back door, where they had full privacy.

Scampering like a lizard along the thorny plants and perilous rocks behind the house, searching for that perfect vantage point, I soon angled myself to gain the best hidden view of that rear door. A sparse clump of bushes with small, sharp-edged leaves was where I found cover. There I softly snapped the branches of neighboring shrubs, creating a decent blind for my secret mission. This was something I hadn't done in a while. Inasmuch as I was more of a journalist, the writerly end of the paparazzi, someone else was usually assigned to do the protracted photographic stakeout. As the minutes ticked, I became reacquainted with this tedious side of the job. By two o'clock, after the first hour in those thorny bushes, I had drunk half the water and wished I'd bought suntan lotion. After the second hour, though, while eating the chicken and jalapeño sandwich, I was chewed down by an army of ants and finished off by an aerial assault of black flies. Just a smidgen of insect repellent would've made all the difference. Small blue-bellied lizards and occasional snakes slithered by. I passed the time by playing memory games, trying to revisit parts of my past where I had made bad pivotal decisions: job opportunities I had missed, guys who had been interested in me and I'd dismissed, men who swiveled up to the air-conditioned economic pyramid points while I squatted, sweaty and bug bitten, shrouded in thorny foliage. At four o'clock, after sneaking out of my rat hole to take a leak in another thorny bush, I returned to my nest and wondered if my nice new iPod was still in my bedroom in Hell's Kitchen where I'd left it. It took me forever to download all those songs on it.

I tried sleeping, but it only made me more anxious, so I started scratching my fingers through that hard and arid dirt to submerge myself even deeper in the hot earth. Soon I felt as though I was digging my own grave, and without thinking I laughed at my little joke. The one thought I kept consoling myself with was that massive encampment of paparazzi still outside of the Scrubbs house in Memphis, while I was all alone here at the heart of the story, south of the border.

Sometime around five o'clock I drifted into a shallow sleep . . . until I felt something wiggling through my hair—a small snake had slithered up next to me.

As it started approaching six, I dreaded that this was going to go into a two-day operation. The rendezvous site where I was supposed to get picked up was roughly ten minutes down the hill. I was intent on staying here as long as I could. After hours of lying in that scorched, itchy earth, I felt cramped and dehydrated. I began to fear that I was jeopardizing my little pregnancy. It was around this time that I spotted what I thought was a vulture circling high overhead, ready to finish off me and my baby. The huge brown bird quickly descended, passing low over the ocean, then soared high up like a roller coaster. Later I found out it was a ferruginous hawk. When I tried pointing the camera, I realized exactly how heavy and unwieldy it was. Taking it in both hands, I braced my elbows against my knees and pointed it as the raptor sailed down along the rolling surf. Digging its talons into the glistening waves for just a second, it managed to yank out a huge fish. I snapped pictures as the fish writhed and twisted before it finally broke free and splashed back into the sea. At least I could sell something to *National Geographic*.

The bird glided around in the limitless sky, swooping down again, looking for a more manageable prey. Just as I positioned my camera again, I heard a sharp click behind me, like the trigger of a gun. Totally naked under a gleam of sweat, Roscoe had pulled open the back door and was stepping outside holding a smoldering spliff. He too was staring over at that distinguished cousin of the penguin and pigeon.

"Baby, you've got to see this!" he shouted behind him.

Also in her glistening birthday suit, covered in a few tiny, tacky tattoos, was the missing child bride who owned the headlines, little Missy Scrubbs. On her slender shoulder, under a shimmering layer of vaseline, I saw her latest ink.

ROSCOE
U
L
E
S

I click-click-clicked every precious moment with my camera as the holy couple focused on that beautiful bird of prey. At one point, as the hawk glided right over, they looked directly at me but didn't register a thing. Seconds later the raptor was gone, and the nude duo dipped back inside their little love nest. Their entire outing probably lasted no more than a minute, but it would be an eternity on digitalia.

My prison sentence in sunny Mexico was over. I jotted down some reportorial notes for later, when I finally got around to writing the story. Then, slowly extricating myself from those painful bushes, I hiked back down the road to my rendezvous point and made a mental note to make a large donation to the Central American Audubon Society.

As I circled the road, I could see a lone vehicle just sitting there, but it was a new green car, not the older blue one I had arrived in. For a moment I worried that I was being set up. It didn't matter. I was baked and glazed and couldn't walk much further.

"Julio sends me to get up," called out the young stranger who saw me approaching in his rearview.

"He did?" I vaguely recalled that the driver's name was in fact Julio.

"He say he no can get out of a job, *pero* he sends to me."

"You'll do fine," I replied. My trust in Puerto Vallartan cab drivers was completely restored.

Although there was no air-conditioning, the drive back to town was one of the most wonderful trips I ever took. I spent the time inspecting the twenty-two focused, well-lit nude photos I had snapped of America's most missingest and trashiest Romeo and Juliet. It was then that Gustavo's recurrent point jabbed me: of all the vital things that required attention in the world today, this was at the very bottom of the pile; yet since it was the slop that the masses wanted, I was going to charge the price of caviar.

While reviewing the photos on the small camera display, I realized that I had indeed seen Roscoe before. He was one of the pigfuckers who slugged and tried to rape me on that first drunken and frosty night in the Blue Suede parking lot. These pictures would be adequate payback.

When we reached my motel, I popped out the flashcard and asked the driver if he'd wait for me while I went upstairs to get something.

"Sí, señora."

In my room, I carefully wiped down and repacked the state-of-the-art camera and the high-powered lens in their Styrofoam casings. Then, after locating the receipt, I carried it all out to the taxi and headed to the camera store with fifteen minutes to spare. I gave the substitute driver a twenty and thanked him earnestly.

As I filled out the refund form, the balding clerk asked, "Was there anything wrong with the equipment, madam?"

"No, I'm sorry, I went way overboard on the cost," I said. "I don't know what I was thinking."

"Perhaps you might consider one of the more affordable models?"

I was going to say no, but then I decided that I had gotten good use of their expensive equipment. I didn't want to leave them feeling bitter about returning such a large amount, particularly since I couldn't exactly come back to Mexico to argue with them if my refund didn't arrive, so I bought the cheapest digital camera they had. The clerk seemed at peace with this as a kind of consolation prize.

When I got back to my motel, I found out that the next plane back to the States was leaving in two hours, so I settled my account and caught another taxi to the Gustavo Díaz Ordaz International Airport. Once there, I began making calls to get the numbers of the editorial offices for the three major U.S. tabloids where I was going to pitch the story. I would wait till I was north of the border to actually call the publications since I didn't want anyone tracing me back to Mexico, only to have them turn down my offer and send a stampede of staff reporters to take the photos themselves. By nine o'clock I had cleared customs and was on a window seat over the wing of a half-empty plane heading back to the States.

CHAPTER TWENTY-ONE

The George Bush Intercontinental Airport in Houston, Texas, detained me for the next two hours while I awaited my connecting flight to Memphis, ample time to make three big pitches. Cellless, I got a roll of quarters and commandeered an antiquated bank of pay phones in a far-flung corner of the terminal. I had been considering my pitch during the entire flight: Missy Scrubbs is alive and well. She wasn't kidnapped and her husband didn't kill her. I have spicy softcore proof.

It was midnight Houston time, one a.m. New York time. Whatever editors were on duty could certainly call their bosses and get immediate approval. I didn't want to be spiteful, but I decided to only contact Jericho Riggs, asshole editor, as a very last resort. One by one I called the three biggest tabloids—the *Weekly World News*, the *Enquirer*, and the *Star*. When I learned that most of the people who I knew were either not on duty or no longer around, I asked for the ranking editors before finally pitching my scoop: "I got tastefully nude photos of Missy Scrubbs, still alive with her lover/abductor, and I am giving you an exclusive one-hour option to make an offer on this story. At that point I'm going to another paper." I gave all three periodicals the same message and left different side-by-side pay phone numbers, so that each paper would be calling me back on a separate line.

Over the next half an hour, all three insomniacs on duty checked with their bosses and called back. We loosely had the same Q & A:

They: You worked for us in the past, no?

Me: That's why I'm giving you the first shot.

They: Where are Missy and her lover?

Me: You'll find out when you buy the story.

They: Does the couple know you caught them?

Me: No, not yet.

They: Exactly how current is the item?

Me: A few hours old.

They: Who else knows about this story?

Me: Absolutely no one, it is definitely an exclusive.

Only the *Star* asked if the pictures demonstrated beyond a shadow of a doubt that she was not being held against her will.

Me: Yes.

Each of them wanted more time. Five minutes later the editor at the *Star* called back to say he had learned that I had been fired from an editorial post at the *WWN*.

"True, awhile back, but I had no problems with credibility," I replied.

Two minutes later the *Enquirer* called to ask, "You're married to Fox News producer A. Paul O'Hurly, aren't you?"

"Yeah, but we're separated and he has nothing to do with any of this." I regretted that his name had to be brought up, but it strengthened my reputation. When he asked me where the notorious lovebirds were, I again said I'd tell him once I had the money. When asked about the content of the photographs, I gave him precise details about the anatomical nature of the naked couple.

"Is there any proof that these photos weren't taken prior to her being kidnapped?"

"Yes," I replied. "It appears she has a fresh tattoo."

"Okay," he began, "if you can get the photos in here before tomorrow's deadline and the chief can see them, and they are as you describe them, and you write us a decent two-thousand-word piece about how you found them, and the issue comes out, and it is indeed an exclusive, and proves upon publication not to be fraudulent, then he authorizes me to cut you a check for two hundred thousand dollars. Take it or leave it."

Another phone had already begun to ring while he was giving his lengthy offer and conditional.

"One second please." I switched over to the pay telephone I had reserved for the *Enquirer*. An old friend, Joe Fontaine, was their news editor. He also interrogated me for about five minutes, trying to get as much free info as he could before opening negotiations at a hundred and twenty-five thousand dollars.

"I already have two hundred thousand from someone else." I didn't reveal the other paper as I feared them calling each other and reaching a compromise to kill the bidding.

"Show us the photos and we might go to two-twelve."

I went back to the *Star* and told them another news service had just offered two hundred and twelve thousand dollars.

"We're authorized to go to a quarter million—*if* we *really* like the pictures."

I told him to hold on and, switching over to Joe at the *Enquirer*, I said that I just got a quarter-million from the *Enquirer*.

"We'll go to two hundred and fifty-two," he quickly replied.

"Hold on." I went back to the *Star* editor, to whom I boldly said, "I just got offered three."

"They can have it," the *Star* said. I had pushed too hard. That was when *WWN* finally deemed it a good time to call and coolly announce that if they really liked what they saw, they would buy the pictures for fifty thousand dollars.

I told them the bidding was up to two-fifty. The editor chuckled, so I went back to Joe at the *Enquirer* and told him that I could be in their office sometime in the middle of the night to show them the pictures.

"Why don't you just bring them at nine when Barney comes in," said Joe, referring to his clear-eyed publisher. "You'll still make our deadline."

"And you'll have the check?"

"You bring the photos and story, and if we like them, you'll sign a contract and get half upon delivery and half upon publication."

"See you for breakfast, Joe."

"Actually, you won't see me. I'm on vacation in France. They asked me to speak to you cause I knew you." Smart.

Photos like this sold papers, bundles at a time. Grabbing my little knapsack, I raced out past airline security to the front desk and changed my destination. Instead of Nashville, I needed the next flight to New York—the headquarters of the Enquirer.

It turned out I had just missed a flight to JFK, but I only had to wait another hour for the next one. Exhausted and fuzzy-headed, I used the time to catnap at the gate. When I finally got on the plane, I began reviewing my notes and eventually wrote out a draft of the story on the back of unused vomit bags I collected from empty seats. It was the only time I recall ever writing a piece in longhand.

It was a hot and muggy night when we landed at JFK. I caught a cab and by six a.m., forty-seven dollars poorer, I was in Park Slope, Brooklyn. There I would be able to rest a few hours at my friend Kara's apartment.

"Are you parked on Seventh Avenue, cause—"

"My car's still down in Tennessee," I cut her off tiredly. Kara was a single mom I had known since college.

She let me flop on her couch and I fell right to sleep. An hour later, Kara's kid Ajax woke me up. It was seven-thirty. Since all my clothes had been stolen, I was wrinkled with dirt indelibly ground into my once attractive pants and beautiful new shirt. Kara lent me some of her things as well as fragrant toiletries. Then she poured me a cup of freshly ground, freshly brewed, free-trade coffee and asked, "What's going on, Sandy?"

I promised I'd tell her everything later, but was barely able take a sip before I saw that I was late and had to rush right out the door. I squeezed into a packed F train and headed over to the midtown offices of the Enquirer.

When I walked in the door a little after nine, they were all waiting for me, half a dozen men and women dying to see the exposé. It wasn't all just curiosity; a photo analyzer and computer graphic experts were summoned to assess whether their quarter-million-dollar purchase was the real deal. I felt their cold skepticism blow through me. For the few minutes it took me to open my bag and locate the flashcard, I feared that I might've lost it . . . or had I had left my lens cap on and only imagined I saw them? How was the light? Though they looked good on the tiny monitor, I obviously hadn't developed any photos from that borrowed camera before. What possibly could've gone wrong? Everything.

When they put the little plastic square into the card reader and the photos popped up, they were even better than I thought. One by one, each image flashed to the borders of a monster monitor where they were thoroughly scrutinized. No one doubted for even a second that they were looking at the genuine article.

"Where's your story?" the editor in chief asked.

When I unfolded the four vomit bags that I had written the story on, he looked at me as though I were insane. He tried making sense of my illegible handwriting.

"Someone stole my laptop. If you have a cubicle, I can copy them out for you."

"I'd be grateful," he said, leading me to an available desk.

"Can I see the check first?" I asked, neither forcefully nor timidly.

He handed me a large, crisp manila envelope. Inside was a contract, a blank 1099 tax form to be filled out, and the check for one hundred and twenty-six thousand dollars. Half the agreed upon sum.

The piece was going to be the cover of the next issue. Because of the magnitude of the story, it would be coming out three days early, on September 3—as a special edition. After finishing the piece, I went back to the top and added Gustavo Benoit as the lead writer in the byline and put my name second. Without him, I couldn't've and wouldn't've done it.

The editor read the piece and asked me half a dozen questions, which I sensed were just more tests of my credibility. Afterward, he asked if I'd do some rewrites. It was one of the few times I was ever asked to expand a tabloid piece. When I finished my rewrites roughly an hour later, it was three times its original size.

"You're a good writer," said the editor inspecting my final copy. "You looking for work?"

"Always."

"Joe says you have a drinking problem but he has always liked you."

"I haven't touched a bottle in over a year," I lengthened my week of sobriety.

"Well, I'll give you a chance. Assignments like this one come up every few months."

I thanked him and left. Two hours later, after some quick shopping and a trip to my bank to deposit the check, I returned to Kara's to make reservations on the next flight to Nashville. Then I told her the whole story, grabbed a bite, returned her borrowed clothing, took a quick shower, and was back out the door.

The short plane trip was surprisingly calm considering the pilot's casual rambling that a new storm was brewing just south of Nashville. After landing, I picked my car up in the parking lot and drove two hours to my mom's place. Bella and her kids had left, but Ludmilla and her mannerly clan were still packing.

"So, is your friend buying the place or what?" she asked impatiently as she and her boys loaded the last of the family photo albums and boxes of knickknacks into the back of her SUV.

"I still have to show her the place and go over the details with her. What's the rush?"

"Another storm is coming tonight," she said, "and the humidity is just playing absolute havoc with my hair."

After about an hour, when she was done, she gave me the keys to the old castle and said goodbye. She was returning home to Atlanta. Assuming Vinetta would go for it, I was hoping that she could put the trailer park down as collateral and take out a mortgage for the house. Whatever the discrepancy might be, I could supplement it with the cash I had made from the Scrubbs scoop. As I drove the short trip to her trailer park in Daumland, the rain started falling.

CHAPTER TWENTY-TWO

S he's back!" Vinetta yelled out as I stepped out of the car in the darkness. A gathering of little people converged on me at the trailer door.

"Did you find 'em?" the eight-year-old asked. Vinny had acquainted the older kids with my plight beyond the Rio Grande. Though I was exhausted, I gave them the suspenseful ten-minute version of all that had happened, right up to selling the spicy photos to the highest bidder. Rain began pouring down more heavily as we shared rice cakes and Diet Cokes. When the winds kicked up, Vinetta turned on a radio and heard that the weather was supposed to get even worse.

"There's no chance of us getting washed away, is there?" I asked half-jokingly as the rains pelted the roof.

Though she said we were just above the flood zone, only the storm cellar was up on the part of the property that seemed to have some real height. As the winds blew, the kids filled me in on their latest little victories and adventures. I tried not to act worried when water began dripping through the raggedy seams of the compartmentalized trailer. Vinetta and the kids made a game of putting bowls and buckets under the increasing leaks around the trailer. They had all been through this before.

"Floyd used to say being here during a storm was kind of like being in a leaky sub," Vinetta commented as together we repositioned the beds. She tried to get the kids to lie down, but the lightning and thunder was a little too scary. Some of the younger ones started crying.

"Hey," I said, "what's the worst that can happen? We'll all get a little wet."

"What if a tornado hits?" one of the twins replied.

"We'll just go into the storm cellar," Mom said.

Around 11 p.m. the electricity went out. Shortly afterward, though, the storm seemed to blow itself out; exhausted, everyone was soon snoozing. Since I had been running up a sleep debt, I too slept like a log.

Early the next morning, Vinetta's fumblings woke me up. I looked out the window, and, though the skies were clear, we appeared to be in the middle of a lake. When I went into the bathroom, Vinetta spoke through the door: "I can't tell you how relieved I was to see you coming in last night."

"I told you I'd be back," I said, wiping.

"I really thought you had taken his money and gone south of the border."

"I told you, he didn't give me any money."

"I thought maybe after spending the night with him, something had changed . . ."

"No. He said he didn't do anything to Floyd and he refused to pay what he called extortion."

"But when you called me from Mexico didn't you say—"

"Before we go into all the details, let me ask you something. Roughly how much are you worth?"

"How much?"

"Yeah, this property? Any idea of its worth?"

"This place was purchased by a pig farm conglomerate."

"Do you rent it from them?"

"We're squatting here till they tell us to leave. But what does any of this have to do with anything?"

"I was hoping you could get a mortgage on this property and I could get you all a really nice place to live."

"Right now, we just better find a dry place," she said softly. When I came out of the bathroom, I saw Vinetta staring at what used to be the tiny laundry room. The wooden shed at the end of the trailer appeared to have floated away.

"I know where we can go," I said.

"Where?"

"My mother's home in Mesopotamia is up for sale. You can stay there."

She put eight bowls down, poured cereal and milk, woke up the kids, and stepped back. After they ate, I helped them wash and dress while she packed a few things to take with us.

"Oh gee, I'm going to need more diapers," she said as she walked ankle deep through water, bringing things out to her truck.

"I'll get them," I said and headed up to the storm cellar.

"Get two packages," she asked.

"You better bring a flashlight if you're going down there," Floyd Jr. wisely advised, so I went into the office and grabbed one.

Barefoot, I headed through the shallow pond uphill to the rear of the property, then down into the storm cellar. The water there was also ankle deep. After a bit of fumbling and splashing, I grabbed two new packages of disposable diapers all the way against the far wall. Near the pile of new diapers was the lone filing cabinet pivoted against the wall that I had never opened. It had been bothering me since I first left it. Hauling it to one side, I was able to pull the top drawer out and tuck the flashlight under my chin. More papers. It when when I opened the second drawer that I saw them. About a dozen new bottles of cough medicine with singed and burnt labels.

"Fuck!" I yelled. Vinetta had lied to me. Pseudoephedrine, the magical ingredient in methamphetamine, is distilled from cough syrup. Floyd was cooking the stuff. Hearing the distant cries of the kids, I realized that this was just not the time. I grabbed the diapers and left the storm cellar.

Except for the two youngest, who Vinetta and I carried, all

slogged through the brackish waters of last night's storm to our vehicles, where we divvied up her clan and she followed me as we slowly drove down Makataka Road toward my mother's place.

Despite their ridiculous youth, all Vinetta's little urchins applauded when they saw the luxurious house in Mesopotamia that they had been so eager to leave just a week earlier. After the sinking bread box, I think they would've been pleased to be anywhere else. Once inside, the Loyd children raced and roamed through the empty rooms of the cavernous home.

"How long will we be able to stay here?" Floyd Jr. asked.

"Well, I have to ask my sisters, but I think you can stay until we get a buyer. It might be weeks, might be months."

"The water around our home should drain in just a few days," Vinetta said, as if to suggest that they shouldn't get too comfortable.

That first night, I decided to just cut Vinetta a check for fifty thousand and be done with her forever. She could stay the rest of her life in her leaky, sinking trailer for all I cared. Tomorrow I had a long drive back to New York, where I had to rebuild my own life, which was still a sizable mess.

While Vinetta was dealing with the kids, I went into the store to say hi to old Pete. We chatted briefly, then he asked when I was next going to see Ludmilla next. I said I was heading to Atlanta to visit her tomorrow on my way back to New York. He asked if I could drop off some things she forgot to bring with her and handed me a large file of receipts and other accounting. My busybody nature led me to snoop inside. While inspecting the various records, I was stunned to see that the store had been earning roughly two thousand dollars a month of pure profit for the past several years. Rodmilla had always given me the impression that she was only getting by, not actually profiting.

Some of the older kids broke out of the house and began foraging in the store for treats. Vinetta soon followed the racing twins so I introduced her to Pete. They chatted a bit and discov-ered that forty years back, Pete had worked with Vinetta's father at a local factory when they were both young men.

"You're not buying the place here, are you?" he asked hopefully.

Vinetta smiled and looked down. Pete smiled too, a bit em-barrassed. Leaving the kids there, Vinetta brushed right past me without making eye contact. I followed her out to the driveway.

"Why did you bring me here?" she asked as soon as we were alone.

"Because you needed a place."

"You've been acting pretty weird since we left the trailer."

"I found your little drug stash," I revealed.

"What are you talking about?"

"The burnt bottles of cough medicine. That goddamn sheriff, Carpenter—they all told me! Snake didn't do shit! Floyd blew himself up, didn't he?"

"He was cooking drugs awhile back," she said, "and there was a fire, I don't deny it. But that was earlier. After that he stopped cooking. But we both know that if I had told you this, you wouldn't've helped me."

"Not acceptable," I said coolly. "You used me to get money."

"It was never about the money," she said haltingly. "Not really."

"Then what was it about?"

"It was about seven children not living with the belief that their father died making meth."

"But he *did* make meth!"

"Not when the shack blew up! *They* did that. I only kept the cough medicine because I figured the kids might need it some day."

"What are you saying?"

"He did it to make money to start this whole project. I mean, for the first time he seemed interested in something, buying the Elvis outfits and stuff; it pulled him out of a real funk and he finally started acting like a real dad . . . so . . ." She began weeping. "Look, I don't want no money, okay?"

Hearing her pardon Floyd's shortcomings by his improvement as a father revealed so much about her. Vinetta's two oldest children were inherited from Floyd's prior marriage. Two others dropped down the chimney when her sister suddenly died. Only three kids were actually hers, yet I never saw any difference in her concern or affection. She totally devoted herself to the life that fate had more or less bestowed upon her—the consummate mother. How could I fault her for having an idiotic husband? I brought Vinetta into the dining room and sat her down.

"Look, you have two choices. I can just give you fifty thousand dollars, as we discussed. Or I'll make you a one-time offer. The store here, ZigRat's, nets about twenty thousand a year—that's all profit. What I'm thinking is, you can get a loan for as much as you can and I'll lend you the rest to pay for this place. Keep living off whatever you have been living on, you can use the store's profits to pay the mortgage, and whatever you have left over, you can pay me."

"You know that no bank is going to gamble on our future."

"I can cosign the loan with you."

"How much is this place?"

"They'll take about a quarter-million."

"You'd cosign a loan with me for two hundred and fifty thousand dollars?"

"Actually, since I own a third of the place, you'd only need a loan for a hundred and eighty thousand. You can pay me back at your leisure."

"So I won't get the fifty thousand dollars," she said.

"That's true, but I'll be taking the entire risk. So if you default, I'll be paying five times that amount."

"Sandra, I don't think . . . What I mean to say is, with the kids and all, I just don't know if I can run a store."

"Pete's getting older. He has maybe another five or so years, but that might be just enough time for Floyd Jr. and some of the other children to learn the business."

"I gotta talk to the kids," she said, and dashed out of the room.

I really couldn't afford any Oprah-size acts of generosity— like loaning her the money myself—but I couldn't abandon her either. If Vinetta hadn't put me up and guided me along that Elvic rainbow, I wouldn't have gotten the pot of gold at its end. I just couldn't go back to New York knowing Vinetta and all those damn kids were living in that leaky, sinking bread box that they might get evicted from at any moment. As long as she slowly and steadily paid the bank back, I'd be fine. And if worse came to worst, I could cover her for months that she was in the red.

Suddenly, Vinetta and all seven kids rushed back into the room. "Tell her what you said," she prompted little Floyd.

"Mom said you offered her a deal to live here and work in the store, and we all cheered. Then she said you were heading back up to New York City, but I remember you saying you lost your place, so I said why don't you just stay here with us because to us you're now kind of a co-ma."

Without a relationship or even a home, it was actually a decent offer, but moving back into my childhood home with all those kids, I'd yo-yo between maternal flashbacks of my combative childhood and Vinetta's current screechfests. "Thanks so much, Floyd, but my life is up there."

"Well I don't need to tell you that no matter how old you are or sick or whatever," Vinetta said, "this will always be your home, and we'll always be your family, and I'd be willing to put that in whatever contract you want."

I told her I might just take her up on it if I couldn't get my kid in a good New York school, then I revealed my own little blessing: "I'm pregnant."

"I'm so sorry," she replied after a slight gasp.

"No, I'm going to try to keep it," I said, and explained to her how I chronically miscarried, so even though I was hoping for the best, I was braced for the worst. I was familiar with all the bleak statistics for older parents, whose babies have higher rates of birth defects. Still, I had to give it a shot.

"Edwina's husband works at the International Savings and Loans over at Murphy County Mall, I can give him a call." I told her that would be fine. I could probably download my financial records online in order to cosign with her.

Over the next few days, when the *Enquirer* hit the stands, breaking the Scrubbs story wide open, reporters flooded into Daumland like starving dogs fighting for final scraps of meat. Since the story also involved Snake Major's evil son Roscoe, I was glad we were over in Mesopotamia. My phone kept ringing with endless calls from reporters wanting to talk to me, but my job was over and I felt no duty to give any interviews. Let them do their own dirty work.

I suggested that Vinetta lie low for a while, just in case any impulsive friends of Roscoe's came looking for revenge. Even so, it wasn't like anything awful was going to happen to Snake's son. When the story broke, I learned that the Mexican authorities in Puerto Vallarta, acting on behalf of American law enforcement officials, kicked in the door of their little beachfront hideaway. They arrested both Missy Scrubbs and Roscoe Major to extradite them to America for faking her kidnapping. On that day, Thucydides Scrubbs, the Monster of Memphis, officially became the latest victim of the press. Charges against him were immediately tossed out and he was clearly grateful to slip back into obscurity.

After working out all the financial agreements with my sisters, I watched the kids while Vinetta went out to the Murphy County Mall. When she returned to the house that afternoon she was beaming.

"This is a little difficult to ask, but if I don't need you to cosign my loan, would you consider giving me the fifty thousand dollars?"

"I suppose, but you don't have a job or any equity. You can't even put down a deposit, how would you be able to get a loan for that much?"

"Gavin says there's a way to do it. And I won't need no cosigner."

"I'd be very careful, Vinetta. That's a lot of money."

"He says I'd have to exaggerate some facts and figures, but lots of people do it and no one ever checks."

"Vinetta, do you really want to take a chance on some nefarious loan? I mean, if something goes wrong and they can foreclose on you . . ."

"I'd rather do it this way if that's okay."

A bank that would loan an umemployed mother a quarter-million would be an intriguing investigative piece, but unless Ben Affleck was screwing yet another celebrity named Jennifer in the bank's lobby, I wouldn't be going anywhere near it. I cut her the check and wished her good luck.

Since Vinetta was nervous about returning alone to her water-logged trailer and retrieving the rest of their things, we drove back together late the next day. By then the electricity was back on and she played a message that Minister Morton Beaucheete had left on her machine. It was to me, asking that I call the Blue Suede pronto.

I would've just drove over to the pub, but fearing retribution from Roscoe's friends, I called and introduced myself.

"When Mr. Carpenter took sick, he asked us to tell you just in case," said one of the bored barflies.

"Tell me what?"

"In case he died. Which he did two days ago."

"Course he did," I said tiredly. This was what I half suspected he would do—go back into hiding, confirming my suspicion that he was the real Elvis.

"He didn't leave you nothing so don't get your hopes up."

"I wouldn't take anything even if he did," I shot back, trying not to sound too skeptical.

"Case you're interested, he had a heart attack."

"Well, if he happens to miraculously come back to life, you can tell him—"

"Lady if you think I'm lying you can go down and see his body for yourself, but you best hurry up. They bury him tomorrow."

"Where exactly can I pay my respects?"

He gave me an address for the Cunningham Funeral Parlor in the next county over. I called it to confirm that this was the last full day of viewing for one John Carpenter.

"Do you know how he died?" I asked the funeral director.

"Nope."

"Can I ask what he looks like?"

"Day-ed." His Southern accent made the word two syllables.

"Is he an older white gentleman?"

"Frankly, I haven't seen the deceased."

That night, I told Vinetta I was leaving early the next day. She asked me what my plans were for Thanksgiving. When I told her I had none, she made me promise to come down; this year they had a lot to be thankful for. Since it would be just a few days before the unveiling of my mother's headstone, it was well timed. I told her I'd be there. Knowing it was my final night with the kids removed all the usual anxiety. I really enjoyed just talking and playing around with them.

Early the next morning, she and the kids gave me a lifetime of little kisses and one big group hug, then I drove across the county to Cunningham Funeral Parlor. A line of shiny black cars were parked out front. Without even trying to look mournful, I marched inside to see most of the assholes from the bar huddled around the lobby with Sheriff Nick, who was explaining the route through town for the funeral procession. Before anyone noticed me, I dipped into the viewing parlor. The coffin lid had already been closed.

"You've got to let me see him one last time," I pleaded with someone who seemed to work there. The man quickly opened the polished maple box. Looking inside at that elderly white-haired man, I saw him plain as day for the first time, now that life's veil of fractures and scars had been lifted: Elvis Presley, dead at seventy-one years of age. At least that's who he looked like.

"Did you know him?" I asked the undertaker.

"Kinda."

"What happened?"

"Just passed away in his sleep, I hear," he said simply. "We all will someday."

"Where is he being buried?"

"The new cemetery over near Mesopotamia, Patriot Hills."

"All are sleeping, sleeping on Patriot Hills," I paraphrased Edgar Lee Masters's beautiful *Spoon River Anthology*. It truly comforted me that he would be up there with others I loved. In a world where so many people wanted to be the King, this was the one person who vowed he wasn't. What better proof that he was real thing.

When I hurried out of the building, I virtually knocked into the gang of good old boys, who seemed naked without their rifles or their beers, standing out front in their ill-fitting suits. They eyeballed me menacingly as I headed out to my car. I fired up the engine, flipped on the radio, and drove east. According to the news, yet another hurricane was heading into Florida. Although Hurricane Katrina was only a category one, I wanted to stay ahead of it. With a little luck, I'd hit Atlanta by late afternoon and get to spend a little time with the sisters. Then I could return to New York a few days later where I'd have to find a new apartment and ponder the distant possibility of a whole new life as a mother. Even if I did miscarry, which was still all too likely, I could always feel genuine comfort about helping the one lost family that I did find.

RUNAWAY BRIDE!

BY GUSTAVO BENOIT AND CASSANDRA BLOOMGARTEN
SPECIAL TO THE ENQUIRER

WHERE'S MISSY SCRUBBS?

THAT'S THE QUESTION THE MEMPHIS POLICE DEPARTMENT HAS BEEN ASKING FOR THE PAST TWO MONTHS!

All eyes are on Thucydides Scrubbs, Missy's husband and presumed abductor.

The Monster of Memphis, as he's called, has been indicted, and though his trial date is set for two months in advance, his lawyer says, "I'm going to be hard-pressed finding an impartial juror in the English-speaking world." Luckily for him Missy isn't dead, she isn't even missing. She's sequestered in a love nest two thousand miles away on the western coast of Mexico, just south of sunny Puerto Vallarta. As this spicy photo taken less than a week ago indicates, the former child beauty pageant winner is alive and well, if not a bit pooped from all the lovemaking with her bad boy paramour, Roscoe Major. The two are having the time of their lives, living off the bogus million-dollar ransom that the tax lawyer quietly paid, money that the Memphis Police mistakenly believed was paid to hire a hit man.

Before notifying the proper authorities both in Memphis and in Mexico, this reporter paid a visit to the lovebirds, hiding out in a secluded beachfront bungalow in Puerto Vallarta, Mexico.

WITH NUDE PHOTOS OF HER AND LOVER IN SUNNY TROPIC HIDEAWAY!

Acknowledgments

Ibrahim Ahmad
George Solimine
Mary K DeVault
Scott Shephard
Aram Saroyan
Jon Resh
Becky Gordon
Barney Rosset
Kara Gilmour
Arthur and Abraham Temple
Jonathan Ames
Toby Sailing

In Memorium

Ruby
Ellen Miller
Ellen Sisk
Susan Woolf

Also by Arthur Nersesian

The Fuck-Up
Manhattan Loverboy
dogrun
Suicide Casanova
Chinese Takeout
Unlubricated
East Village Tetralogy (plays)
The Swing Voter of Staten Island
The Sacrificial Circumcision of the Bronx